LAW AND ADDICTION

ALSO BY MIKE PAPANTONIO

FICTION

Law and Disorder

Law and Vengeance

NONFICTION

*Closing Arguments: The Last Battle
with Fred Levin and Martin Levin*

*Clarence Darrow, the Journeyman:
Lessons for the Modern Lawyer*

*Resurrecting Aesop:
Fables Lawyers Should Remember*

*Air America:
The Playbook with Robert F. Kennedy et al.*

LAW AND ADDICTION

A Novel

MIKE PAPANTONIO

Waterside Productions

ISBN-13: 978-1-939116-46-8 print edition
ISBN-13: 978-1-939116-47-5 ebook edition
ISBN-13: 978-1-939116-49-9 audio edition

Waterside Productions
2055 Oxford Ave.
Cardiff-by-the-Sea, CA 92007

www.waterside.com

To all the mothers, fathers, sisters, and brothers
who have lived through the opioid nightmare.

ACKNOWLEDGMENTS

I wish to thank my team of outstanding trial lawyers,
who are putting it all on the line in this case.

AUTHOR'S NOTE

As I write these words, somewhere in America an individual is dying of a drug overdose. During the next twenty-four hours, there will be at least 115 deaths from the same cause. In 2017, more than 72,000 people in the United States died of a drug overdose. To put that in perspective, during our seventeen-year involvement in the Vietnam War, there was a total of 58,220 American casualties.

When I was first approached about representing plaintiffs in an action against the major corporate opioid distributors, I knew little about the opioid epidemic. There was part of me, I suppose, that preferred to look the other way. It was only when I started peeling back the opioid onion that I had no choice but to confront its ugliness. The more I discovered, the more outraged I became. The opioid crisis didn't occur as some kind of happenstance, but as a direct result of corporate greed.

That isn't my opinion, and that isn't hyperbole. My legal team has documented these claims . . . and more. We have roomfuls of paperwork showing that these distributors knowingly and willfully opened Pandora's Box, and the evils and misery that sprang out of that box are still plaguing our society. Over the last twenty years, thousands of children have grown up without parents (a result of parental death, neglect caused by drug abuse, and/or incarceration). The human toll has been terrible; the collateral damage, heartbreaking. Still, people often forget that although all seemed lost when Pandora opened her box, the last thing to emerge from her box was hope. There are lots of people fighting for hope, and I'd like to think I am among their ranks. These days many communities ravaged by the opioid epidemic are bereft of hope. We must change that, and we must make sure these communities get back some of that which was taken from them.

In my more than thirty years of working as a trial lawyer, I have never been as passionate about a case. The more I learned about the opioid epidemic, the more outraged I became. It became a personal cause for me, and then some. I have visited desolated communities, and talked to too many people who have lost loved ones to opioids. The Four Horsemen of the Apocalypse have been busy. Too busy. Anyone who visits areas blighted by this epidemic can see the wake left by these four riders of conquest, war, famine, and most of all, death.

Just as I was initially reluctant to take up this legal gauntlet, neither did I want to write about this subject. I was hoping to write about a different and more uplifting theme, with good triumphing over evil. I started working on that book, but I kept finding my thoughts returning to this topic. Ultimately, I felt compelled to write this novel.

One of the misconceptions about opioid addicts is that they're "lowlifes." That simply isn't the case. The truth is that many opioid addicts were unwittingly hooked by their own doctors. For every addict, there's a story. Opioids have claimed victims, and continue to claim them, from all walks of life.

In this novel, I have created many composite characters. Their stories bespeak the tragedy that has befallen too many. I have also

xi / **Mike Papantonio**

cribbed from my professional life. When you read about subjects such as the ARCOS data, that is not something I made up. (Unlike what occurs in my novel, there was no trial to obtain that data, but the metaphor remains all too valid—getting information from the corporate drug distributors has been a daunting task.) The "death map" that Deke introduces—which tracks drug deaths throughout the country—*does* exist. If you ever want to see a sobering series of snapshots of our country, just watch a time progression of that map. I introduced that map in one of the depositions I was involved with, and as people watched the epidemic overtake our country, you could have heard the proverbial pin drop.

My hope in writing this fictional account was to both edify and entertain. I wanted to provide readers with a front-row account of this epidemic, but not bludgeon them in the process. While I didn't try to gloss over the human suffering, I still remain a believer in the power of the human spirit to prevail. At the same time, I am hopeful about getting meaningful justice out of this terrible and sad epidemic caused by corporate greed. I hope this novel *does* spark outrage in readers. As a nation, we *need* to be outraged.

In my legal career, I have been a trial lawyer in cases ranging from asbestos to tobacco litigation to litigation of harmful chemicals and products that have maimed, killed, and injured far too many. That said, I can say in all certainty that the opioid catastrophe has created a class of suffering all its own. The opioid epidemic is an American tragedy, but it is one we must examine so we never repeat it again.

— Mike Papantonio,
April 9, 2019

PROLOGUE
LITTLE BLACK TRAIN

Blake snuck a glance over his right shoulder, trying to see into the darkness. There were three of them—no, now there were four. He vaulted over a streambed and raced up the hillside. That didn't deter them. Their pounding footsteps marked their close pursuit. So far, he hadn't been able to shake them, nor had they shown any sign of giving up their chase.

His shoes dug into the dirt path, pushing hard with each step. The way was slippery, and for a moment Blake lost traction. He fought for balance, and with a sharp intake of breath, steadied himself. He didn't dare slip. They'd be on him if he did.

Blake reached the top of the rise and began sprinting. There was no way his pursuers should be able to keep up with him. Blake was fast. Few individuals could stay with him in a footrace. So how was it that he couldn't shake them?

He shifted his head and dared another quick look behind. The pack seemed to be gaining on him. Blake yelled, "What do you want?"

Their silence was more frightening than an answer. He knew then that he was running for his life.

"Help!" Blake screamed. "Help!"

No one responded to his screams. Maybe they'd heard too many screams just like his. They were afraid to try and help, and for good reason. Oakley was looking more and more like a ghost town, especially at night. The citizens hunkered down when it got dark. Except for the ghosts and ghoulies. They came out at night.

The streetlights were few and far between. Most were in disrepair. Blake ran through the darkness, trying to find the light. Even though he'd grown up in Oakley, it was hard to figure out exactly where he was. The darkness muted the colors, offering up a stark black-and-white landscape. The shadows had to be playing tricks with his eyes. The once-familiar roads and woods and hollows seemed to have changed. Skeletal branches from trees reached for him, snagging his clothing.

The whistle of a train made him start. The sound was alien and out of place. You didn't hear trains in Oakley. The nearest train tracks were ten miles to the west. That didn't explain the whistle he was hearing, or the music. A man with a deep bass voice was singing. Blake could hear the words through the pounding footfalls of his pursuers.

"There's a little black train a-coming, better set your business right . . ."

Blake realized the singer must have a toy whistle that sounded like a train. The whistle sounded again.

"Help!" he screamed, but the man just kept on with his song.

Blake thought the lyrics sounded familiar, but he couldn't place them. The whistle screeched again. Now it sounded as if it were directly behind him, almost like it had joined the pack trying to run him down.

Run, run, run. He couldn't slow down. They'd catch him if he did. But the race was taking its toll on him. His breath was getting ragged. He dared not stop. Death was right on his tail, and death didn't even seem to be winded. The train whistle sounded once more, and it was accompanied by the singer's words:

"God sent to Hezekiah, a message from on high, you better set your house in order, for you must surely die."

"Little Black Train," thought Blake. He'd grown up hearing that tune. But why was someone singing that song so late at night? And where was the singer?

The shadows finally opened up enough for Blake to see that just ahead was the turnoff to downtown Oakley, marked by a familiar sign that read WELCOME TO OAKLEY. The sign had been around for all of Blake's twenty-five years, but someone had defaced it the year before. The word *Oakley* had been X'd out with spray paint and replaced with *Zombieland.*

Blake was in the race of his life, yet he felt disembodied, no longer in control of his person. He needed to run, but he could never outrun what was chasing him.

Flight hadn't saved him. Maybe he'd do better to fight.

Blake slowly turned to face his pursuers. There was a part of him that was afraid to see exactly what was there. It was as if he knew it would be worse than he could even imagine. The pack was on all sides of him now. They were getting closer. He gasped at what he saw, at what was reaching for him. There was no wind in his lungs for him to scream.

Zombies.

Their faces were white, with huge dark circles, and their heads hung to the sides, jerking straight and then going slack, as if they were in between waking and nodding off. Eyes without pupils, and with no souls behind them, stared at him. Fingers with blue nails were aimed his way. The zombies reeked, and itched obsessively.

Blake knew there was something off in all of this. How had these lumbering zombies been able to run him down?

The train whistle called, and the singer called to him: "Death's dark train is coming, prepare to take a ride."

Blake knew he should grab a weapon or pick up a rock or branch, but he couldn't move. He swayed back and forth; it was all he could do to not fall. As he steadied himself, he had a moment of clarity. The zombies didn't exactly disappear, but they morphed—into the bodies of the four people sprawled around his own living room.

Everyone was wasted, including Blake.

He saw their pinpoint pupils and pale skin, watched them scratch at imaginary itches with blue-tinged nails, and forced himself to take a deep, shuddering breath. *What a nightmare,* he thought. He raised an unsteady hand up to his face. His nose and mouth were wet with a frothy fluid that had the consistency of snot.

Shit, thought Blake. He'd taken what he thought was oxy, but it must have been fenny. Maybe that explained him imagining the zombies. Or maybe the reality of his life was even worse than his hallucination. He'd heard from others who had experienced the willies that you could have an opioid-induced hallucination.

The train was whistling again.

Blake sank a little lower into his chair. He needed to get off this shit. It was time to clean up his act. In just a few days he'd be going to Jake's graduation. Luckily for him, Jake had visited only once in the last year. Blake had done his best to hide his addiction; he didn't want to worry his brother or take Jake's eyes from the prize. Good old Jake had done it. He was going to be a lawyer.

In his stupor, Blake smiled. He was so damn proud of his twin brother.

The thought of Jake's success eased Blake's mind. His panic subsided, as did his pain. He no longer heard the train whistle, no longer felt compelled to try and outrun the zombies, no longer strained to catch his breath.

Blake's lungs slowed to a stop, but his mind didn't know it.

"Jake," he tried to whisper, but didn't even have breath enough for a last word.

1
WELCOME TO ZOMBIELAND

Out of habit, Jake Rutledge kept glancing beside him for Blake.

The fraternal twins had been inseparable for most of their lives and had relied on each other growing up in Oakley, West Virginia. They'd had to. When they were boys, their father had succumbed to his years working in the coal mines and had died when they were nine. Their mother had held on until their eighteenth birthday; the doctor said she'd died of a brain aneurysm, but Jake was of the opinion that it was despair and tiredness that had done her in. Mom had held on just long enough for her sons to graduate from high school.

He and Blake had talked of leaving West Virginia, but it wasn't the Rutledge way to cut and run. They were the fourth generation to call the Mountain State home, and their Appalachian ties were deep. Blake, in particular, seemed bound by the Rutledge roots. Their family, now small as it was, was everything.

"I got your back, brother," one would say to the other.

"I got your back, brother," was always the reply.

Jake steered his car onto the exit from State Route 19. The sign that Jake had grown up with that said WELCOME TO OAKLEY had been defaced so that it now read WELCOME TO ZOMBIELAND.

Growing up, he and the other kids had often referred to Oakley as "Smokeley." That was usually good for a wink and a snicker. After all, there was a lot of dope smoking in town. And it was kind of an inside joke, because even the adults sometimes called it Smokeley—a nickname that didn't refer to weed but to the time when coal stoves and fireplaces had blackened the winter sky. But now the name Smokeley seemed almost quaint, especially in light of its new nickname.

Still, Jake wasn't surprised. Even before he'd left town for college, then law school, the long death throes of the coal industry had been pushing Oakley toward the edge of poverty. But the town had held on. Jake had grown up with a downtown that had its Ma-and-Pa businesses and restaurants. They'd even had a small movie theater. Over the course of a decade, though, more and more businesses had failed. Oakley's infrastructure had crumbled along with the closings. The local library had cut its hours and days, and then shuttered altogether due to budget cuts. It had been the same with the park service. Even the Elks Club was gone.

Now, more than half of Oakley's downtown storefronts were empty. Only the drugstore seemed to prosper. Of course, there were fewer than five thousand residents in Oakley, so it was no wonder it felt small, but that wasn't the only thing. The town felt dispirited, and dark. Bruce Springsteen's song "My Hometown" seemed to describe the place perfectly—everywhere there were signs of troubled times.

Jake drove past the Rutledge home, not ready to stop there just yet—he had another destination in mind. Fresh in his thoughts was the memory of the day he'd graduated from Marshall and was accepted into law school.

"Imagine that," Blake said. "You're going to be a lawyer."

"That's a long way off," said Jake.

"How are you going to pay for it?" asked Blake. "Half this house is yours. We can sell it to help with your schooling."

"Not on your life," Jake said. "WVU is offering me a partial scholarship. Still, there's nothing keeping you here. If you want, we could share an apartment in Morgantown."

"That sounds like a great idea," Blake said.

It was a great idea that never materialized. Blake stayed in Oakley. He worked in what he said was "construction," but mostly it was part-time demolition. There weren't any new buildings going up in town.

The good thing about law school and his part-time jobs was that the three years passed quickly for Jake. The last time he'd gone home to visit Blake had been just a month before graduation. Jake was concerned about his brother; it was at least the third time that year Blake had gotten sick.

"Don't worry," said Blake. "It's just stomach flu. Wild horses couldn't keep me from your graduation. I'll be the one in the audience screaming the loudest. I got your back, brother."

"I got your back, brother," Jake said.

The twins weren't carbon copies of each other. Blake was darker and stockier, an inch taller than Jake, and the older brother by twenty minutes. That was something he frequently pointed out to his "little brother."

Both were good students, but it was Jake who put a real effort into academics. Blake was more happy-go-lucky. He'd settle for a *B*, when only an *A* was good enough for Jake. And so, it came as no surprise to anyone when Jake ended up the valedictorian of their class at the five-hundred-student Midway High School.

After their mother's death, and with money tight, it was "big brother" who insisted that Jake continue his education at Marshall University upstate, though it would be the first time in their lives the two brothers would be apart. To Jake, moving to the tristate area, with its three hundred and fifty thousand residents, meant he was truly going off to the big city.

Blake had promised to visit him, but something always seemed to come up.

Jake navigated the car around a corner, and his destination was in front of him. He drove through the wrought-iron gate and parked. At fifty acres, the Oakley Cemetery wasn't overly large, but it might very well have been the most scenic spot in town, especially with its profusion of black oaks, live oaks, basswood, beeches, and its many varieties of maple trees. The cemetery grounds had been selected as a historic area by West Virginia's State Historic Preservation Office.

The dead, however, were not immune from the slings and arrows of the living. The upkeep of the cemetery was no longer a community priority, and vandalism seemed to be ever more of a problem—addicts, everyone assumed, looking to rob the dead of whatever jewelry and keepsakes they'd been buried with. It didn't help that the cemetery was also a popular spot for the young to party.

As Jake headed in the direction he'd walked in only a few weeks before, he whispered to the universe, "I got your back, brother."

Walking down the row toward Blake's grave, his thoughts on the past, Jake saw a figure working in front of a headstone. He paused, not wanting to intrude, and as he did so, she got to her feet and began to move away.

"Anna?" he said, shocked by the familiar face.

She turned. "Jake?" she said, her voice unsure.

Anna Fowler looked much the same as she had in high school. Her blue eyes sparkled, and her long chestnut-brown hair swayed against her shoulders. The two of them walked toward each other and then embraced in a big hug. As they disengaged, Anna's gardening basket hooked on Jake's shirt.

"Don't move," she said. "I don't want to tear your shirt."

With careful fingers—did Jake imagine it or were her fingers trembling?—she disentangled the shirt from her basket. "Sorry about that," she said.

"You could always hook 'em without even trying," said Jake. He hoped his smile said he was kidding—sort of.

"Listen to you," said Anna. "It's so good to see you. How is it that we both live in the same town and we never run into one another?"

She seemed to be struggling to speak and smile at the same time; he could see the sweat trickling down from her forehead, though the day wasn't very hot.

"I've been gone," he said. "For a while, actually. And now that I'm back, all I plan to do is work."

"Then nothing has changed," Anna said. "I knew I never had a chance to be valedictorian with you in the mix."

"That's not how I remember it," Jake said, grinning. "I recall you were always matching me grade for grade."

"Blake thought we were both crazy to study like we did." A cloud passed over her face; then she said, "My kryptonite was Algebra II. You deserved to be valedictorian."

"I didn't have your social demands," Jake said with a wink. "I was more the nerd while you were doing cheerleading and student council. You even played volleyball, if I remember correctly. Not to mention how you were always working at Fowler's."

She laughed. "Don't remind me about my misspent youth. See where it got me? Still right here. On the other hand, I hear you're a lawyer."

Jake nodded. "Hard to believe, right?"

Anna shook her head. "It's not hard to believe at all. I'm really proud of you, Jake. And even though Blake and I didn't keep in touch much after high school, I know he would be, too."

Jake tried to deflect her praise. He didn't want to feel like a fraud. "It's not as glamorous as it sounds," he said. "I'd probably be making more flipping burgers."

"I don't believe that."

"Sadly," he said, "it's true. But that's partly because of my own stubbornness. I'm about to start working on this long-shot case. I hate to think I'm tilting at windmills, but I probably am. You can call me Don Quixote."

"It sounds like you're doing something courageous, Don," she said.

That got a smile out of him, along with more head shaking. "I wish I was that noble," he said, "but the reason I'm pursuing this case is because of Blake's death."

Anna's voice was unsteady. "I am so sorry about that," she said.

Jake nodded. "His death really threw me for a loop. I never saw it coming, so it was a real shock."

She didn't speak for a moment, and he could see that she was blinking away tears. He hadn't meant to make her sad.

"What about you?" he asked. "I heard you went off to college but then came back."

"A dream deferred," said Anna, nodding. "My mom got cancer, and I came home to help her fight it. Unfortunately, it was a fight we lost. And right after her death, Daddy had his stroke. I've sort of been a recluse myself since Momma died. And for a while there, Daddy needed round-the-clock care. Luckily, he's better now. That's allowed me to go out and work a part-time job."

"Doing what?" asked Jake.

"I've been modeling."

"That doesn't surprise me," he said, "as pretty as you are. What kind of modeling?"

"I've been an art model for Clint Smith for a while now," she said. "Oakley's native son made good."

Jake nodded. In high school he'd had a crush on Anna, but then again, just about every male in his class had. Back then, he'd thought Anna was out of his league. She was classy, always doing and saying the right thing. Whenever he found himself in her presence, he had the hardest time uttering a complete sentence. In his daydreams he wasn't tongue-tied; in *them*, he dared to ask her out. But that never happened. Besides, she'd always been arm candy for Blake. The two of them had looked great together. In fact, the school had voted them homecoming king and queen. They had dated a few times before mutually agreeing they were better off as friends. Jake wondered if Blake had sensed how he felt about Anna, and backed off to give him a chance. He guessed he would never know.

"This morning I made some floral bouquets to put on gravesites," Anna said, gesturing to her basket. "I made one for Blake's stone, assuming that's okay with you?"

"Okay? At this very moment, Blake is strutting around the clouds, saying, 'The prettiest woman in all of West Virginia is leaving me flowers.' And loud enough for me to hear, he's saying, 'What do you think of *that*, little brother?'"

"You were the younger twin?" She laughed. "I don't think I ever knew that."

"By only twenty minutes," said Jake. "But he loved lording that over me."

Anna's hands rose to her face, and a frown creased her expression.

"Are you all right?" he asked.

"I'm afraid I'm not feeling well," she said. "If you don't mind, I'll give you Blake's bouquet."

As Anna passed him the flowers, Jake couldn't help but notice her shaking hands. Pale red blotches had formed on her fair skin.

"I better walk you to your car," he said.

"That's not necessary," Anna said, her voice sharp. Then she softened it. "I'll feel better after a warm bath and a little rest."

She smiled for him and began walking away.

"It was great seeing you," Jake called after her.

Anna paused in her escape, waved to him, and said, "It really was. Don't give up on your dreams, Jake. Or should I say . . . Don? Keep dreaming those impossible dreams. I hope you'll call me."

Her words, and her invitation, made Jake smile. "I will," he said.

Anna waved again and kept walking. Jake watched her go. Her illness would give him a reason to call to see how she was doing.

Maybe he wouldn't even wait until tomorrow to call her.

2

REMEMBER WHY THE GOOD LORD MADE YOUR EYES

It turned out that tomorrow never gave him a chance.

There were plenty of impediments to Jake's trying to make a livelihood as a lawyer. In addition to not having a client, he also lacked an office, secretarial support, and financing. Most of his classmates at WVU had spent a good deal of their final year canvasing potential employers. Unlike his peers, Jake hadn't interned with a law firm during that time. Between his UPS warehousing job, law school, and working on the Law Review, there just hadn't been enough hours in the week. He had gone to a few job fairs, where it had quickly become apparent that lawyers with no experience and no connections weren't exactly in high demand.

With limited options at hand, Jake set up his law practice out of the Rutledge family house in Oakley. His laptop and his cell phone comprised the totality of his legal research sources as well as his legal support team. He made the dining room table his desk, setting it up with photos, knickknacks, and mementos. His immediate family might be gone, but he put up a display of family photos, keeping their pictures and memories close.

Then, through word of mouth, he announced to the world that he was ready and willing to give advice to clients. The world didn't exactly beat a path to his door, but Jake used the quiet time to learn more about the opioids that had killed Blake, and their impact on communities like his. He didn't need to remind himself that he was on a mission. Blake's absence was a continual reminder to him.

Jake blamed his own self-absorption for not noticing his brother's addiction on the few occasions he came home. His time away at school had blinded him to everything except his own situation. Anyone with eyes and ears should have seen that Blake was in a death spiral. It seemed as if everyone but Jake knew that for more than a year, Blake had taken oxycodone—a drug some called Hillbilly Heroin—for pain relief. Blake had started taking opioids after an old brick chimney fell on his leg. Someone had given him some oxy for the pain. That had been the beginning of the end for Blake.

Jake talked to everyone in Oakley who had known his brother, including neighbors, old family friends, former teachers and classmates, and law enforcement. Blake's story, he learned, was anything but unique. A plague had descended upon Oakley, and its swath of destruction was nowhere near done. Many were afraid it was even getting worse, if that was possible.

Walter Hughes, their longtime neighbor, talked about how it broke his heart when the local Elks Club had to close down. "All the break-ins at our building," he said, shaking his head. "It got so that it became too scary to hold meetings at night. Our wives didn't want us to be away because they were afraid to be alone. What happened to our hometown? Most days it feels like I'm now living in some kind of scary third-world country."

Some residents whispered the word *zombie*, as if afraid to say it aloud, as if voicing it might turn their harsh reality into even more of a horror film. It was a reality where residents saw hundreds of addicts walking the streets in a daze. Former family members and friends . . . now transformed into barely recognizable beings.

Unlike zombies in films, though, Jake knew these zombies hadn't sprung up as a result of a scientific experiment gone wrong. That's what he needed to get to the bottom of—why did it seem as though his community, and his brother, had been targeted? How had the government become overwhelmed by the catastrophic problems caused by this plague?

During his three years in law school, Jake had used a voice-activated digital recorder to make notes. It wasn't only a study technique—he often spoke into the recorder as if he were preparing for a case. The technique allowed him to better analyze a problem. By stating the problem multiple times, along with its potential solutions, he found that it improved his ability to arrive at a correct resolution.

Jake spoke into the recorder, pretending to talk to a fellow law student. "When Blake died, they blamed the neighborhood dealer who sold him heroin. There are a thousand neighborhood dealers, though. That's the low-lying fruit for law enforcement. I need to show who was behind the oxycodone that originally got him addicted. They say the road to hell is paved with good intentions. I'll need to show a court every SOB profiting from the opioid epidemic—from the corporate greed that permeates manufacturers and distributors, making them turn a blind eye to human carnage, to the personal greed of doctors and pharmacists preying on their own patients. I'm going to have to build a case showing all the opioid interconnections, and all the lies."

Jake reached for another memento, an old picture of him and Blake wearing Halloween costumes. They'd been ten that year, and Jake had called dibs on Harry Potter, which hadn't sat very well with Blake. At the time, the twins were both obsessed with the books and movies, but only one of them could be Harry.

Looking at the picture now, it almost seemed as if Blake's choice had been prophetic. Mom had fixed him up with a white shirt covered in goo that made it look as if he'd just eaten a plate of bloody brains. It was Blake, Jake recalled, who'd gotten most of the compliments that night. Jake had thought he'd be the cool one, with the scar on his forehead and his wizard's wand and his robe, but as it turned out, he couldn't compete with an old-fashioned zombie.

He spoke into the recorder: "In court I'll need to make the point that the new breed of opioid zombies don't eat brains. It's their brains that get eaten away. You'd think that would make them sympathetic, but that's a problem I'll have to face up to. Most jurors will think they brought on their problems themselves. But I'll need to demonstrate how opioids didn't magically appear. I'll have to show how thousands of rust-belt communities—communities like Oakley that experienced loss of jobs and industry—were specifically marketed to and targeted. Corporate predators looked for communities with a high despair index, and the distributors then told the people in those communities, 'We've got just the thing to help.'

"Suddenly, doctors began prescribing their new wonder pills like candy. Every year the Big Pharma manufacturers produced more and more opioids, and every year their distributors found creative ways to sell more and more of the product. Sales doubled, and tripled, and then went up tenfold. It's all there in their corporate accounting and annual shareholders' reports. Corporate profits depended on increasing demand, so they did all they could to create that demand."

Jake stopped talking. There were a lot of moving pieces in the opioid epidemic, and stating them aloud helped him understand those pieces.

"The corporations hired scientists and doctors and field reps who were willing to be their mouthpieces and claim that studies showed these new, breakthrough opioids were nonaddictive. They took that one right out of the Adolf Hitler playbook: *Tell a big enough lie, and tell it frequently enough, and it will be believed.* Those studies have since been debunked."

Jake clicked off the recorder. It was one thing building his imaginary case, but it was another to do it for real. First, he had to get the right client, and then he would need to file actual pleadings. Only then would he have a crack at making his case in front of a jury instead of his tape recorder.

He took one last look at the Halloween photo of him and Blake, then reluctantly put it away. For old time's sake, he wanted to say, "Trick or treat." But now he knew better. What Blake had fallen for—what had murdered him—wasn't a treat.

"Trick," Jake said.

Very few lawyers practiced in Seneca County. The nearest firm that Jake was aware of was in the town of Melton, twenty miles northwest of Oakley. He didn't know anything about Fitzhugh, Hodges, and Wolfe other than that the firm had been around for a long time. He hoped he would find a lawyer receptive to his questions, someone willing to mentor him. In his mind's eye, Jake imagined an avuncular sort addressing his concerns and revealing a few tricks of the trade. There had to be some brotherhood among lawyers, right?

Melton had always been a more affluent community than Oakley. The opioid crisis had made that even more apparent—anyone with any money had fled the towns most affected by the blight. But during his drive, Jake could see that the blight was spreading, and he didn't doubt that Melton was also feeling the pain of illicit drugs. A plague doesn't respect borders.

The law firm of Fitzhugh, Hodges, and Wolfe was housed in a converted Queen Anne Victorian just off the main road. Old sugar maples and red maples lined the street. Jake passed through a wrought-iron gate and started up the path. He hesitated at the front door, unsure whether to ring the doorbell or walk in. There were lights on inside, so he tried the doorknob. It was unlocked, and he pushed the door open.

A reception desk dominated the space, but judging from the pile of old papers and junk mail piled on it, the desk had long been in disuse. Although the building didn't appear to be deserted, it was *quiet*. The office nearest to where Jake was standing looked dark and vacant. In fact, only one of the offices appeared to be occupied. Colorful light filtered into the hallway through a stained-glass window. On the door was a sign that read ALTON HODGES, ESQUIRE.

"Hello," Jake called.

There was no answer.

He walked up to the door and knocked gently on the wood frame, taking care to not shake the stained glass.

"What?" a voice called out.

Jake decided that was an invitation to come in. He opened the door and found himself being stared down from behind a desk by a glowering man who reminded him of an older and meaner-looking version of Mr. Potter in *It's a Wonderful Life*.

"Mr. Hodges?" asked Jake.

"What do you want?" the man said.

"I came by to introduce myself. My name is Jake Rutledge, and I'm a lawyer who lives in Oakley."

"Oakley?" said Hodges. "That town has become a den of thieves. Are you a thief?"

"No, sir," said Jake. "Like I said, I'm a lawyer."

Hodges laughed, but it sounded more like a dismissive snarl. "As if those two things are mutually exclusive." His eyes were as cold as his words.

As Jake approached the desk, he tried to smooth a few of the wrinkles out of his blazer. While Hodges remained seated, Jake extended his hand across the desk and said, "It's nice to meet you, Mr. Hodges."

"Oh, God," said Hodges, shaking his head but not Jake's hand. "Is this the Ted Mack amateur hour?"

"I'm afraid I don't know what that is." Jake retracted his hand. Without asking permission, he took a seat, pretending not to hear the old man's sigh.

"You say you're a lawyer?" said Hodges.

"Yes, sir."

"You don't even look like you've gone through puberty."

"Well," Jake said, not sure how to answer, "I have." Then he added, "As I said, I'm a lawyer who practices in Oakley."

"Let me head you off from the get-go: I'm not hiring, and Melton doesn't need another lawyer. There's not enough business for *me* in this town, and that's even after my partners had the good sense to finally die."

"I'm not looking for a job," Jake said. "But I wouldn't mind asking your advice, sir."

"So this is a consultation?"

"Yes, sir."

"And you're prepared to pay my consultation fee?"

Jake looked away from the man's probing eyes. As old as he was, Jake thought, this miserable misanthrope deserved to have cataracts. Instead, his blue eyes were sharp and probably hard enough to cut glass.

"I was hoping for some professional courtesy," he said.

"Ah," said Hodges. "What you're saying is I can call on you for the same, should the occasion warrant. Is that it?"

Jake started nodding, until Hodges said, "That will happen when hell freezes over."

"You might be interested to know that I did graduate at the top of my class—"

"Bah."

Jake shut his mouth, wondering if the old man would add "humbug." But he did not.

"I don't care if you graduated first in your class from Oxford Law," said Hodges. "At this stage of your career, you don't even know how to properly hold your dick."

This conversation wasn't going the way Jake had imagined. He thought about standing up and walking out, or asking Hodges whether his mother had been a mutt or a purebred, but insults wouldn't help his situation. Despite how unpleasant Hodges was being, Jake didn't doubt he could be of help if he were willing. His arrogance came out of confidence; he knew the law well. That explained it, even if it didn't excuse it.

"I came here hoping you might be able to answer a few of my questions," Jake said. "My brother recently died of an opioid overdose. I'm trying to figure out a way to sue those responsible."

"What did you say your name was?" asked the old lawyer. "Don Quixote?"

"I'm not tilting at windmills," Jake said. Unbidden, Anna Fowler popped into his mind. He couldn't afford to get distracted from the case, but he remembered that at the cemetery she had called him Don. Jake had planned on calling her, but working on Blake's case had consumed him. "My goal is to make the Big Pharma players pay for what they did to my brother, and thousands just like him."

"If that's the case, you should stick to jousting with windmills, because I can assure you that jousting with silk-stocking corporate lawyers is a much tougher enterprise."

"How would you proceed with such a case?"

"I wouldn't," said Hodges. "I'm not a fool."

"How about pretending for one moment that you're young and idealistic?"

"I much prefer being old and cynical."

"Please," said Jake.

Hodges rolled his eyes and said, "You are a wide-eyed babe in the woods, aren't you? Let me acquaint you with some hard facts: you can't be naive and be a lawyer. Or I should say, you can't be naive and be a *successful* lawyer. Do you understand that?"

When Jake didn't answer, Hodges sighed. "I was never as stupid as you're apparently determined to be. I knew better than to contemplate such a pie-in-the-sky case. But if you're dead set on making a fool of yourself, then you'd better practice copycat law. I'm sure there have been other lawyers as irrational and imprudent as you."

Jake wondered if he'd heard correctly. He was pretty sure Hodges had said *copycat law*, not *copyright law*. He was also pretty sure WVU had never offered a course on copycat law.

"Copycat law?" he asked.

"Yes, yes," Hodges said impatiently. "Lots of young lawyers have gotten their starts with copycat claims."

Jake was afraid to look as stupid as Hodges seemed to think he was, so he gingerly attempted a fishing expedition. "And how do they typically go about this?"

"They don't reinvent the damn wheel," said Hodges. "They find out what kinds of similar claims have been filed. Do you think you're the first lawyer to want to take on the pharmaceutical companies? You find out who's filed what, and where."

"That makes sense."

"Of course, it makes sense. You save a lot of time by knowing what's out there and how it was done." The old man cleared his throat and added, in singsong cadence, "'Remember why the good Lord made your eyes, so don't shade your eyes, but plagiarize, plagiarize, plagiarize.'"

Jake's mouth must have dropped open a little—Hodges looked pleased. He seemed to enjoy throwing Jake off his stride.

"Tom Lehrer sang that. It's from his song 'Lobachevsky.'" At Jake's blank look, Hodges rolled his eyes. "There was a time when this country produced the greatest satirists in the world. Of course, there was also a time when there used to be a national sense of humor."

Jake nodded. "Right. So what you're saying is that I look at these other claims, find out what's worked and what hasn't, and then build my case accordingly in state court."

"That's one way to do it," Hodges said, leaning back in his chair, "if you want to have your case dismissed."

"Dismissed? Why?"

"This is West Virginia, sonny. It is not exactly a bastion of liberal law. You have no chance of prevailing in court on the state level. The politics of big money will eat you alive before the ink even dries on the half-ass pleading you intend to file. In federal court, you might have at least a snowball's chance in hell."

Jake's pulse started racing; he could see the wisdom in that. "And how would I be able to make a federal case?"

"For starters, if you think that bringing a case on behalf of a bunch of long-dead drug addicts is going to open those doors, then you're exactly the fool I thought you were." At Jake's blank look (he was beginning to feel déjà vu), the old lawyer grew impatient. "Your best chance at success is to represent a county or a city that has lost millions of dollars from this drug epidemic of yours. Of course, you'll have to figure out how to show specific damages to that kind of client. In fact, you'll have to figure out a lot of things as you waste the first three to five years of your career."

"I guess one thing I need to figure out before I can start wasting that time is how I go about getting hired by a county or city in the first place."

"You know what they say," said Hodges. "It's not *what* you know, it's *who* you know."

That wasn't exactly reassuring advice, thought Jake, to someone who didn't even own a Rolodex.

Hodges gave a few underhand waves of his right hand, gesturing for Jake to "shoo."

Jake stood. "You've been a big help, Mr. Hodges."

The lawyer snorted. "For your sake, I hope that's not true. Now don't come back unless you make an appointment. And unless you bring money."

3
LAWYERS, GUNS, AND MONEY

Jake sat in the waiting area near the reception desk. The law firm of Paul Vogel and Associates took up the entire fifth floor of the six-story brick River Building located along the Ohio River. The former warehouse had been revamped in the seventies for commercial office space. From its upper floors you could look out on the states of Kentucky, Ohio, and of course, West Virginia.

The law offices were adorned with marble flooring, ornate glass chandeliers, and antique doors. Jake couldn't help but feel out of place, despite the receptionist's friendliness. He only had one suit to his name, but since he saved that for special occasions, today he'd worn his backup professional garb: a blue blazer and khaki pants. He'd declined coffee out of fear that he might spill some on his clothes; he wanted to avoid a dry-cleaning expense.

In the months since speaking to Hodges, it had been the rare day when he hadn't gone to bed exhausted. Blake was always on his mind, always spurring him on, but while the case was moving ahead, Jake wasn't sure if he was getting somewhere or if he was just spinning his wheels. He'd heard that Walt Disney once remarked, "I must be successful; I owe seven million dollars." That's how Jake felt. Like the emperor with his new clothes, he was just waiting to be called out by someone who'd noticed he wasn't really the lawyer he was pretending to be.

"Mr. Rutledge?"

The words didn't register at first.

"Mr. Rutledge?"

Jake realized the receptionist was talking to him, and he jumped to his feet.

"Mr. Vogel will see you now," she said.

Paul Vogel's office reflected the lawyer. There were more pictures than diplomas, and mementos from Vogel family trips stood out more than the room's legal library. Along the walls were historic black-and-white photographs of the Ohio River, and old nautical memorabilia. Beyond the large windows was the river itself.

The two men shook hands, and then Vogel motioned Jake to a chair and said, "Please have a seat, Mr. Rutledge."

As he took a seat, he said, "Jake."

"And I'm Paul."

Paul Vogel was in his late forties but moved with an exuberance that made him seem far more youthful. He was medium-size and wiry, with alert blue eyes that didn't seem to miss a thing. Jake's glance kept drifting over to a framed picture of a younger iteration of him standing next to a musician.

"I got that taken with Warren Zevon two years before he died," Paul said. "Do you know his music?"

Jake thought about it and came up with a title: 'Werewolves in London'?"

"Good one," said Paul. "But my personal favorite is 'Lawyers, Guns, and Money.' It's sort of become this office's anthem. When people are desperate, they call for all of the above."

"I don't know the song," said Jake.

"If you get a chance, give it a listen. It's an office tradition to play the song loudly every Friday at the end of the workweek."

"Good tradition," said Jake.

Next to a picture of Zevon was another photo. Jake knew its subject, then turned from the picture to Paul. "When I first walked into the office, I could see your resemblance to your father."

The lawyer tilted his head back, his face showing his surprise. "You knew my father?"

Jake nodded. "He represented my mother in a wrongful-death claim against the coal company where my father worked for almost thirty years. The coal company claimed my father's cigarette smoking killed him. No one else would take the case."

"That sounds like Dad," said Paul. He didn't hide his proud smile. "He favored tough cases."

"He won a settlement for my family," said Jake. "It wasn't a lot of money, but we were in sore need of anything we could get. My mother used to say that Hank Vogel was heaven-sent."

"I can't tell you how many times I've heard that," Paul said, "but it never grows old."

"I was sorry to learn he died," Jake said. "To be honest, when I found myself in this pickle, the first person I thought might be able to help me was Hank Vogel. It was only after I tried to track your father down that I learned about his death. That's how I found out about you."

"That's what recommended me?"

Jake nodded. "I was hoping the apple didn't fall too far from the tree."

"That's been my lifelong hope as well."

"I'm certain I never would have become a lawyer if it weren't for your father. When I was a kid, we talked a few times; I liked it that he didn't talk down to me."

"Judging from the email you sent me," said Paul, "I think my father would have approved of your career choice." Paul picked up a printout of Jake's email and studied it for a moment. "Just to make sure I'm not missing something, let me clarify a few things."

"Shoot," said Jake.

"You have no affiliation with any law firm, and are in fact a solo practitioner?"

Jake nodded.

"And you don't have an office, but you work out of your house?"

"Correct."

"You haven't worked for any other law firm, or even interned anywhere?"

"That's right."

"And yet county commissions in two different states hired you to represent their interests against some of the biggest corporations in this country?"

Jake shrugged. "I suppose I should point out that Wirt County is the smallest of West Virginia's fifty-four counties; Vinton County also happens to have the smallest population in Ohio."

"When I received your letter asking for this consultation," Paul said, "I wondered if someone was having a little fun at my expense. I don't mean to be rude, Jake, but lawyers with your inexperience don't get these kinds of cases."

"No joke," Jake said. "I think I was so persistent that they decided hiring me was the easiest way to get rid of me."

"And I assume you don't have the kind of deep pockets typically needed to engage a case like this?"

"Guilty as charged," said Jake. "I'm flat broke."

"I'd like to hear how you've gotten as far as you have," said Paul.

"It probably helped that I agreed to work on a contingency fee of only fifteen percent," said Jake.

Paul whistled softly. "Most lawyers would never consider working for a percentage that small," he said. "But then again, I suppose you have to get the horse out of the barn."

"I never took on these cases to make my fortune," Jake said.

Paul looked at him, his eyes warm but shrewd. "Anything else help land you these counties?" he asked.

"I had contacts," Jake admitted, to which Paul started nodding—as if he must have struck some inappropriate backroom deals that explained his hiring.

"But those contacts only got me in the doors of the county commissioners," Jake said. "I was lucky to have an uncle who was well thought of in Wirt County, and my Marshall roommate vouched for me to his father in Vinton County."

"That was the extent of your contacts?" said a surprised Paul.

"Less than six thousand people live in all of Wirt County," said Jake. "And I think everyone there knows my Uncle Bill. Vinton County is bigger, but it feels like a small town."

"And you only knew your roommate?"

"Quinn Barnett might have overstated my qualifications to his father."

"What did he say?"

Jake shrugged. He didn't like talking himself up. "Quinn was very complimentary. He told his father that if I hadn't tutored him as much as I had his last two years of college, he never would have graduated."

"Anything else?"

"He might have mentioned that I worked almost a full-time night job along with taking a heavy course load, but still managed to pull down good grades."

"What were your grades at Marshall?"

"I graduated with honors."

"Mostly *A's*?"

Jake shrugged, and then nodded.

"And let me guess, Law Review at WVU?"

Instead of answering, Jake said, "Most people don't know WVU has the fourth-oldest Law Review in the country."

"And you still managed to work a part-time job all three years?"

Jake nodded. "It seemed like I didn't sleep for three straight years. I was so busy I didn't keep in contact with my twin brother, Blake, like I should have. That's why I was oblivious to his opioid addiction. Two days before I graduated, I got the call that Blake had died of a drug overdose."

"I'm sorry," said Paul.

"In a roundabout way, that's why I'm here. I came home and buried my brother, and then I began asking questions. This opioid problem is devastating the country, but I knew nothing about it. Blake's death prompted me to become fully aware of the circumstances killing hundreds of people every single day. I didn't set out with some kind of crazy vendetta in mind, but the more I learned, the more I began to treat my brother's death like it was a homicide investigation. Have you ever seen those police flowcharts with string and lines connecting individuals and events?"

Paul nodded.

"If you visit my house," Jake said, "you would see how I used an entire wall to map out the collusion between the manufacturers, the distributors, the medical community, the government, and basically the entire opioid pharmaceutical business. The opioid epidemic did not occur naturally, Mr. Vogel. I'm not overstating my case when I say there was a classic RICO-type conspiracy and subsequent cover-up here."

"That's a bold theory."

"There is ample evidence to prove it."

"Let's say that's true. Let's even say you have a case. What do you honestly think your chances of survival are in that predatory world you just described?"

"I'd like to think the Bible is right when it says the truth shall set you free."

"I'm more of a believer in the song lyrics that say 'Praise the lord and pass the ammunition and we'll all stay free.'"

"I think I have the ammunition to make my case."

"You better have, because you've targeted a wake of vultures that will try and pick your bones clean before you even know you're dead. I can promise you that, merely based upon what you've already filed. Right now, there is a bounty on your head, and these particular bounty hunters are two-thousand-dollars-an-hour corporate lawyers who will seek to take your scalp."

Jake suppressed a shiver, but only just. "That's why I'm here asking you for advice," he said, "and what I hope will also be your help. As you know, the McQueen Health Corporation has filed a motion to dismiss in both the West Virginia and Ohio courts where I filed claims. I need advice as to how to proceed. And since I've got my hat in my hand already, I'm hoping you'll consider being my co-counsel in court, at least to fight their first motion to dismiss in West Virginia."

Paul raised his brows. "You do understand that beating the motion to dismiss will be the easiest part of your case?" he said.

"I hope you're right."

"Trust me, I am right."

"Intellectually, I understand that, but it scares me to think MHC can stop me at the starting gate and end the race before it begins. I've already done so much work and learned so many things. It would kill me to not be able to tell this story in a courtroom."

"I'm assuming you're not surprised that MHC responded as they have?"

"No," Jake said, "but . . ." The word hung there as he thought out his answer. "I guess I didn't expect such a vigorous response."

"Welcome to the Big Leagues," Paul said.

"What do you mean?"

"MHC's motion was designed to scare the bejesus out of you, as well as anyone who might consider coming to your aid."

"It did. In comparison, I'm sure my plaintiff's pleading was amateurish."

"Claims can be amended," said Paul. "Understand that their response was calculated. They threw every conceivable legal and personal attack into their motion because they wanted to create shock value. So how shocked are you?"

"Let's just say it got my attention," said Jake. "And that's why I'm here seeking out some advice, and maybe a little courage."

"I don't know if I can deliver either," said Paul, "but on a positive note, I can assure you after twenty years of lawyering that overkill and overreaching on a motion to dismiss shows genuine fear on their part. And it also shows not a little loathing directed your way. They hate you for daring to question their tactics. Goliath—and by that I reference MHC and other Fortune 500 Companies they are in league with—can't even tolerate the notion of a David challenging them. From the onset they'll want to squash you."

"You mean they won't just play nice with us?" said Jake.

Paul met his eyes. Jake was smiling. "Us?" asked Paul. "If you don't mind my asking, Jake, how much money did you make this past year?"

"Just under thirty thousand dollars," he said. After a moment's hesitation, he decided to be totally forthcoming: "But almost half of that was doing part-time census work. The rest was from offering legal advice."

Paul nodded, and then very gently said, "Jake, do you understand that movies featuring the scrappy lawyer taking on the corporate bad guys are not based on reality?"

"Are you saying it's a rigged game?" asked Jake.

"Let's just say it's not an even playing field. It's not David going up against Goliath. No, he's going up against Goliath *and* the fifth infantry. And at the end of the day, David ends up bankrupt, with his life in shambles."

The lump in Jake's throat prevented him from breaking the silence. In so many words, Paul Vogel had just told him he thought the case was hopeless. He bit down hard on his lip. He didn't want to shed bitter tears, or tears of any sort.

"Thank you for your time, Mr. Vogel," he managed to say.

As he rose, Paul said, "Whoa, my young warrior. Sit down."

Jake sank back into the chair.

"I just wanted to make sure you understood what you're going up against," Paul said. "Or I should say, what *we're* going up against. I'll be your second chair in the motion-to-dismiss hearing."

Jake let out pent-up air and even managed a smile. He reached across the desk, and this time shook the hand of his co-counsel.

4
JAZZ HANDS

The Robert C. Byrd Courthouse, named after the eight-term U.S. senator, took up an entire city block in Charleston, West Virginia. The two men followed the deserted sidewalk around the impressive—and to Jake's eye, intimidating—nine-story courthouse. The building incorporated a combination of neoclassic, Egyptian, and art deco designs, including forty-foot marble walls inset with tall stained-glass panels.

"Some building," said Jake with an admiring nod.

"This is the right place for us to make history," said Paul, offering a subtle reminder about why they were there.

It certainly wasn't Paul's first rodeo; during his years practicing law in West Virginia, Jake knew, he had won some of the largest verdicts in the state.

"I like the sound of that," said Jake, his breath visible in the morning chill.

Their steps were unhurried; Paul made sure their conversation was as well. He knew how much this proceeding meant to Jake, and how worried he was.

"Did you stay with family or friends here in town last night?" Paul asked.

Jake shook his head. "I knew I was too worked up to be fit company for anyone, so I got up early and made the drive from Oakley. And when I say 'got up,' that means I got out of bed after hours of not being able to sleep."

Paul looked him over and nodded with approval. "Your youth serves you well. I don't see any dark circles. What I see is a confident lawyer ready to kick butt."

"Thanks," said Jake. "Out of curiosity, though, when was the last time you saw your ophthalmologist?"

Paul smiled. The more the two had worked together, the more Jake had come to appreciate Paul's easygoing sense of humor—and Paul himself.

"I'm a firm believer in having a prescription for rose-colored glasses," Paul said. "You'll find them helpful if you're going to be a good trial lawyer."

"I thought justice was supposed to be blind."

"Lady Justice does wear a blindfold—but that doesn't mean she never peeks out from under it."

"I did my due diligence on Perry," said Jake, shifting topics. Judge Willard Perry was sixty-four years old and had been a U.S. District Court judge for the last five years. "He's conservative. I don't think anyone would characterize him as a plaintiff's judge."

"It doesn't matter if he's conservative or liberal," said Paul. "What matters is if he's fair and follows the letter of the law. From my experience with him, Judge Perry will do that."

"What else can you tell me about him?"

"He was born and raised in West Virginia. I'm sure you'll have known individuals much like him. He likes to cut to the chase and sometimes has fun doing it. What you'll need to remember in this proceeding is that less is more. You excel when it comes to the facts, figures, and statistics surrounding this case, but most of those things are not germane to a motion to dismiss. Remember the acronym KISS—keep it simple, stupid. This is a relatively straight-forward hearing. The corporate mouthpieces are going to come in and make those same three basic arguments they laid out in their pleading. We're going to hear that every word in the complaint you filed failed to state a legitimate legal claim that the court can grant any relief for. And then they're going to argue that even if you did succeed in providing a legitimate legal claim, it's all for naught, as they had no control over any of the bad things that doctors, pharmacists, and drug dealers did with their perfectly safe product. And, finally, they're going to argue that it's impossible for you to prove exactly how much money Wirt County lost because of costs related to EMT services, county hospital services, extra police services, and court costs. And the first words out of your mouth will be . . ."

Jake replied with the words Paul had made him memorize; it was the same response most lawyers used to refute any motion to dismiss: "Your Honor, West Virginia law is clear on the guidelines for granting summary judgment: The court must treat as true all well-pleaded facts stated in the complaint in a light most favorable to the claimant."

Paul nodded his approval. "Perfectly said. And you will repeat it over and over to the judge, all the while intertwining it with ugly facts. One of my favorite sayings is: *There is nothing uglier than reason when it is not on your side.* Remember, we don't need to win our case here. We simply need to be the voice of reason and remind the judge what the law is, while filling his ears with the kinds of facts that will predispose him to dislike our opponents. Our goal is to live so we can fight another day, and maybe in the process tilt the judge's attitude ever so slightly against these pred-ators. Roger that?"

Jake nodded. Paul made it sound so simple. He'd learned a lot from Paul's mentoring; at the same time he felt like an athlete who'd heard enough coaching and just wanted to get out there and play.

As they rounded a corner of the building, they saw a uniformed deputy approaching the front doors of the courthouse. In his hand was a set of keys.

"Looks like the bailiff is here," said Paul. "What do you say we get out of the cold?"

Jake's heart was pounding so hard he could only hear half of what Paul was saying. He tried looking at the typed notes he'd spent so many hours preparing, but reading them was like trying to understand a foreign language. For one panicked moment, Jake even had trouble remembering his own name.

Maybe I should write it down, he thought, *so that I don't forget it.*

Even though court employees had gone about making preparations for the first case to be heard, the courtroom had remained quiet. Voices had been respectfully lowered; greetings had been muted. Jake was reminded of the hushed activities preceding the start of church.

That quiet came to a sudden end with the appearance of the defendants. Paul and Jake had both made guesses as to the size of the lawyers' contingent. Now was the moment of truth.

"It will be as much about show as anything else," Paul said. "In a motion to dismiss, you don't need more than two attorneys. That means they'll probably have four. And of those four, I'm guessing at least two will be female. We can also expect at least one minority attorney. That will send a supposedly subliminal message demonstrating how fair and evenhanded the defendants are."

"Five attorneys," Jake had guessed, arguing just to be contrary.

As it turned out, the defendants marched in with four attorneys and a paralegal. Two of the attorneys were female. One of the male attorneys was black; one of the females was Asian. The paralegal was Latina. All were impeccably dressed.

"Wolves in sheep's clothing," whispered Paul, "and by that, I mean Oxxford and Armani worsted wool suits."

One of the two male attorneys was clearly in charge. His subordinates, who carried enough items for them to qualify as Sherpas, were tending to him as if he were a potentate. The attorney looked their way, flared his nostrils as if smelling something questionable, and then approached their table. He offered a wide smile that showed teeth bleached to an unnatural whiteness, and extended a hand. "Mr. Rutledge? I'm Nathan Ailes."

Paul shook his head along with Ailes's hand. "I wish I was the more handsome and youthful Mr. Rutledge," he said, "but I must confess that I am only the second chair, Paul Vogel."

An apparently chagrined Nathan Ailes said, "My mistake." Then he turned to Jake and appeared surprised—if not somewhat aghast—at what he saw. With an expression bordering on disbelief, he looked Jake up and down. The worn state of Jake's shoes brought on a momentary smirk.

Jake hoped he wasn't blushing. His entire body was suddenly hot, and his stomach felt as if he'd been hit deep in the solar plexus.

"I apologize, *Mister* Rutledge," Ailes said, though it sounded as if he were questioning the use of the word *Mister*.

The two men shook hands, and then Ailes made a point of rubbing his hand dry before withdrawing.

It was bad enough to feel like a fool, Jake thought, but worse to hear Paul laughing. He turned, ready to tell Paul off, but the other man spoke first.

"What an asshole," Paul whispered. "And what a bad actor the way he pretended he didn't know who you were. I guarantee you MHC had their investigators find out everything they could about you. This Ailes guy probably even knows your favorite brand of toothpaste. I guess he thought by holding his nose up in the air and acting like you were a mere mortal, you would be intimidated."

Jake's sweats suddenly vanished. He was breathing again. The pit in his stomach had mostly filled in.

"You ever see that movie *A Knight's Tale?*" Paul asked.

Jake started nodding. It had been a favorite of his and Blake's.

"You remember what that self-satisfied prick of a count said after he beat the knight in their first joust? 'You have been weighed, you have been measured, and you have been found wanting. In what world could you possibly beat me?'"

And now Jake answered it with the knight's words: "'In this world,'" he said, "'and at this time.'"

"My feelings exactly," said Paul.

Jake felt a fire rising from deep inside him all the way to his eyes. He was a knight errant on a Holy Grail mission. This was the first battle in his crusade to avenge Blake.

"I got your back, brother," he whispered.

The bailiff called everyone to rise, and Judge Willard Perry entered the courtroom. Perry wasn't a big man, but he exuded authority. His salt-and-pepper hair was cropped in a military cut. He wore black-rimmed glasses that seemed to have the dual purpose of vision enhancement and prop. Paul had told Jake that whenever the judge heard something he didn't like, or he thought an argument was going on too long, he would move his glasses down his nose so as to better glower at the attorneys. Many judges liked the sound of their own voices, Paul had said, but not Perry. Jake quickly saw this demonstrated in court. Perry made it clear he was not in love with anyone's oratory, not even his own.

That included Nathan Ailes, who prided himself a poet. He'd hardly started his opening remarks when the judge told him, "Get on with it."

Ailes smiled and said, "Yes, Your Honor," pretending that he was fine with being forced to rein in his verse. Ailes looked at his notes, then back up at the judge.

"There are ten valid reasons to dismiss this claim," he said, holding up both hands to signal the number ten.

The finger waving was not to Judge Perry's satisfaction; he pulled his glasses down his nose, and Ailes dropped his jazz hands.

"Those ten reasons are included in our response to the plaintiff's pleading. It is our belief that each and every one of those reasons demonstrates that what was alleged by the plaintiff cannot be proven."

Jake's original pleading had been all of twelve pages long. Its brevity, he'd told Paul, was a result of his not being paid by the hour. The truth of the matter was that because Jake had never written such a document before, he'd been more comfortable keeping it succinct. Besides, he'd known he could add to the claim in the future. Paul had tidied up the pleading but had added only one more page to its length. Their opponents weren't as pithy. The defense's motion to dismiss had run twenty-five pages.

"Mr. Rutledge asserted in his claim," Ailes said, "that my client caused widespread addiction, along with many other ills in this world, because of their having *lawfully* distributed medicinal opioid products."

Ailes shook his head and looked over at Jake disparagingly. That was enough in the way of dramatics to bring the judge's glasses down over his nose again.

"That allegation cannot be proven," said Ailes, "but let's say for the sake of argument that their claim *could* be proven. There still is no case because there is no cause of action under West Virginia law.

"Further, the plaintiff's claim implies that my client is somehow responsible for the drugs after they are distributed. I don't think we have to remind this court that the defendant is in the business of health care, and not law enforcement. As such, my client is not empowered, nor does it have any legal duty, to provide any form of law enforcement in regard to the products marketed, nor is it encouraged to do so.

"The claim also states that my client should have foreseen the consequences that would result from its having distributed these drugs. If it please the court, health care companies are not in the psychic business. Not only is MHC innocent of malfeasance, it is also innocent of anything that could be characterized as negligence. What the McQueen Health Corporation does is simple to understand, even if Mr. Rutledge misses the obvious. It distributes a product designed to improve the lives of people suffering from pain. What the rest of the world does with that product after MHC has lawfully circulated it is beyond its control."

The judge began impatiently tapping his index finger; there was something gavel-like about his action, but Ailes pretended to ignore the tapping and continued speaking.

"Also, Your Honor, contrary to what this young man hints at in his complaint, my client can't tell doctors who they should be writing prescriptions for, or for how many pills. That is the responsibility of physicians; it is not the responsibility of my client."

Ailes looked over at Jake and did some more head shaking. "And yet the plaintiff's pleading insists that MHC, an exemplary health care science firm, is guilty of a number of ludicrous assertions. Because of those outrageous claims, which go so far as to allege criminal conduct, we intend to bring personal and professional sanctions against Mr. Rutledge. Specifically, it is our goal to seek monetary sanctions, as well as bar sanctions that should result in his suspension and/or disbarment."

"Objection," said Paul, rising to his feet.

Judge Perry nodded. "I get it, Mr. Vogel. There is no need to argue."

He motioned for Paul to sit down, but the lawyer remained standing. Turning his gaze to Nathan Ailes, it was Paul's turn to shake his head. "Before this case is over, Mr. Ailes, it will be my goal to make sure that it won't only be a civil jury hearing the facts of this case. For today, though, I would advise you to focus on the business of this proceeding."

Judge Perry barely tapped his gavel, but that was enough to command complete silence.

"Lecturing lawyers is *my* job, Mr. Vogel. Now, be seated."

Paul nodded contritely, said, "I am sorry, Your Honor," and took a seat. Even Jake could see, though, that Judge Perry's mild admonition spoke volumes. The consensus of the court, he was sure, was that Nathan Ailes was an asshole.

"It is also my job to determine the facts of this case," said the judge. "And I will make it clear for the record, Mr. Ailes, that nothing I saw in the plaintiff's pleading would merit sanctions."

Jake let out a little sigh of relief that only Paul heard.

Judge Perry turned his gaze to Ailes. "Although you have had the floor for some time, Mr. Ailes," he said, "I have yet to hear anything that wasn't already detailed in your lengthy written response to the original plaintiff's pleading and its subsequent amendments. Do you have anything new, some novel argument, perhaps, with which to acquaint me?"

"No, Your Honor," said Ailes.

"Then rather than waste any more time," said Judge Perry, "I will commence with my own questioning."

For more than an hour, Judge Perry grilled the lawyers. As he'd been coached, Jake stuck to his script, reiterating the law governing motions to dismiss. Whenever the opportunity presented itself, Jake also provided damning information against the defendants.

When Judge Perry's direct questioning ended, he asked Jake what his helicopter view of the case would be if the litigation were allowed to proceed. Jake had hoped for a question of that sort. It was why he'd spent so many hours standing in front of a mirror and talking into a microphone. Now was his chance to shine.

"Judge Perry," said Jake, "in his brief, as well as in open court, Mr. Ailes stated that none of the consequences from the opioid epidemic were *foreseeable*. He said that the manufacturers and distributors of opioids had no way of knowing the drugs they were selling by the billions would be overprescribed by doctors. That they could never have predicted that gangsters would move in, and that so-called pill mills—medical establishments that allowed doctors to write countless prescriptions to anyone wanting opioids—would simply become the middlemen for street pushers. And over and over again, Mr. Ailes insists that none of this is MHC's problem, and that they had no legal duty to do anything except distribute pills and make a profit.

"Let's accept that supposition. Let's say at the onset of MHC's distribution of opioids that the consequences *were* unforeseeable. We'll take them at their word for that first year, and even the second year, when their profits were only in the two hundred-million-dollar range. Let's even throw in that third year as well. What then, though? After that time, it's absolutely inconceivable that Mr. Ailes's client didn't know exactly what was going on. From the documents I presented the court, you can see that in the first year of opioid sales in the small county of Wayne, West Virginia, only five thousand opioid pills were sold to a population of twenty thousand people. However, four years later, more than *eight million* opioid pills were sold in a calendar year in that same small county. To paraphrase Shakespeare, 'Something is rotten in West Virginia.' How can such a small population be taking so many pills every single day? That wasn't just good marketing, Judge. That was legalized and reckless drug peddling."

Nathan Ailes jumped to his feet. "Objection, Your Honor." Ailes wagged his index finger as if he were poking holes in the air. "Haven't we heard enough rabid conjecture? This wannabe lawyer is impugning the good name of my client and making them sound like gangsters. His wild speculation is turning this whole proceeding into a circus."

"And that would make me the ringmaster, would it not, Mr. Ailes?" Judge Perry's little smile belied the hardness of his gaze. "Since that is the case, I would suggest you tread carefully on your high wire. Now, please have a seat. And Mr. Rutledge, let's finish up."

"Yes, sir. I haven't even yet addressed the matter of corporate profits. Between year one and year four, MHC's profits skyrocketed from one hundred million dollars to well over two billion dollars. And though MHC is the largest distributor, there are two other Fortune 25 companies making similar profits. And these same results have occurred in small counties all over West Virginia.

"Your Honor, if you allow this case to proceed, we intend to pursue a host of claims against MHC and its ilk, where we will provide data showing how these companies were complicit in creating the opioid epidemic. The figures are irrefutable. What is also irrefutable is that the three major drug distribution companies were well aware of what was going on. Every day their own employees were witness to droves of West Virginians lined up first thing in the morning in front of the pill mills they helped create. These pill mills would never even have existed if not for the corporate pushers who supplied them."

Unseen to anyone but Jake, Paul made a cutting motion with his hand. Jake had more than made his point.

"Thank you, Judge," said Jake.

He took a seat next to Paul. Although he did his best not to smile, Jake wasn't sure if he succeeded. Making his case in a courtroom was everything he'd hoped it would be . . . and more.

Judge Perry turned to the defendant's table. "Mr. Ailes, I've heard from you already, but I will give you exactly two minutes to respond to Mr. Rutledge."

Ailes stood up. He put two fingers on his ear and pretended to be hearing something. "Is that an ambulance I hear?" he asked. "Because if it is, Mr. Rutledge might consider trying to chase it down, as it seems that's the kind of indiscriminate finger-pointing law he wants to practice. Mr. Rutledge continually claims this so-called epidemic was foreseeable, even though he hasn't shown that to be the case. The health corporation I represent has no legal duty other than to deliver its products according to the drug distribution laws of both the federal government and the state of West Virginia. It complied with those laws while at the same time delivering a product that brought relief to individuals suffering debilitating pain. Given those facts, I am hoping you won't encourage the opposing lawyers. If it comes to it, in the long run they will not prevail."

Ailes used all ten of his dancing digits to make his point. Jake found his waving hands incredibly annoying.

"It's time to shut this little garden party down," said Judge Perry. "Thank you, one and all, for your contributions in this matter. Please know that I'll take everything under advisement and have an order out to you in a timely fashion."

The judge rose from his bench, then disappeared through the door behind him.

The defense team quickly followed suit. Studiously ignoring Jake and Paul, they filed out of the courtroom, their noses held high as if trying to avoid smelling something base and disgusting.

5

TIME TO COWBOY UP

It had been a long time since Jake could leisurely sip his morning cup of coffee. He was actually sitting down at an old vinyl padded dining table that had been in his family for as long as he could remember. For once, his laptop wasn't on. It wasn't as if he was taking a morning off work, but he wasn't doing three things while gulping down a cup of coffee. The respite would be brief, Jake knew. He was already thinking about what needed to be done.

His cell phone sounded. Before answering, he looked at the display and saw that Paul Vogel was calling, which brought a smile to his face. He knew Paul was responding to the email sent out that morning from the district court in Ohio, which informed them that they had prevailed against MHC's motion to dismiss for a second time. The courts in both West Virginia and Ohio had given the green light for their lawsuit to proceed.

"Good morning, Paul."

"And it *is* a good morning for the young barrister, isn't it? Congratulations, Clarence Darrow! Are you celebrating with champagne?"

"Instant black coffee," said Jake. "Maybe I'll splurge and pick up some milk today. But I'd like to offer a toast to you with my imaginary glass of champagne."

"I'm all ears."

"Okay, then: To West Virginia's best trial lawyer, who somehow managed to prevent me from making too many stupid mistakes."

"I didn't want you to get disbarred on my watch," said Paul.

"I think Jazz Hands was hoping he could provoke me enough for that to happen."

Jake and Paul had taken to calling Nathan Ailes "Jazz Hands" after he'd used his fingers a second time to enumerate the ten reasons why the case should be dismissed. Even in front of a different judge, Ailes and his ten fingers hadn't had any better luck.

"I expect you'll be hearing from Jazz Hands in the next day or two," said Paul. "Despite all his noise and posturing about this being a minor nuisance suit, I'm sure he'll make some kind of inadequate and insulting offer to settle the case out of court."

"Good luck with that."

"If he makes the offer in person," said Paul, "right after you tell him 'Hell no,' you ought to close with the jazz hands."

Jake laughed. "How about I just wave goodbye to him?"

"That lacks the drama of all ten digits," said Paul.

"All right," said Jake, "I'm all in." After a moment, he added, "I'm hoping you are, too. I've been giving a lot of thought to what you said about litigating this case like it should be done. I know you're right when you say it will be outrageously expensive."

"I believe I said outrageously and prohibitively expensive," said Paul. "The other side will make sure of that. They've got the deep, deep pockets. You don't."

"And because of that, I know you still think I should join forces with a big firm."

"Not just any big firm," said Paul. "You need a firm that has a history of not being afraid of a tap-out kind of brawl against mega corporations and all the resources they bring; it has to be a firm with lawyers who don't blink first."

"What if I can deliver that, Paul? What if I can get one of the best firms to join us in this case? Would you help see the case all the way to the end if I could deliver that?"

There was a long silence on the telephone line. Jake held his breath while waiting for a reply.

"When you came to me, Jake," Paul said, "I didn't tell you that I was already more than familiar with the opioid problem our state was experiencing. In fact, I was friends with, and an unofficial adviser to, the former state attorney general who tried to crack down on the proliferation of opioids. That made him the enemy of Big Pharma, and when it came election time, they put a big bull's-eye on his back and poured money into the coffers of the candidate running against him. Long story short, my friend was voted out of office, and the new attorney general is a pathetic puppet for the drug companies.

"That's when I got involved with politics on the local level and started talking to county commissioners so that I could get some idea about the trail of carnage left by opioids. In the county where I live, there are around one hundred and fifty overdoses every week. The fallout has been enormous. Because of that, for the last three years my firm has been helping financially to shine a light on the fact that the pill bottle has become even more dangerous than the crack pipe."

"Why didn't you ever tell me that?" said Jake.

"I wanted to get to know you first," said Paul. "I'm selective about who I go to war with. Let me point out that when we first met, you were a very young lawyer who showed up in my office with an idea that most people would have thought was crazy. Now you're looking crazy like a fox."

"I sure hope you're implying what I think you are."

"My firm doesn't have the resources to go up against this industry alone," said Paul, "but if you find the right legal warriors to help you out with this, then I'm all in."

"I already know what firm I want," said Jake.

"Tell me they don't carry alligator briefcases and wear Armani suits."

Jake chuckled. "That would be a deal breaker."

After Paul hung up, Jake felt better than he had in a long time. His mentor was *in*, as long as Jake landed his fish. Jake's thoughts turned to Blake. In his absence, any victory felt bittersweet. *You put me on this path, brother,* he thought, *but I'm afraid we still have a long way to go in our journey.* In some ways Jake felt as if he'd traveled far. But he was still living in the same rundown home, barely getting by, with a nonexistent personal life. That didn't matter, though. There were lots of people like Blake out there who needed him to succeed, and that meant he had to pull a rabbit out of a hat. No, not a rabbit. Something much bigger. Something with sharp teeth. Less than five minutes later, after writing out a little script, Jake was making the call.

He took a few deep breaths to steady himself. The law firm of Bergman/Deketomis was located in Spanish Trace, a coastal city on the Florida Panhandle. Jake knew they were one of the most successful personal injury law firms in the country, and that they'd collected somewhere in the vicinity of $5 billion in jury verdicts and settlements. They were big-time, and Jake needed them.

"Thank you for calling Bergman/Deketomis," said the receptionist. "Where may I direct your call?"

"Nick Deketomis, please," said Jake.

"One moment, please."

Jake's heart pounded in his chest while he sat on hold listening to Euge Groove blast away on his sax. The jazz buildup proved anticlimactic; the next person who came on the line wasn't Nick Deketomis.

"Nick Deketomis's office. This is Diana Fernandez. How may I help you?"

"I'd like to speak to Mr. Deketomis," said Jake.

"Who is calling?"

"My name is Jake Rutledge, ma'am."

"And what is this regarding, Mr. Rutledge?"

Jake realized that Diana was the gatekeeper. Unless you had Nick Deketomis's private number, there was likely no getting around his assistant. He looked at his short script, then set it aside and took his chance.

"Thank you for asking, Diana," he said. "It's about Zombieland."

"Zombieland?" she said.

"That's correct, ma'am."

Not hiding her amusement, she asked, "Is that one word or two?"

"One word, ma'am."

"Anything else?"

"Well, Diana, I'd appreciate your mentioning that I'm a lawyer in West Virginia. I'll give you my cell phone number. Please tell Mr. Deketomis he can call me day or night."

The whirlwind that was Nicholas Stavros Deketomis—known by most as Deke—stopped by Diana's desk to collect his messages. Deke was always juggling multiple cases. "Look," he said into his cell phone, "the figures don't lie. The glyphosates—they use cause cancer. That's the only explanation for all the cancer cases springing up in garden-ers and agricultural workers and groundskeepers." Deke listened to the other speaker for a few moments, shook his head, and then said, "That dog don't hunt." He went on to rattle off statistics about the many cancers attributed to the herbicide in question, a product man-ufactured by one of the largest agrochemical companies in the world.

That was Deke through and through. He looked professional in his tailored suit but would have been more at home in a rolled-up flannel shirt and jeans. Deke spoke in a folksy, unhurried way. There was no artifice to him. That was why juries liked him and opposing lawyers hated him. To use his own words, when it came down to the clinches, Deke was "tougher than a two-dollar steak."

He finished the call and turned to Diana. "That man doesn't know whether to check his ass or scratch his watch," he said.

Diana laughed. She'd heard all his sayings in the many years they'd worked together, but he never failed to make her laugh.

She reached for Deke's messages, anticipating his extended hand a moment before he stretched it her way. Even though Diana logged all calls into a computer file, Deke was old school and preferred to have his calls written out on message pads. The pile she handed him was more than an inch thick.

"Did I ever tell you that you're the best thing since sliced bread?" Deke asked.

"Not for at least an hour."

"Shame on me," said Deke, tipping an imaginary hat.

He headed into his office, then a minute later buzzed Diana on the intercom.

"What is Zombieland?" he asked.

"I believe it's a Woody Harrelson film," she said. "I think Mila Kunis was in it as well. In my humble opinion, it was a B minus or C plus."

"So this"—Deke paused to find the name on the message pad—"this Jake Rutledge called me to talk movies?"

"No, I didn't get that impression. Mr. Rutledge said he's a lawyer in West Virginia."

"This is a teaser," Deke said.

"What's a teaser?" asked Diana.

"It's a tactic to get someone to call you back," he said. "When I was a young lawyer, I used to use teasers all the time."

"Mr. Rutledge did sound exuberantly youthful."

"His teaser isn't going to work that easily," said Deke. "I'll need to find out more about him."

"He sounded like a polite young man."

"That's a good reason to not call him back. I'm sure he wants something."

"He used my first name several times during our conversation," said Diana. "I deal with some people who have never used my first name, and I've been taking their messages for a decade or more."

"He's probably raising money for some politician."

"In West Virginia?"

"Call me skeptical," said Deke.

"I thought you said teasers were an old tactic of yours."

In the sanctity of his office, and out of sight of Diana, Deke smiled. There had been a time when his name hadn't opened doors or gotten him any callbacks. His teasers had been one of his first successful techniques for getting people to take notice of his name.

Deke called out, loud enough so that Diana could hear without the intercom, "I'll bet you he calls again within the hour, and I'll bet he has a brand-new kind of bait."

He looked at his watch and was sure Diana was looking at hers. She liked to remind him when he was wrong. But he was pretty sure about his time frame. It was his spot-on reads of people, as much as anything, that had helped him succeed in his career and his life.

An hour later, Deke walked out of his office, looked at the message Diana was writing, and said, "I told you he'd rise to the challenge."

Jake Rutledge had called back, as Deke had predicted, and he'd also offered up another come-on. But Diana wasn't about to credit Deke's gift of prophecy. "If you'd have just called him back the first time, he wouldn't have had to call back."

"But I wouldn't have gotten a look at his alternate strategy if I'd done that," said Deke. "And I wouldn't have been able to join in his cat-and-mouse game. The truth is, he's managed to get my interest."

Diana couldn't help but notice the smile on Deke's face. "Interesting message," she said. "And he was very specific about it. Tell Mr. Deketomis, 'Cowboy up.'"

"Cagey character," said Deke.

"Excuse me?"

"I mean that in all sincerity. This kid has promise."

"In what way?"

"His new pitch was a clever way of telling me he's done his homework. I kind of like him already."

"Then I think you should call him," said Diana.

"I think I will."

When Jake answered his cell phone, Deke didn't offer any pleasantries. He entered the conversation in trial-lawyer mode.

"Okay, you win," he said. "What is Zombieland?"

"Visit me in West Virginia and I'll show you Zombieland. I'll be your tour guide."

"You're not answering my question."

"Some things need to be seen. And you need to see Zombieland, Mr. Deketomis. My hometown has become Zombieland, but there are thousands of other towns just like Oakley. Big corporations created these drug addicts—these zombies. And now these towns are struggling to stay alive."

"Opioids," guessed Deke.

"Poison dope," said Jake. "It's now our national nightmare."

"Agreed. But how do you intend to make that into a lawsuit?"

"That's what the defendants I've sued—I started with the biggest corporate drug distributor, and now I've upped the ante to include the biggest three—have been doing their best to argue. They've tried to shoot me down not once, but twice, in West Virginia and Ohio. And guess what? Two incredibly conservative federal judges sided with me, and both times have allowed my cases to continue. So to answer your question, Mr. Deketomis, I don't *intend* to create a lawsuit. I already *have* created a lawsuit."

Deke covered the phone with his hand. He didn't want the kid to hear him laughing. Then he called out to Diana and said, "I want you to listen in on this conversation."

With Diana on the line, Deke said, "Our firm has no doubt crossed paths with the defendants you've sued, so I already have a pretty good idea about what you have to do to get where you want to go. Who are you representing?"

"I convinced county commissions in West Virginia and Ohio to let me represent their interests in an action against the biggest three Fortune 50 pharmaceutical companies."

"You must be a good salesman."

"It's easy when you're selling the truth."

"If only that were true," said Deke. "Okay, Mr. Rutledge, what's your case? Just give me the quick CliffsNotes version."

"These defendants targeted communities like mine. First, they laid the groundwork by creating a myth that they had revolutionized the way that both acute and chronic pain could be safely and nonaddictively treated. They did that with deceptive literature created by the best doctors Big Pharma money could buy, as well as doctored-up clinical studies put together by highly paid physicians and scientists. Those efforts made it appear that their specific kind of opioid wasn't addictive. By the time this information was debunked, they had a ten-year foothold. Doctors all over the country believed their fantasy science and began liberally prescribing opioids. But once people's addictions got out of control, they began having to turn to less ethical doctors—pill mills. And because the pills were so easy to get, people started reselling them on the black market to make money. The pharmaceutical companies kept feeding the demand far beyond what anyone could have thought was being legitimately sold. What most people miss about this case is that both federal criminal statutes and state criminal statutes specifically required these companies to have a distribution review program to prevent excess numbers of narcotic opioids from reaching the market. But here's the kicker—the industry itself was the only gatekeeper. It should come as no surprise, then, that they turned a blind eye to all the abuses going on. These so-called gatekeepers created an all-out cash-cow criminal enterprise. It wasn't only that they didn't monitor or restrict their legalized dope; they failed to intervene and correct problems of systemic addiction as they were required by law. That resulted in their knowingly and intentionally opening up the floodgates and selling as much as ten thousand percent more drugs than what they were legislatively permitted to sell. I know that individuals wearing three-thousand-dollar Brioni suits don't look like bottom-feeding drug pushers, Mr. Deketomis, but that's exactly what they are."

Toward the end of Jake's impassioned talk, Diana had positioned herself so she could be seen by Deke. She offered a big thumbs-up and an enthusiastic nod. Deke shrugged, pretending to be unconvinced, but what he'd heard made him as impressed as Diana.

"At this point, I imagine you've been exposed to their three-monkey defense," said Deke.

"Haven't I?" said Jake. "See no evil, hear no evil, and speak no evil. Their counsel swears they couldn't see anything that looked like a problem, says they never heard anything that sounded like a problem, and now are unwilling to declare they created a problem."

"And how have you responded to all of that?" asked Deke.

"I've told them that monkeys don't hunt."

This time Deke wasn't the only one who had to cover up the phone to hide his laughter. Diana did the same. Both of them knew Jake was paraphrasing Deke's old standard of "That dog don't hunt."

"Cowboy up," he said to Jake. "Tell me about that particular message."

"I'd rather hear it from you," said Jake. "As I understand it, you weren't much older than I was when you helped take on Big Tobacco. Everyone said there was no way you and that team of lawyers you were working with could win that case, but that didn't seem to faze you or your partners. I wrote a paper about you at WVU and used you as an example when I wrote about innovation in the practice of law."

"It's gettin' kinda thick in here," said Deke.

"How about I produce that paper for you?" Jake said. "In it, I quoted what you told all the lawyers in your firm. You said, 'We all cowboy up or we all go home.' What they didn't know at the time was that you were focusing on one particular cowboy."

Deke was beginning to think the kid might actually have written that paper.

"Before you put a former Marlboro Man on the stand," said Jake, "you showed commercials of him that had aired, footage of him roping cattle and working the range and smoking his cigarette, and looking like the rugged all-American man. And then a dozen years after that ad campaign had run, you called that honest-to-goodness cowboy as a witness. Everyone saw how the Marlboro Man was now skeletal and sickly and wasting away with emphysema. You shocked the world with a different connotation of the Marlboro Man."

"I'm flattered you remembered that," said Deke, "but these days, that's ancient history."

"I couldn't disagree more," said Jake. "It was a landmark case with all sorts of legal innovations. And now it's more relevant than ever because there are so many parallels between Big Tobacco and Big Pharma. There is one major difference, though. With tobacco, it takes most people thirty years to die; with opioids, it usually happens within five years."

Deke felt something stirring in him. His plate was full, and he had more work than he wanted to handle, but the kid reminded him of what it meant to be a young trial lawyer on a mission. Deke liked to go "all in" with every case he worked, but nothing had ever motivated him as much as going to war against Big Tobacco. He'd known how important that case was, and that successfully pulling it off meant saving millions of lives. This opioid case, he realized, had the same kind of life-and-death consequences.

"I'm just guessing," Deke said, "but it sounds to me like you might have a personal stake in this fight. "What is it?"

"My twin brother, Blake, was an opioid addict who overdosed and died."

Deke sighed and then said, "Sorry."

"Thanks."

This conversation hadn't played out as Deke had expected. He'd thought he would listen to an eager young lawyer's pitch and then politely tell him that he would find someone to help him, but that he and his firm would have to take a pass.

Deke considered his too-many commitments and said, "Tell you what, why don't you send me some of the information you have on your cases and what you're hoping Bergman/Deketomis can do to help."

"No," said Jake.

The kid surprised him again. Deke had thought he'd be delighted that he would even consider his proposal.

"Excuse me?" said Deke.

"I know how busy you are, Mr. Deketomis, but once you see what I'm talking about, you'll be as moved to action as you were in the tobacco wars. This isn't something that can be put off till next week or next month. Nearly one hundred and seventy thousand people will die this year, all because of Wall Street's corporate greed."

"I've been a lawyer for many years, Mr. Rutledge," said Deke. "During that time, I've learned the old axiom is right: Act in haste, repent in leisure."

"That old axiom will kill a lot of people," said Jake.

From outside his office, Deke could hear Diana's intake of breath. By the sound of it, she approved of the kid's not backing down an inch. Deke found himself nodding in approval even though his answer remained guarded. "I'll think about what you've told me," he said, "but right now all I can do is promise you that I will get back to you very soon."

"Thank you for taking my call, Mr. Deketomis," said Jake. He wasn't completely successful in hiding his disappointment.

Right after their call ended, Deke punched in the extension for Carol Morris, the head of Safety and Security and Investigative Services for Bergman/Deketomis.

"I'm still waiting on the chemical results," she said, assuming that he was calling about the weed-killer case they were working on.

"I've got something else to put on your plate. I'd like you to do a background check on Jake Rutledge. He's a West Virginia lawyer who hails from the town of Oakley. I don't want anything extensive; just give it an hour and tell me whatever you can."

"Will do," she said.

"I just finished talking with Mr. Rutledge," Deke said. "He called the town of Oakley 'Zombieland.' I'd like to take a look at this Zombieland firsthand. And I'm thinking the best way to do that is for you to schedule me a ride-along with the local cops up there."

"For when?"

"Tomorrow afternoon. And I don't want to be touring a place called Zombieland by myself. Can I have Bennie Stokes for all of tomorrow?"

Bennie was part of Carol's investigative staff. He also acted as bodyguard when needed. The full-blooded Seminole Indian had played football at Florida State, and few people were as intimidating in person. Unless provoked, Bennie was a mild-mannered family man. Still, even the flesh-eating kind of zombies might think twice about trying to take Bennie on.

"I'll arrange that," said Carol.

"Thanks," said Deke. "And I'd appreciate it if you could call Bennie and tell him we'll be flying out midmorning."

Deke hung up the phone and decided it was time to take a walk. He exited his office and casually strolled over to Diana's desk.

She looked up from the monitor, smiled, and said, "I told you he was persuasive."

Diana was a second-generation Cuban; her parents had fled the Castro regime in the sixties.

"It's your fault," Deke said.

"Is that so?"

Diana had been organizing Deke's life for most of her adult life. She was his efficiency expert. On her watch, nothing fell through the cracks.

"Yes," he said. "You were the one who insisted that I call the kid."

"Even *you* thought his 'Cowboy up' pitch was clever."

"Too clever by half."

"I'd call that a good thing," Diana said.

"Good thing or not, come tomorrow it's wheels-up for West Virginia."

"Tomorrow?" she said.

Deke nodded. "Good luck clearing my calendar. What do I have? Seven appointments?"

"I think it's nine," she said. Despite that, Diana was smiling.

So was Deke. His juices were flowing. This case already had him revved up. He always had a gut feeling about cases that compelled him to get involved. The kid had sure gotten his attention.

"Sounds like a good day to play hooky," he said, even though both of them knew he'd be doing anything but that.

"Should I offer an explanation when I'm rescheduling your appointments?"

"Sure," said Deke. "Tell them the last time you saw me I was on my way to a place called Zombieland."

6
SPECIAL DELIVERY

Jake spent the evening second-guessing himself. Instead of trying to ingratiate himself with Nick Deketomis, he'd essentially challenged him.

"I need to know you're all in," Jake had said. Even now he cringed at his temerity. He could have welcomed the opportunity to arouse Deketomis's interest and then done his best to get the lawyer to commit to visiting him in West Virginia. But no, what he'd done was challenge him to an all-or-nothing proposition.

Nick Deketomis had been the youngest lawyer ever inducted into the Trial Lawyers Hall of Fame. He probably had forgotten more about the law than Jake ever knew.

Tomorrow I need to call him up and apologize, thought Jake. *I need to tell him that I thought over his words and am willing to accept his terms.* But the idea of saying those words roiled Jake's stomach. The truth of the matter was that he would need a committed Nick Deketomis and the resources of his law firm in order to win.

Mr. Deketomis had told Jake that he would call back very soon. But what if his definition of *very soon* was a month from now? There was no way Jake could remain on tenterhooks for that long. The wait was already agonizing, and only hours had passed.

The sound of a car pulling into the gravel driveway surprised him. He wasn't expecting anyone, and Oakley was no longer a place where you welcomed surprise visitors at night.

Jake pulled up a shade and looked out into the darkness. There was enough light for him to make out two men in suits, one white and one black, getting out of a late-model sedan. Jake's first impression was that the men were federal agents, but even with the less-than-optimal light, he changed his mind. The suits looked tailored, the men wearing them not so much. They were big and muscled and deliberate. The black man was carrying a briefcase.

Stepping away from the light and into the shadows, Jake tried to hide from any prying eyes. From his front door he heard knocking. Instead of going to the door, Jake waited. "Mr. Rutledge?" called a voice. "We know you're inside. We're here with a delivery."

"Who sent you?" Jake called.

"A friend wanted you to have a gift. But you'll need to sign for it."

"What is it?"

"I'm not at liberty to say. And I'm not comfortable conducting business on your doorstep talking through a door."

If the two men had wanted to break in, thought Jake, they could have already. He went to the door and unlatched the dead bolt. Both men smiled—or gave their best attempt at it—as they came inside. Their frowns were part of their faces and seemed to have been formed by a gravity not easily overcome.

"Mr. Rutledge," said the white man, "today is your lucky day."

"You two don't look like you're from Publisher's Clearinghouse," said Jake.

His visitors tried to laugh, but that exercise was even less successful than finding their smiles.

"Not exactly," said the black man, "but that's not to say you haven't won a grand prize."

"What kind of prize are you talking about?"

"The contents inside this briefcase," he said, extending it toward Jake.

Instead of taking the case, Jake said, "What's inside?"

It was the white man's turn to speak: "A whole lot of Benjamins. They add up to one hundred and twenty-five thousand dollars. And if you sign some paperwork, you'll receive a second briefcase within the next ten days."

"So altogether we're talking about a quarter of a million dollars," said Jake.

The men nodded; their sneers looked more at home on their faces. Greed was something they understood. Offering bribes was part of their everyday handiwork.

The briefcase was still outstretched, waiting for Jake to take it. That much money would help launch him into a real law practice. And for a few fleeting seconds, Jake couldn't help but consider everything he could do with a quarter of a million dollars. He could get an office with a copy machine, and maybe even a secretary. And with that kind of cushion, he could do lots of pro bono work. Jake thought of a favorite quote of his from St. Francis of Assisi, who'd said, "All the darkness in the world cannot extinguish the light of a single candle." Jake could be that light in Oakley and beyond.

"What paperwork do I have to sign?" he asked.

There was a momentary consultation of eyes, and then the black man opened his mouth to speak. Everything about the men was in sync. They spoke with the same low voice and had the same hard, brown eyes. The men were of similar height and weight, although one had been cut from black granite, and the other, white.

"Basically, it's a contract which says that you agree to not pursue the lawsuits you filed in West Virginia and Ohio, now or in the future."

"Game over," Jake said, mostly to himself. "So I'm supposed to just walk away and disappear?"

"No," said the white man, "you're supposed to walk away a rich man."

His partner added, "Of course, these earnings are never to be discussed, and part of your paperwork is signing a nondisclosure agreement to that effect."

"Why the unorthodox method of payment?" asked Jake. "Why not a company check?"

"That could be arranged, if you prefer," the white man said, "but it would not be to your advantage. Since you're working on a contingency fee, the lion's share of any settlement money would go to the counties that you represent. The paltry amount you'd be left with would be subject to taxes. By giving you the money this way, we protect your best interests."

"A quarter of a million dollars, with no questions asked?"

The two men nodded.

"I guess it's a no-brainer, then, isn't it?"

Knowing smirks reappeared.

"But then there's that pesky contract I have to sign," said Jake.

"You'll see in the paperwork that there's a promise of confidentiality for both parties," said the white thug.

"Will I be provided a copy of that contract?"

"The money you receive now and the cash you receive in ten days should serve as all the paperwork you'll ever need," he said.

"Take the money and run, is that it?"

"Much better than that. You don't have to run. You can stay put and thrive right here in your little town."

"Stay put in Oakley?" said Jake.

"Why not?" said the man.

The veneer of pleasantness in Jake's voice vanished as he unleashed all that had been building inside of him. This was the living room of his family home. This was where he and his brother had grown up. He thought of Blake, and how he'd died. These two men actually thought he would take their bribe.

"Why not? Well, for starters, I'm thinking it would be much more rewarding for me to build a case that results in the creeps you're working for getting indicted. Tell them if they think that's far-fetched, they can revisit the many civil court cases that have historically ended with criminal prosecutions. And to that end, tell them I'll happily be a witness for the prosecution." Jake pointed a finger from one man to the other. "I'd be remiss in not asking your names so that I can offer them up during my testimony."

The extended briefcase was retracted. Unsurprisingly, neither man offered his name. Their expressions didn't change; they appeared unfazed by Jake's rejection.

"You're under no obligation to take the money," said the white man, "although it's the safest thing to do—on a purely personal level."

"I assume your use of the word *safest* constitutes a veiled threat?" said Jake.

"It's just a word," he said. His smile said otherwise.

"So, what'll happen when I see you the next time?" asked Jake.

"Since you seem to be a man of great imagination, we'll leave that to your speculation."

"Tell you what," said Jake, "I'm using that imagination to envision both of you standing in front of a police lineup."

"Enough talk," said the black man. "Either accept the payment or say bye-bye to your easy money."

Jake shook his head. "Like good old Ralph Waldo Emerson said, 'Money often costs too much.' And easy money costs even more. You can tell your bosses that's what will put them in prison before this is all over."

The black man turned to his partner and said, "We're done here."

"I'm wondering something," said Jake. "Did your bosses tell you anything about my brother? Did they mention he got hooked on the poison they helped put out on the street? And did they tell you he died from that poison?"

The black man tucked the briefcase against his side. "You'll wish you'd taken the money," he said.

"Like we give a shit about your junkie brother," said the white guy. "Good riddance, I say."

He kissed his hand and blew it Jake's way. "Can't wait to see you again, son."

Equal parts valor and stupidity propelled Jake forward. He took a swing at the white guy, a move both his opponents were waiting for. They were counterpunching before Jake's blow ever landed; he was hit just to the side of his right eye with one fist, and to his stomach with the other. Slamming into the floor felt like a third blow.

His mouth opened, but no air seemed to be traveling to his lungs. The wind had been knocked out of him. What made everything worse was the sensation that he was going to be sick, but he lacked the air to even throw up. Jake could do nothing but flop around on the floor.

Getting to one knee took a lot of gasping. Inch by painful inch, Jake fought his way to his feet. Putting a steadying hand on the sofa, he was able to take a faltering step toward the door, and then another. He propped himself up on the door, leaned on the front-door handle, and then found the strength to turn it.

As he feared, there was no sign of a car, and no license plate to write down. The two men were long gone.

7

ABANDON ALL HOPE

The flight by private jet from Florida to West Virginia took only two hours. Deke used that time to read up on what was being called the "Epidemic of Despair." Opioids had been able to do something that even AIDS and wars hadn't—beginning in 2015, American life expectancy had actually declined. Drug-related overdoses were now responsible for 2 percent of annual deaths, with most of the victims in their twenties.

Being aware of the opioid epidemic was one thing; digesting the frightening statistics associated with it was quite another. But maybe that was the problem. In the courtroom, as in life, large numbers were difficult to envision. Deke was only too aware of the saying that the death of one person is a tragedy, while the death of thousands is a statistic. Nationwide, there were almost one hundred million people taking prescription painkillers. An estimated ninety thousand of them were dying every year. During the long and protracted Vietnam War, the United States had suffered a total of fifty-eight thousand fatalities. It was as though the U.S. were losing a war—this time, the war on drugs—all over again each year.

Those numbers weren't likely to change for the better anytime soon. As far as Deke could determine, the opioid epidemic was like a hydra—you struck one head off and two more surfaced. Whenever a pill mill was shut down, heroin pushers moved in. In fact, the heroin epidemic was referred to as "the tail" of the opioid epidemic. Attempting opioid withdrawal was potentially a death sentence, with the risk of seizures and cardiac failure, so for most addicts, there was little choice but to stay hooked.

The sound of wheels being lowered on the Cessna Citation Excel made Deke stop reading. Below him he could see the West Virginia landscape drawing ever closer. He looked across to the other seat and saw that the noise hadn't yet roused Bennie, who was fully reclined in his leather chair. Bennie's mouth was open, and he was lightly snoring.

If I had three kids under the age of ten, Deke thought, *I'd probably be doing the same thing.* Deke's two children were pretty much grown. His son was in college, and his daughter was a lawyer who worked for his firm.

"Hey, Sleeping Beauty," he said, "it's time to wake up. We're about to land."

Bennie opened his eyes, stretched, and then brought his seat to an upright position.

"You must have the cleanest conscience of anyone I know," Deke said.

"Why do you say that?" asked Bennie.

"The sleep of the just always overcomes you within five minutes of our taking off."

"I hate to say it," Bennie said, "but I sleep a lot better on business trips than I do at home. Of course, I know better than to tell my wife that. She thinks these business trips must be miserable for me. If she hears about how well I sleep when I'm away, she'd probably insist on going on a girl's weekend while I look after the kids."

"Your secret is safe with me," said Deke. Bennie's wife was about half his size, but she definitely ruled the roost.

"I've never been to West Virginia," said Bennie. "What about you?"

"I tried a few environmental cases here years ago. After one victory, I made the mistake of celebrating with some West Virginia moonshine. Boy, did that have a kick."

"Cleared your sinuses?" asked Bennie.

"It pretty much blew off the top of my head."

A welcome committee awaited Deke and Bennie on the tarmac. Two uniformed sheriff's deputies approached; the older one, with thinning salt-and-pepper hair, took the lead. "Mr. Deketomis and Mr. Stokes? I'm Todd Poole from the Seneca County Sheriff's Department."

Deke extended his hand. Bennie's huge mitt followed. Then the fourth man joined in the pressing of hands. "Jackson McCrumb," he said. The deputy was about thirty, with a bantam strut that was offset by his quick smile.

"Good flight?" asked McCrumb.

"My friend slept through it," said Deke, "even though we had to deal with a bit of turbulence."

"That's what comes with flying anywhere near the Appalachians," said Poole.

He pronounced the mountain range *Ap-uh-latch-uns.*

"I hope you notice how he pronounced that, Bennie," said Deke. "I'm told the fastest way to lose a case in this part of the woods is to mispronounce *Ap-uh-latch-uh.*"

"For a Yankee," said Poole, "that pronunciation sounds pretty good."

"That's the first time I've ever been called a Yankee," said Deke. "Usually my Florida Panhandle accent gets me categorized as a cracker."

"Anyone who's not from around here is a Yankee," said McCrumb.

"We're at your disposal, gentlemen," said Poole. "My orders from above are to take you to wherever you want to go. Deputy McCrumb is from these parts, so he'll be able to give you local insights that I can't. We'll be driving in a state trooper vehicle that was especially selected since we were told that Bennie was about as big as—"

"The Ap-uh-latch-uhs," Bennie said.

Everyone laughed, and Poole said, "Yeah, just about that big."

The four men walked over to a black-and-white Chevrolet Tahoe. Once again Deke found himself indebted to Carol Morris and her extensive list of contacts. People who didn't know Carol were always surprised to find that the grandmother of two was the lead investigator and head of security for Bergman/Deketomis. Before joining the firm, Carol had been both a cop and a private investigator. Law enforcement is typically a haven for macho men; Carol's femininity and brains had always proved much more of an asset than brute force. With all her contacts, Carol was always able to smooth the way for Deke.

"We appreciate your hospitality," said Deke. "If you don't mind, we'd like Deputy McCrumb to take us to Zombieland."

McCrumb's brows rose. "Never thought I'd hear visitors make that request. That's like asking to go to a war zone." He got behind the wheel. "Y'all better buckle up."

They were five minutes into the drive, and everyone was beginning to get comfortable with one another, when Poole said, "I know these parts, but not nearly as well as Deputy McCrumb does. Still, we're not exactly touring one of the Seven Wonders of the World. Is there anything in particular you want to see when we get to Zombieland?"

"I'm not sure I'll know what I want to see until I see it," said Deke. "But what I'm looking for is how the opioid epidemic is impacting, and has impacted, your state."

Poole did some nodding and thinking, and then said, "You ever see how blight hits the trees in a forest?"

Deke and Bennie nodded.

"Well, that's just how it is," Poole said. "In the forest you see a few dying trees, and then you see a few more. Then it's like there's this whole patch of forest that's dying. And before long the rot is more common than not. Sometimes parts of the forest try and resist—you hope they'll be able to hold out, but that doesn't usually happen. Eventually the contagion overwhelms everything."

"How do you stop the blight?" asked Deke.

"I assume we're talking about the human blight now," Poole said. "Lord knows, there are no easy answers. Like trying to put toothpaste back in the tube."

McCrumb turned the black-and-white at a sign that said OAKLEY TOWNSHIP PARK. As they followed a road that led toward playing fields, Deke looked to his right and left at the bucolic setting. There were walking down paths lined with trees.

"Nice-looking park, isn't it?" said McCrumb. "Look closer."

Deke and Bennie looked around them, trying to see what the deputy was talking about.

"If the two of you were wearing boots," McCrumb said, "I'd consider taking you on a walk. You'd get my point then, probably all too literally. The thoughtful junkies toss their needles into the trash cans. The bad-off ones don't give a shit and leave them everywhere. You get stuck, you run the risk of AIDS or hepatitis A, B, or C."

"I'd hate to pick my poison," Deke said.

"Me, too," said McCrumb. "Disposing of needles in these parts has become a major health hazard. Junkies flush needles down their toilets. In the past year, the sewage system has had to be shut down twice because they clog up the pipes."

He steered the black-and-white into a parking lot, and its presence didn't go unnoticed. Two of the six vehicles turned on their engines and started to pull away, clearly seeking to avoid a run-in with the law.

"Do you want me to light them up?" asked McCrumb.

Poole shook his head. "If they were aware enough to notice us, they've probably already stashed their drugs out of sight."

They made a circle through the parking lot, getting a good look at the empty baseball field.

"Are the sports fields still used?" asked Deke.

McCrumb shook his head. "Night games are a thing of the past. The fields still get some use on the weekends, but not before a safety committee clears them for play. Needles," he added.

"Last year the softball league disbanded after more than twenty years of play," Poole said.

To the casual observer, Deke thought, the park looked like any other in the U.S. That's what made the hidden tragedy so insidious.

"Next stop, Dresden," said McCrumb, swinging the car toward the main road.

"Where's Dresden?" asked Deke. "Or *what's* Dresden?"

"One of the old-timers around here came up with that name," said Poole. "You ever hear about the firebombing of Dresden during World War II?"

"I saw some pictures in a history book," said Bennie. "It was like seeing the aftermath of a nuclear blast."

"No bombs in our little Dresden," McCrumb said, "but it's been just as ravaged."

The area of Oakley known as Dresden consisted of around fifty houses. Perhaps half the residences were still occupied, but it was hard to tell—Dresden was dark even in the light of day. Fires had blackened the walls of several homes. There was no pride of ownership; there was no pride at all.

"Ten years ago, it was a pretty nice place to live," said McCrumb. "But around five years ago, almost all the families that were holding on here gave up. Now you have the squatters. That's why everything looks so dirty. There's no gas or propane deliveries, so people cook with wood and coal."

Dogs barked at the SUV; most of them had ribs showing. Dresden was even more overrun with feral cats. Sickly eyes of green and yellow looked out from behind piles of trash and from under rotting porches. Deke wondered if the scrutiny of the almost-wild animals made the other men feel uneasy as well.

The deputy slowed the car down. An older man in a faded green John Deere cap was walking toward them.

"Here comes Victory," said McCrumb.

The nickname, Deke was sure, was a result of the way the man held up his index and middle fingers, almost in a victory sign. When the man spoke, though, the reason for the pose became obvious.

"Got a cigarette?" Victory asked.

"None of us smoke," said McCrumb.

That didn't deter Victory, or maybe it just didn't register with him. "Got a cigarette?" he repeated.

"No," said McCrumb. "How are things going, Victory?"

"Got some money for a Vietnam vet?"

"Victory wasn't born until the late sixties," McCrumb advised. "I think either '68 or '69."

With a start, Deke realized he was about the same age as Victory, though the man looked at least twenty years older.

"And since the Vietnam war ended in 1975," said McCrumb, "you can do your own math as to Victory's military service. I'm sure that claim's helped you get a little more money when you beg on corners, hasn't it?"

"Got a dollar?" Victory asked.

Even without a cigarette in them, his fingers rose to his mouth. Not finding the fix they were looking for, they detoured to scratch his facial hair.

"I know he'll just use it for drugs," Deke said, "but I'd still like to give him something."

"Go ahead," McCrumb said. "A couple times a month he catches me in a weak moment, and I do the same, even though I know what he's using the money for."

Deke extended a five-dollar bill; it disappeared in a sleight of hand worthy of a magician. Victory apparently didn't want anyone to see he had money.

"God bless you," he said, the words rote—zombielike.

Then he asked, "Got a cigarette?"

As they drove away, Deke heard how things used to be in Oakley, how things were now, and how it appeared things were going to be. Neither of the cops was optimistic.

"It's this vicious cycle," said Poole. "It started when the economy, and the community, was down. Doctors began prescribing opioids like they were candy, for treating everything from pain to the dismals."

"No shortage of people with the dismals," McCrumb said. "But then that's always been the case. What's different is suddenly there was a pill for it."

"Jobs disappeared, the economy got worse, and our little Zombieland began to take form," McCrumb said. "A doctor would set up shop, run an all-cash operation, and never spend more than five minutes with any patient. It was howdy-do and here's your prescription."

"Is the pill mill still in operation?" asked Deke.

"Not that one," said McCrumb. "Operated long enough to get about half the town hooked; then it closed its doors, and the heroin pushers moved in. But there's another town exactly like ours just a hoot and a holler from here."

Poole translated the phrase with a smile: "That's about two miles. If it was a 'fur piece,' it would be maybe five miles, and 'over yonder' is less than a mile."

"What's the source of the pills?" asked Deke.

Poole shook his head. "The magic question. Straight from the manufacturer, but no one seems to point a finger at those corporate distributors supplying these doctors."

"Is anything getting better?" asked Deke.

The two cops looked at each other, and then they both shook their heads.

"There's a saying in these parts," McCrumb said. "We started out with nothing, and we've still got every bit of it. I'm thinking maybe we should now say we've got less than nothing."

"What do you mean by that?" asked Deke.

It was Poole who fielded the question. "Take little Dresden, for example. Used to be there were homeowners and businesses who took care of their property and paid property taxes. When the drug blight hit and the area was abandoned, it was a blow to the town's economy. And the double whammy was all the new expenses associated with drugs that hit the town and county. It seems like every week we're having to remove children from the homes of addicted parents. Then there's ambulance services, hospital costs. You think it's expensive to run a township? What's expensive is the *disintegration* of that township."

"Welcome to the world of the Native people," said Bennie. "Alcohol and drugs took away our way of life. The poison took over the world around us. We've been dealing with the vicious cycle you speak of for the last century, until despair has become all but institutionalized. Now the white nan is joining us in this hell."

"Dante wrote a pretty good book about the inferno I'm seeing here," said Deke.

Abandon all hope, he thought, *ye who enter here.*

The squawk box sounded, and McCrumb listened intently to the dispatch. He picked up the transmitter and offered a short response.

"Got an overdose," he said.

He turned on the red-and-blue light show and hit the gas.

8
TRANCE AND DANCE

The house stank of human neglect. There were plates with old, moldy food, and the ground was littered with trash. But Deke couldn't take his eyes off the surreal dancing girl.

She was moving to music that only she heard. He wasn't sure if she was actually dancing, or if she was trying to keep her balance in slow motion. She swayed and dipped, raised herself, and then swayed and dipped. She reminded him of a Gumby toy, twisting like her limbs weren't flesh and sinew and bone.

Across the floor, Deputy McCrumb and another deputy were trying to revive an unresponsive male who was naked except for a WVU T-shirt. McCrumb said something to the other deputy and shook his head. Then he raised himself up, sighed, and rejoined Deke and Bennie. Poole was out in the car—left unattended, it would have been a magnet for junkies to try and break into.

"Is he going to make it?" asked Deke.

"It's not looking good for Shotgun," said McCrumb, "but Lazarus—that's what we call Deputy Lawrence—has raised more junkies from the dead than the rest of us put together."

"And Shotgun?" asked Deke.

McCrumb glanced toward where his fellow deputy was working on the unresponsive man. "I don't know his real name. Everyone around here calls him Shotgun because of the way he liked to shotgun a beer. Then he learned that he preferred heroin."

"So what's Lazarus's secret?" asked Deke.

"Naloxone," McCrumb said, "whether by injection, nasal spray, dermal pads, or any and all of the above. Whatever it takes, Lazarus knows how to kick-start a heart."

Deke had read about naloxone, a drug more commonly referred to as Narcan. When administered in time, it blocked the effects of the opioids. To date, it was the only known antidote that was effective in combating opioid overdose.

"These days it seems like we're being called out on overdose cases more than anything else," said McCrumb. "Last week I was working a shift and had to administer four separate naloxone blasts."

"Why is there water all over the floor?" asked Bennie.

"Half an hour ago that water was ice," said McCrumb. "Junkie cure. His friends forced ice cubes up his rectum because they were convinced that would reverse his overdosing."

Deke and Bennie exchanged a glance. "You're not pulling our chains, are you?" Bennie asked.

McCrumb wearily gestured toward the water on the floor. "Exhibit A." Then he pointed to a pair of pants nearby. "Exhibit B. And if you want to get close enough to Shotgun to see his inflamed red ass, that's Exhibit C. I suppose Exhibit D would be the anonymous caller who phoned this in, and how all of Shotgun's junkie friends have disappeared from this shooting gallery."

"Deke, I got to go outside and get some air," said Bennie.

"I'll be joining you in a minute," Deke said, noticing that his bodyguard was looking pea-soup green.

Then again, thought Deke, *I'm probably not looking any better.* His gaze shifted from the ongoing saga of life and death, to the dancing woman.

"What's her story?" he asked.

The young woman was still swaying, her movements sloth-like. The thick makeup around her eyes gave her the appearance of a raccoon, especially when her eyes were closed.

"One of the nicknames for Fentanyl is 'Dance Fever,'" said McCrumb. "When Coco uses, she starts doing her shuffle. I've seen it in a lot of women who use."

McCrumb turned toward the dancer. "How are you doing, Coco?" he asked.

Coco continued her swaying, not acknowledging the deputy.

"Trance and dance, we call it," said McCrumb. "In ten minutes or so, she'll start coming out of it. Then she'll probably try and run away from the crime scene."

"How old is she?" asked Deke.

"Eighteen or nineteen," he said.

"I've seen enough," said Deke.

"I wish I could say the same," said McCrumb.

When Jake saw the name on his cell phone display, his grip on the phone involuntarily tightened. For the last twenty-four hours he'd been agonizing over whether he should call Nick Deketomis to apologize, or just wait to hear from him. Paul had advised him to sit tight, saying it wouldn't be wise to enter into a potential business relationship from a position of weakness, but it had taken all of Jake's willpower to not make that call.

"Mr. Deketomis," he said, doing his best to sound calm, "I'm so glad you called."

Instead of picking up where the two of them had left off, Deke surprised Jake by saying, "I've been sitting here trying to remember the name of that diner you were so keen about."

"You mean Mom's?" Jake asked.

Jake heard part of Deke's exchange with another man—he thought he heard the man say, "Fifteen minutes"—but he couldn't figure out what was going on.

"How soon can you get to Mom's?" asked Deke.

"Twenty, thirty minutes," said Jake, suddenly making sense of the situation, as hard as it was to believe. "Are you saying that you're in West Virginia, Mr. Deketomis?"

"I am. And I'll be flying out two hours from now. What would you like me to order you from Mom's?"

"I'd like the chicken-fried steak with gravy," said Jake, "and a side order of ramps. They sprang up all over the state just in time for your visit."

"Very hospitable of them. I'll see you soon, Jake," Deke said, and he clicked off.

Jake arrived at the restaurant just before his order did. Even now he was in a state of shock. Yesterday he'd been trying to talk Nick Deketomis into visiting West Virginia, and today the lawyer was here. For Jake, that was even better than Santa Claus coming to town.

He opened the faded red entrance door and walked into Mom's. The diner smelled of all the comfort food it had been serving for almost seventy-five years. The old wooden flooring, uneven in a few spots, groaned under Jake's shoes. He walked by the chalkboard that listed the day's specials. Today there were two entries: *Meatloaf* and *Ramps*!

All the seats at the counter were taken, as were most of its twelve tables. Jake scanned the faces of those there and paused at a table where he saw a familiar face. Edward "Paint" Dunn— so-called because his name made people think of Dunn-Edwards paints—was the sheriff's deputy who had been called out to the scene of his brother's overdose. Dunn hadn't provided many insights into Blake's death and had seemed wholly unconvinced that Oakley's opioid problem might be worse than anywhere else. Jake remembered he'd begun thinking of him not as "Paint" but as "Whitewash."

Dunn's attention seemed focused on the conversation at a table across from where he was sitting. There were four men at that table. Jake recognized sheriff's deputy McCrumb, who worked Oakley and the surrounding area of Seneca County. There was an older man in uniform Jake didn't know, and sitting across from him was perhaps the biggest human being Jake had ever seen.

The fourth man at the table was Nick Deketomis. He was sipping coffee and looked at ease with both the company and the surroundings. The lawyer was dressed casually. He had on jeans, boots, a faded green linen shirt, and a brown leather jacket.

Deke must have felt eyes on him; he looked up and then acknowledged Jake with a smile. With his coffee cup, he motioned to the empty seat next to him.

Jake made his way over to the table. Deke was already up on his feet before Jake could tell him to stay seated. To the other men, Jake said, "Please keep your seats."

He shook hands with Deke and said, "It's an honor."

"Likewise," said Deke.

And to Jake's ears, it sounded like the other man meant it. The two of them sat down.

"This is Jake Rutledge," said Deke.

While the hand shaking and introductions went on at the table, Deke said, "Yesterday I talked to Jake for the first time. I remember that one minute I was telling him that over the next month I'd carve out some time and take a look into two cases he was working, and then the next minute I was being told by him that wasn't good enough and that I needed to get to West Virginia ASAP. I'm pretty sure Jake is a heck of a fisherman. There I was in Florida, like a big old largemouth bass squatting down in the depths, and Jake knew just what bait it would take to get me to rise up and bite."

The men at the table laughed, and so did Jake. But then he passed a sheaf of papers over to Deke and said, "I wish I was the fisherman you think I am, Mr. Deketomis. But as you can see, sometimes there's just no improving on telling the truth."

Deke looked at the cover page and shook his head. "Forgive me, Jake, for doubting you."

He held up the law-school paper for all at the table to see. The title was *Nick Deketomis: LEGAL INNOVATOR*.

Deke flipped to the back of the paper and saw the circled red *A*. He winked his approval to Jake, but to the rest of the table, he said, "How Jake wrote a ten-page paper from a subject that should have merited a sentence or two at most, I'll never know."

Along with everyone else, Jake smiled. At the same time, he recognized a pattern to Deke's self-deprecating nature that put people around him at ease, including himself.

By the time the food arrived, table talk had touched on everything from deer hunting in West Virginia ("Best in the U.S.," according to McCrumb), to the state's many underground waterfalls, to ghost stories (in particular, the "ghost girl" who was said to walk Fifth Street Road in Huntington). Service at Mom's wasn't exactly prompt, but Jake could tell that the others at the table thought the wait was well worth it. As for Jake, his stomach was too tied up to enjoy the food. He was desperate to find out if Deke had come to any decision as to whether he and his firm would be joining Jake in his action.

At any other time, Jake would have enjoyed Deke's company. The lawyer was a natural raconteur and had everyone laughing throughout the meal, but Jake would have actually preferred talking business.

When all their plates had been cleared, Deke leaned back in his chair and shook his head thoughtfully. Then he turned and looked at Jake, catching the younger lawyer's eye. Jake wondered if this was the moment of truth.

"I must admit," said Deke, "that when Jake told me the name of this restaurant, I was more than skeptical. You see, I try to abide by Nelson Algren's three rules of life. Algren said you never play cards with a man called Doc, you never sleep with a woman with more troubles than your own, and you never eat at a place called Mom's."

Jake found himself holding his breath. Did Deke approve of his restaurant choice? Did he approve of his case? The man's face looked pensive, and for a moment Jake feared the worst, but that was before Deke winked at him and smiled.

"Now I'm pretty sure Algren was right about his first two rules of life," said Deke, "but I've decided to revisit my lifelong bias against restaurants called Mom's. The food here has proved to be just as good as young Jake Rutledge said it was."

Jake joined in the table's laughter. The smile of approval told Jake everything he needed to know. Nick Deketomis was in.

9
THE HOMECOMING QUEEN

Anna Fowler stepped outside onto the porch and inhaled deeply. When she let out the pent-up air, it was cool enough that her breath was marked by a condensation trail. She looked around, taking in the night sky. Seeing the North Star, she recited:

> "Star light, star bright,
> First star I see tonight,
> I wish I may, I wish I might,
> Have this wish I wish tonight."

The wish that followed was as simple as it was heartfelt: *I want something good to happen in my life, something to get me out of my rut, something that puts me on a positive path.*

She was reminded of another Starry Night that had occurred ten years before. Starry Night had been the theme for Midway High School's homecoming dance. The ceiling of the school's gymnasium had been adorned with reflective spray-paint stars. In the darkness, they had glistened and glittered like real stars.

It had been the best night of Anna's life. She remembered how a spotlight had penetrated the darkness, with the light moving from one side of the gym to the other, until its beam had found her and Blake Rutledge. The two of them, the homecoming queen and king, had walked arm in arm. Everyone in the gym had applauded as they made their way out onto the dance floor. Her classmates had thought that she and Blake looked like the perfect couple, and no one could understand why the two of them weren't more than friends. What Anna had never told anyone was that she carried a secret torch for Blake's shyer and much more studious brother, Jake.

Still, homecoming was a magical night. Anna thought back to the song the royal couple had danced to: Lady Gaga's "Poker Face." That had been one of the most popular songs her senior year. When it came to the line "Russian Roulette is not the same without a gun," she'd pretended to spin a cylinder and put a gun to her head.

Everyone had laughed when she did that, including Blake. It had seemed funny back then. Now Anna knew better. You didn't need a gun to play Russian roulette. There were other games just as deadly, other ways to kill yourself.

Even though it was cold out, she didn't want to go back inside. Anna had always thought that by the time she was thirty she'd be a wife and a mother and have a career. As much as she'd cared for Blake in high school, she'd known he wasn't the one she would ever marry. He'd always been devoted to Oakley, while her plan had been to become a dental hygienist and move to a big city in Ohio or Pennsylvania. She was supposed to have gotten away from this town, but here she still was.

It wasn't her fault, though. After graduating from high school, she'd moved away and had been sharing a two-bedroom apartment with three other girls also enrolled in the Sinclair Community College dental hygiene program in Dayton, Ohio. She remembered how she and her roommates had all felt so grown up. But then she got the call that changed everything. Her mother had been diagnosed with lung cancer. Her family was counting on her to come home and help with her mother's care. That was the traditional role of the oldest girl, after all.

When Anna agreed to come home, the understanding was that it would be for just a few months. After her mother got better, the plan was for Anna to return to school. But her mother never got better, just wasted away slowly. Anna remembered how her mother never complained, even though it seemed so unfair that she was the one with lung cancer. Her mother was a nonsmoker; it was Anna's father whose chain-smoking habit ended up killing his wife.

And ended up killing Anna's dreams.

Her mother's drawn-out death should have released Anna from her familial bondage, but three days after her mother was buried, her father had a debilitating stroke. Even now, he only had limited mobility. Once again, it had fallen to Anna to look after a sick and aging parent. What made it even harder this second time around was that no one expected her father to ever get better. It was just a matter of time—his and hers.

Anna knew how frustrated and depressed her father was. Even before his stroke, he'd been living with a partially ruptured disc in his spine that he refused to have repaired. Because of his constant pain, he'd started drinking heavily. Anna was never sure whether his refusal to have surgery was so he could justify his own heavy drinking, or whether it was a self-imposed penance for the death of his wife.

There had been a time when Fowler's Service Station was a respected business in the heart of Oakley. Anna had even worked in the small, attached convenience store throughout high school. For a while, her father had continued to operate the business, but as his health declined, so did his work. Business went from bad to worse, and Anna's proud, independent father turned into a bitter alcoholic. That's what Gary Fowler now was—an alcoholic. Anna had warned her father that his drinking was going to kill him.

"Let's hope that's sooner rather than later," he'd replied.

When he'd said that, Anna hadn't argued. As terrible as it was, that was exactly what she'd been thinking—and perhaps wishing.

Diseases of despair, she thought. So many deaths in Appalachia were the result of what those in the medical and mental health fields called diseases of despair.

Anna tried not to be bitter, but here she was in the prime of her life doing something she didn't want to do. Her siblings were of little help. Her brother, Tim, was in the army, and her younger sister, Lynn, lived in Maryland with three little ones under the age of six who took all her time.

The glamorous life of a homecoming queen, Anna thought with a sigh. She began shivering from the cold but still resisted going inside. Once more, she looked to the stars. What she really wished was to be the same girl she was ten years ago.

I wish I could be that innocent again, she thought.

Jake Rutledge probably thought she still was. She'd thought about him often since she'd run into him at the cemetery. Standing there, talking about Blake, she'd felt like a hypocrite. Even though she and Blake hadn't spoken much since she'd moved back to town, she'd seen him often enough to know what he was going through. She'd feared Jake would see the same signs in her, and so she'd hurried to wrap up their conversation and get away before he noticed anything.

Earlier in the year, a snake had slithered into the garden. No, that wasn't quite right, thought Anna. She had *welcomed* the snake into the garden. Her father had slipped and didn't have the strength to get up off the floor by himself. When Anna had pulled him to his feet, her own back had given out. She'd learned the hard way that bad backs ran in the family.

It was a shame she hadn't learned another lesson from her father or Blake Rutledge: that it was all too easy to become dependent on drugs.

Anna had decided to forgo the expense of a doctor and medicate herself. In Oakley, it was easy to get pain pills. She'd taken a couple for relief, and then a couple more. In the beginning she had tried to limit herself to one in the morning and one at night, but she'd been increasingly unsuccessful. Upping the dosage was the only thing that made her feel better. Still, she continued to convince herself that she wasn't hooked, like so many other people she knew. The pills eased both her pain and her worries, but Anna kept telling herself they didn't have the hold on her that they had on others. *I can give them up,* she thought, *whenever I want to.* At the same time, Anna didn't like to admit that there were times during the day when she found herself thinking about the relief the pills brought. The snake told her things would be better if she just took one, its whispers growing louder and louder until she succumbed to its hissing and took another pill.

Her back was long recovered now, but she had never put away the pills. There was a time when she'd been certain that after her father's death she'd return to school, but now she wondered if she'd be stuck in Oakley forever.

She offered up one last wish to the stars: *Don't let the snake deny me my dreams.*

❖❖❖

Anna checked in on her father before leaving for work the next morning. "Here's a bologna sandwich for you, Dad," she said, putting a plate down on her father's nightstand.

"I don't want any damn bologna sandwich," he said.

His speech was much improved from when he'd first had his stroke. There were some days when Anna wondered if that was a good thing. From what she could determine, his mental faculties were as sharp as ever. If anything, his memory might be *too* good. He'd caught Anna in a few fibs when it came to her explaining the sometimes-slurred speech and slow reactions that came from taking the pills. That's why a recent visit from sheriff's deputy Dunn had come as a surprise to her. Supposedly her father hadn't filed some paperwork that pertained to their family business, or he had overlooked paying some bill. Of course, her father insisted that the government was wrong and he was right. For him, that was the end of the subject. Anna wouldn't be surprised if his heavy drinking was finally catching up to him.

"You might be hungry later," she said, leaving the plate of food where it was.

"Where you going?" he demanded.

"You know very well I'm going to work," she said. "I'll be modeling for Mr. Smith."

"Mr. Smith," her father said in a mocking voice. "I hear your Mr. Smith is painting a bunch of filth nowadays. You'll be taking your clothes off for him, won't you?"

"Dad," Anna said, "you know his work isn't like that."

She wished that were true. When she'd first gotten the job modeling three days a week, she'd loved her work. Clint Smith was renowned in the region for his bucolic rural images. The fifty-five-year-old artist had painted the world he knew very well. Initially, Clint had been a hobby painter while working his small farm. His success had freed him to paint full-time, which he'd done for the past quarter century. Anna's favorite painting of his was one where he'd had her model atop a haystack in blue jeans and a white blouse. She'd been looking up at the clouds while chewing on a piece of hay. (It had sold for a lot of money, she'd been told.) But the job had changed, along with the artist's motifs. His bucolic images had morphed into what Clint called *phantasmagorias*. He liked to say a phantasmagoria was like a dreamscape, but to Anna they looked more like nightmares.

"Uh-huh," said her father. "Well, before you go, get me a beer."

"It's ten o'clock in the morning."

"I know what time it is."

"Our rule is you don't start drinking until noon at the earliest. I am not getting you a beer, Daddy. If it's that important to you, then you'll have to get it on your own." Trading one vice for another hadn't improved his temper. Her father had finally quit smoking after the damage to her mother had been done, and now he sucked on a bottle instead of on a cigarette. It was his liver taking the abuse instead of his lungs.

Her father grumbled something, but Anna chose not to hear it. She would be late for work if the two of them got into an argument. Modeling might not pay much, but it was the only spending money she had.

Clint's farmhouse was a fifteen-minute drive from downtown Oakley. His family had been tobacco farmers. In fact, Clint's studio had been converted from an old barn formerly used to cure tobacco. On warm days in particular, Anna was sometimes able to catch a scent of leaf tobacco wafting down from the rafters. It was almost like being able to sniff a memory—a reminder of how their forebears had been able to endure. That meant *they* could as well.

When Anna had first entered Clint's studio, he'd almost been persnickety about the way everything was set up. Even though it was a barn, he'd laid down oilcloths before setting up his easel. His paints were carefully laid out, along with his brushes. Anna had never known that brushes came in so many shapes and sizes—some were used for broad strokes; others were very fine. As messy as the work could be, the studio was neat and tidy. There had even been times when Clint had joked about getting "ready for surgery," usually while putting on his latex gloves right before painting.

Anna had enjoyed her first two years of modeling, but this third year hadn't been going well. Clint had lost much of his discipline and had let things slip in both his personal and professional lives. There had been a time when he was a stickler about setting up her work schedule so that he could get the lighting he wanted. But now he didn't seem to care much about the lighting. His brushes were no longer as carefully cleaned, and he often wore the same clothes several days in a row.

Anna suspected the cause of his transformation, not only in personality but in subject matter. It was the cause of so much other torment in and around Oakley. Clint had been dealing with severe arthritis for years. His joints were sometimes so inflamed and sensitive that it was difficult for him to hold his brushes, let alone make the exacting strokes his craft often called for. The menthol fragrance of the BENGAY he rubbed into his hands usually greeted Anna when she arrived at work, but one day it wasn't there.

The cure, Anna was convinced, was worse than the disease. His pain had seemed to rein Clint in. He had worked in a very orderly fashion. In the absence of pain, he had lost his structure. Clint tried to explain his altered persona by saying that he was going through a new artistic phase. Sometimes, especially when his painting wasn't materializing as he'd hoped, he'd offer up angry explanations.

"You can't always do the same old shit," he'd rail. "Look at Picasso. He had at least ten different periods. One day he was a cubist, and then he was a surrealist, and then a Postimpressionist. He had his Blue periods and Rose periods and African periods. An artist has to evolve."

Evolve or devolve? Anna was afraid it was the latter.

She drove up the gravel driveway and parked her father's truck next to the old tobacco curing barn. She saw smoke rising up out of a vent and was glad that Clint had been organized enough to start a fire. These days she was glad to even find him awake. Over the last month, there had been a few days when he'd overslept and arrived late to their sessions.

Before getting out of the truck, she took a deep breath. Clint's ever-more-erratic behavior made her edgy. She hated to think about how much more anxious she would feel if she wasn't being fortified by the OX 20 pill she'd taken an hour earlier.

No, she thought, it was possible she'd taken two. Was it that easy to lose count?

Inside the studio, Clint was staring down into his coffee cup. When he looked up at her, Anna could see that his eyes were bloodshot. In the old days, he used to offer her a cup of coffee. She usually accepted, and the two of them often chatted for a few minutes before getting to work. Today he said, "Well, if it isn't my muse."

Anna wasn't sure if she should smile or not. There was an ugly undertone to his words.

"Speak to me, muse," Clint said.

Was he speaking metaphorically? "Good morning, Clint," she said carefully.

"Strip," he said.

"Strip?"

"Get out of your damn clothes."

When Anna had first started modeling, she'd made it clear that she was a life model and wasn't interested in nude modeling.

But over the past year, he'd increasingly asked her to pose without clothes. Afraid of losing the income, she'd agreed. Only two things made it bearable, though: the pills she took, and Clint's distorted vision of her nude body. He drew naked harpies and succubi and maenads—his personal demons materializing in his paintings. The final images looked nothing like Anna, or at least that's what she wanted to believe.

"Isn't it early—"

He silenced Anna with one word: "Strip."

A voice in her head said, "You should have taken another pill. That way you wouldn't care."

Anna wasn't sure if those were her thoughts . . . or the serpent's.

"How do you want me to pose?" she asked, hoping her voice sounded professional.

"Like a fallen angel," he said. "Like the whore of Babylon."

"I'm not sure what you mean," Anna said.

"You're Eve," Clint said. "You're twined around a tree. A snake has entered your little paradise. He's lowering himself from a branch and whispering his sweet nothings in your ear. And what he's saying sounds good to you."

Anna's heart started pounding. It was just a coincidence, she told herself. There was no way Clint could have known about the serpent in her imagination. Still, the fact that he was even talking about the snake scared her.

"Can you hear his hissing? I know you can, Anna. It's like the buzz of a bee entering the flower and stirring up that pollen, isn't it? The bee wants that nectar. And so does the snake. You can hear it whispering its desires."

Clint's words made sibilant hissing sounds. It was altogether too much like the voice of the snake that tested Anna's limits and tempted her daily—no, hourly. How did he know?

Anna had stripped down to only her panties. Clint was pacing in front of his easel, staring at the canvas. He raised a brush, but the naked canvas seemed to ward off his brush. He picked up his palette and jabbed at the paint, but he still couldn't bring himself to apply that first stroke. He looked up, saw that Anna wasn't completely unclothed, and pointed his brush at her.

"Are you planning to pose sometime this century?" he asked.

Anna hurriedly removed the last of her clothing, but it didn't help his mood.

"You think clothing hides the real you? You think you can walk in here wearing a tiara and acting like a beauty queen and I can't see the real you?"

Was it Clint talking, thought Anna, or the snake? She prayed for the pills to fully kick in so that she wouldn't have to feel any of this. But the pills, Anna knew, were a vicious cycle. To get to the elusive calm she desired required more and more pills.

He raised a brush, but once again the blank canvas seemed to repel his efforts to paint. Furious, Clint turned to Anna, and then closed the space between them.

Anna wasn't sure if she should scream, or even if she was able to scream. Clint's wife, Ruth, rarely came into the studio. She knew that Clint didn't like being disturbed. Would she even hear Anna's screams from the house? Looming over her, Clint plunged his brush at her, jabbing paint over her breasts and torso. His intensity frightened Anna; she froze, afraid to move while he grunted and groaned.

Stroke by stroke, the form of his nightmare materialized on her body. He started with a white base, then added blues, grays, blacks, and reds. By the time he stepped back to view his creation, Anna was trembling so hard she thought she might vomit. Then he pulled out his cell phone and began taking pictures. All the drugs in the world couldn't deliver her from her terror, from the humiliation of being treated like she was nothing more than a canvas. She wondered what monstrous image he had depicted.

Clint stopped taking pictures and returned to his easel. He took up a brush and began painting as if she were no longer in the room. With his attention elsewhere, Anna slowly got to her feet. She shuffled over to a full-length mirror in the corner of the studio and looked at her reflection.

Staring back at her was something not quite human. The black, sunken eyes against the white-and-blue face looked dead, as did the black lips. Around her left breast was the appearance of a deep gash; from her heart it appeared that blood was oozing out.

Anna stepped away from the mirror, afraid of the creature looking back at her. Was that how he saw her? Was that what she had become?

"What is it?" she whispered.

Her question managed to get through to Clint. He looked up from his canvas and pointed his brush at her with a cruel smile.

"What is it?" he said, repeating her question. "It's you."

Anna began sobbing silently. Without removing the paint, she dressed herself and then ran out of the studio.

10

STRANGER IN A STRANGE LAND

Guillermo Flores—whose friends back home called him "Guillo"—had lived and worked in America for almost a year now, but there were times when he wondered if he would ever understand the first thing about this strange land in which he now resided.

The motto of the state of Jalisco, located in the western part of central Mexico, was *Jalisco es Mexico*—"Jalisco is Mexico." So many things that outsiders associated with Mexico originated in Jalisco—mariachi and ranchero music, the sombrero. Even tequila originated in Guillo's home state. Geographically, Jalisco and West Virginia were little more than two thousand miles from each other, but Guillo had come to realize that their cultural divides were immense.

Growing up working on his family's small corn farm had molded Guillo's character and instilled in him a strong work ethic. He had a farmer's patience, and the fortitude to persevere even in the wake of difficult circumstances. The gold that had always interested him most was the golden silk of growing corn. Most people never gave a second glance to dirt. But when Guillo looked at it, he saw potential. That was one of the things he liked about West Virginia. Most of the soil was rich, even though it was full of stones. He would often reach down into the dirt and feel it with his hands, then let the soil spill back from between his fingers. He didn't think much of West Virginia's chilly climate, but the dirt didn't lie. It was capable of producing great things.

Guillo hadn't told many people about his dream for the future. He kept quiet, mostly because he was afraid of jinxing it. When he did open up about his dream, though, he liked to say it had been predestined by his last name. *Flores* meant "flowers" in Spanish. And growing flowers was what Guillo wanted to do. With the proceeds from his West Virginia job, he hoped to return to Jalisco with enough money to buy his own plot of land. He was a man with a plan, and there was a woman who shared his vision. Waiting for his return was his Bella. In Spanish, *bella* means "beautiful," and his eighteen-year-old fiancée was as beautiful as her name.

Under the watchful eye of Bella's *abuela*, her grandma, the two of them had often discussed their dream.

"I will build you a rainbow," Guillo promised, "and every day I will bring you a bouquet of flowers."

"Every day?" asked Bella.

He had nodded. "You will know when the flowers are blooming. The breeze will bring to you their perfumed fragrance. And I will look for just the right flower for you to place behind your ear."

"I would like that," she said.

And sometimes her *abuela* would pretend to look away, and that's when Guillo would kiss Bella.

It was only for his dream, and for Bella, that he was in the U.S. Here, he was making far more money than he ever could in Mexico. In another year or two, he hoped to return home with enough money to buy his plot of land and start his family with Bella.

The ringing of his burner phone interrupted Guillo's daydream. Without even looking at the display, he knew Miguel was calling.

The only calls he ever received, except for wrong numbers, were from his dispatchers. Even though there was no one driving behind him, Guillo pulled over to the side of the road and turned off the engine. He knew the use of a handheld cell phone was illegal in West Virginia, so he didn't want to do anything to catch the eye of the authorities.

The conversation with Miguel was brief. Both of them avoided specifics, speaking in a code that identified another delivery. Miguel was the primary dispatcher for Guillo's territory. In the years he'd lived in West Virginia, Miguel's Mexican-accented English had taken on the same mountain twang heard through much of Appalachia. Like the locals, Miguel said "ain't" instead of "isn't," "bin" instead of "been," and "thar" instead of "there." Guillo remembered how on one occasion his car had been disabled with a dead battery. When he'd called Miguel to advise him of the situation, the dispatcher had suggested Guillo pronounce it *bat-tree* so that the locals would know what he was talking about.

Guillo put away the phone and started the car. He did a lot of driving in his job. Before coming to the U.S., the only vehicle he'd driven was a small tractor. He was clean-cut, had no tattoos, had never used drugs, was a devoted Catholic, and knew nothing about the product he sold. "Jalisco boys" like him were considered the perfect employees by the cartel. They worked hard, were polite, didn't complain, and did as they were told. None of them skimmed from the top or used the product they were selling—after all, the young men didn't only represent themselves; they represented their families back home.

Thus far, Guillo's life in America had been uneventful. He and several other Jalisco boys shared an apartment with blow-up mattresses, futon chairs, and a twenty-five-inch TV with rabbit ears. To improve reception, they wrapped tinfoil around the antenna. Their life consisted of working and sleeping. They kept to themselves.

A black-and-white car came up behind Guillo. *Policía,* he thought, tensing up. The man behind the wheel was familiar to Guillo, a deputy referred to by the Jalisco boys as *Pintar,* or "Paint." Even though the policeman hadn't put the *mordida*—the "bite"— on any of the Jalisco boys, Guillo still didn't feel comfortable. Inside Guillo's mouth, secreted in his cheeks and lower lip, were half a dozen balloons filled with black tar heroin. One of the hardest parts of his job was getting comfortable carrying the balloons that way. At first he'd been afraid of inadvertently swallowing them and had felt like a chipmunk with too many acorns in his mouth, but in less than a week, he'd grown accustomed to carrying the drugs that way. Guillo's mouth grew dry being in the policeman's line of sight. He was under strict orders to swallow the balloons if pulled over by the police.

Guillo offered up a silent prayer as the deputy stayed on his tail. He tried not to keep looking through his rearview mirror, but every few seconds he felt compelled to do so. The deputy was wearing dark glasses. *Pintar* seemed to be enjoying Guillo's unease, but after tailing him for several blocks, the cop sped up and passed him. Guillo sighed in relief. He and the other Jalisco boys had been assured there was an "arrangement" with the local police, but no one really knew this for sure. Guillo did his job with no questions asked.

With the cop now out of sight, Guillo continued with his deliveries.

Vernon Johnson was a regular customer. Guillo wasn't sure what Vernon's "disability" was, but Mr. Johnson often referenced the word. The first time Guillo had gone to Vernon's house, he'd been surprised by all the American flags on display. Now it no longer seemed unusual to him. West Virginians loved flying their American flags.

Mr. Johnson usually greeted him with a big smile and asked, "How are you?" The first time, Guillo had tried to be thoughtful in his answer. After a few more days in West Virginia, he'd realized that no one really expected him to answer that question. In America, smiles didn't necessarily mean a person was being friendly. And though it might seem that Americans were considerate about one another's welfare, most of their questions were just a way of saying "Hello."

For at least twelve hours every day, Guillo delivered balloons of heroin. His customers were always relieved to see him, but Guillo could see that the drugs didn't make them happy. He had always thought people took drugs in order to be happy, but that clearly wasn't so. It almost felt as if he were delivering medicine, and that his customers were treating some kind of fatal sickness. One thing he knew is that they were always relieved to get his deliveries.

It was why Guillo was kept busy, very busy, although he would have been much happier delivering flowers of his own creation.

11

WITH FRIENDS LIKE THESE . . .

Less than a month after Nick Deketomis committed himself and his firm to work with Jake Rutledge and Paul Vogel, the attorneys general for the states of West Virginia and Ohio filed a motion arguing that the small counties that Jake had named in his complaint had no legal right to initiate a lawsuit on behalf of the citizens living in those counties. Their argument was that they alone as state attorneys general had the exclusive standing to sue opioid distributors on behalf of the citizens of Ohio and West Virginia.

Deke didn't know if there was a cause and effect between his firm's coming aboard and the AGs filing their case, but it did seem more than a little coincidental.

"Am I wrong in thinking that what's going on doesn't pass the smell test?" Jake asked soon after the filing. Deke had gotten on a conference call with him and Paul. "I took a look at the case law, and it's almost unheard of for state attorneys general to act in such a way. In fact, you can say it's about as rare as a politician with a real job."

Deke felt sorry for the kid—he was so earnest in wanting to save others from his brother's fate, but he hadn't been practicing long enough to realize that the law wasn't set in stone; it was always being challenged. He tried to lighten up the situation. "It's kind of like this," he said. "In 1986 Ronald Reagan said the ten most terrifying words in the English language were 'I'm from the government, and I'm here to help you.'"

Paul laughed at the gallows humor. Jake still seemed too wound up to relax.

"These state attorneys general are saying, 'This is my ball, and my rules, and we'll play my way or not at all.' The good news—or at least it's not *bad* news—is that the appellate courts in both states are split on whether I have the right to sue without the state attorneys general."

"They'll do their best Bigfoot with the judges," said Paul. "While trying to stomp us into the ground, they'll act like they're the best and the brightest, and they'll say, 'We got this.'"

"And while the two state attorneys general are acting like they're the smartest people in the room," said Deke, "I seriously doubt they'll point out that neither of them has ever tried a real lawsuit in their entire legal careers."

"You're kidding," said Jake.

"Hard as it is to believe," he said, "I am not kidding. And I'm not at all surprised by this maneuver. Why should I be? Both these AGs have had their campaign coffers filled by the same people we're suing. And that's only the start of it. However, you can be assured that in the courtroom we'll get our chance to detail the altogether-too-cozy relationship between Big Pharma and their distributors, and these two state attorneys general."

"You sound like you're looking forward to that," said Jake.

"You are a perceptive young man," Deke said.

Jake started laughing, and Deke thought, *Mission accomplished.*

"Before I start feeling too good about this," Jake said, "don't we need to be worried?"

It was Paul's turn to speak. "We certainly need to prepare," he said. "If they win on their motion, then they win the case."

"And the citizens they're supposed to represent, lose," said Jake. "What's with these attorneys general? What's stopping them from doing the right thing and letting us help their constituents?"

"Some seem to understand that duty," said Deke. "Unfortunately, some AGs look at their position as a stepping-stone to the governor's mansion. And to that end, they do favors for the people who can write them fat campaign checks."

"That sucks," said Jake.

"I can't tell you how many times my firm has put in years of work," said Deke, "only to have some half-wit attorney general come in at the last minute and gum up the works. What really hurts is when they're ready to settle for pennies on the dollar just so they can claim 'victory' on behalf of the people who voted for them. They take a win-win situation and turn it into lose-lose. There have been situations where drug companies have scammed hundreds of millions of dollars from a state's Medicaid program, and when the state AG gets a paltry hundred grand back for the taxpayers, that attorney general acts as if it's a huge accomplishment."

Over his speakerphone, Deke could hear Jake whisper to Paul, "Does that really happen?"

When he didn't hear Paul responding, in his mind's eye Deke could imagine him glumly nodding.

"Welcome to the show," said Deke. "But I don't want you to waste your time worrying about this, Jake. You now have a band of brothers and sisters who have your back."

"If that's the case, I'll take all the brothers, sisters, and even family twice removed, and welcome them all," he said. "And I'd also like to say I feel damn lucky to have you and Paul working this case. With the two of you around, I don't feel like I'm in over my head. Still, I don't feel like I should be the lead on fighting city hall."

"Locking heads with state attorneys general is a dance I'm all too familiar with," said Deke. "Do either one of you have a problem with me taking the lead on this?"

"I'd be happy if you would," said Paul. "This isn't what I would call my bailiwick, or my firm's."

"That sound you just heard was my sigh of relief," said Jake. "Still, what can I do to help you?"

"I'm going to need a short-term apartment rental in Charleston starting tomorrow," Deke said. He started typing out an email to Diana at the same time; there were plans to be made. "It doesn't have to be anything fancy, but I'll need it to be three bedrooms, preferably with a huge master bedroom. I'd like each of us to have our own desk in there. What would work best is if there is room enough left over for a conference table."

"Tomorrow?" said Jake. Deke wasn't one for letting the grass grow under him.

"Yes," he said. "I'll be flying in tomorrow afternoon with two paralegals. Those paralegals will be working full-time on this case, and at least at the onset living in the apartment. Bennie will also be earning frequent-flyer miles helping out with legwork and locating witnesses and the like. For the foreseeable future, I'll be spending half my workweek in West Virginia."

"What else do you need me to do?" asked Jake.

"Start working with my office on putting together the best briefing possible on the issue of standing," Deke said. "The focus needs to be on the constitutional arguments that are on our side. I want our team taking the prior cases where the appellate courts have ruled against the attorneys general in favor of the cities and counties. Study the arguments that were used, and make those positions fit our case."

"Are we going to win this, Mr. Deketomis?" asked Jake.

"Deke," he said. "Mr. Deketomis was my father. And I never sign up to try a case with anything less than an attitude toward winning. And lest you think I'm sounding like a politician, Jake, what I can promise you is we're going to be in one hell of a dustup. We'll be making some noise and having some fun, and all the while we'll be doing the right thing."

"If that's the case," said Jake, "it sounds like we can't lose."

"My point exactly," said Deke. "I'll see you two gentlemen tomorrow."

12

WHISTLER'S WIFE

In West Virginia, few faces were as prominently displayed as Eva Whistler's. She could have been a model if she'd chosen to, but instead she held the high-profile job of prosecuting attorney for Davis County. Her decade-old union with Danny Whistler had brought two prominent old West Virginia families together. And even with her demanding job, she found time to be a mother to her two fine-looking children, a boy and a girl.

Naturally, some were envious of her. In West Virginia, the prosecuting attorney for the county was an elected position, and at the age of thirty-five, Eva was already halfway through her second four-year term. Most were certain that her next elected position would be governor, or maybe U.S. senator. After all, she had won her last PA race with almost 80 percent of the county vote. Still, there were some detractors. Despite Eva's down-home ways—she liked to remind voters that she was "descended from bootleggers"—a few in the media chose to portray her as a "steel magnolia." Being perceived as tough didn't bother Eva—that's what you wanted in a prosecuting attorney. What she didn't like was the nickname of "Mother Whistler," which was what her enemies were now calling her. She pretended to be amused by the name, but the truth was, she detested it.

It was Danny's fault, of course. Her husband was ten years older than she was but still acted like a child. His grandfather had been called "Old King Coal," and had owned and operated some of the biggest coal mines in the state. Not content to live off the family fortune, Danny had set up what he called "skilled nursing facilities" throughout the state. These nursing homes were very profitable—or at least had been because of the way Danny operated them.

There was overcrowding and minimal staffing. Danny tried to get by with a rotating selection of visiting doctors (instead of learning their names, he called the lot of them "Dr. Dopers") who believed in keeping their elderly patients in a drug-induced state. In Danny's facilities, lots of vitamin A (Ativan), vitamin H (Haldol), and vitamin X (Xanax) were prescribed. And looking after the residents were a lot of LPNs, or what Danny called "low-paid nurses."

All had been going well with Danny's empire until Health and Human Resources conducted what was supposed to be a surprise audit of one of his facilities. An hour before the inspection, Danny got tipped off to what was about to occur. He raced over to the facility in Davis County and made a series of frenzied calls. Additional staffing showed up just before the inspectors, and some of the more egregious violations were avoided. What they could put lipstick on, they did. A dozen residents had been conveniently transported to the local hospital for a variety of conditions, but that didn't completely solve the nursing home's overcrowding. Ten residents were shuttled to out-of-the-way storerooms, a desperate attempt to make the facility's overcapacity less obvious. The hope was that the investigators wouldn't insist upon looking into those storerooms.

Unfortunately, they had. The staff stonewalled, pretending to not have the keys, but they couldn't hide the voices calling from inside the storerooms. That was bad enough, but what was worse was that the inspectors found a confused elderly woman in one of the storerooms who repeatedly identified herself as Mrs. June Whistler. And what Mrs. Whistler couldn't understand was why her son, Danny, had ordered her to be taken away on a gurney and then left in a dark closet.

The picture of Danny's eighty-seven-year-old mother being removed from the storeroom, with tears running down her face, became front-page news. Danny's treatment of his mother had made him notorious throughout West Virginia, and Eva couldn't escape the guilt by association. She'd been given the nickname "Mother Whistler." There was even a cartoon that had circulated, which Eva had found particularly hurtful. It was a parody of *American Gothic* in which she had been identified as Mother Whistler; her husband, holding a pitchfork, was Whistler; and her abused-looking mother-in-law had been Photoshopped into the painting in the form of Whistler's Mother. It was Eva's vanity that had been hurt the most. She might have been the mother of two, but she was young and vibrant, and she didn't like being associated with an old, puritanical-looking bat.

The scandal had tarnished the golden couple and hit them hard financially. All of Danny's nursing homes were subjected to new scrutiny. The fines and enforced regulations turned their cash cow into a financial albatross. The lavish lifestyle to which Eva and Danny had grown accustomed was suddenly in danger of vanishing. That was about as acceptable to Eva as being portrayed as Mother Whistler.

Eva's forebears hadn't gotten rich following the law; they'd greatly prospered by violating it. Given her financial straits, Eva made the decision to get back in the old family business in an updated way. While nowadays many of her relatives dressed well and no longer spoke with an Appalachian twang, she still had plenty of kin who were part of the so-called Hillbilly Mafia. Controlling that mountainous turf hadn't been easy when they'd plied their trade as bootleggers. It had required the work of a tough, ruthless family. And now there was a new moonshine in town.

To a large degree, the old network was still in place. Eva knew there was no need to be directly involved in the opioid trade—that was too ham-handed and too risky—but there were other ways to exploit the opioid tragedy that could make her rich beyond reproach. It was Eva's dream to be like the Koch brothers, able to finance one public broadcasting series after another and engender all sorts of goodwill. She knew that by paying off the right people, a predatory robber baron could be magically transformed into a philanthropist. That was her goal . . . and her dream.

Eva's hillbilly kin had once created a vast moonshine distribution network, and it had never completely gone away. Over the years, her relatives had updated its inventory and used its trade routes to distribute meth, crack, molly, and smack. When Eva reached out to her kin, they proved receptive to her ideas. Luckily for her, she was blood. That gave her an entrée she would not otherwise have had. Outsiders would not have been afforded the trust given to her. Eva's relatives were receptive to her ideas about how to best deliver opioids nationwide. The family ramped up its "drive line circuit" between Miami and Chicago—stopping at every pill mill and corrupt pharmacy to buy vikes, oxy, and China Girl—fentanyl. Eva got her cut of the profits by providing her family inside information about law enforcement activities in West Virginia. Her protection allowed them to operate virtually unhindered throughout the state. Best of all, Eva didn't have anything to do with the drugs. Her family rewarded her assistance by "selling" her huge tracts of land for pennies on the dollar. No money ever changed hands. As a further buffer, the property deeds were "negotiated" between her husband and the landowners.

The ends would justify the means. You needed to crack a few eggs to make an omelet—Eva was convinced of that. And every farmer knows you need manure to grow great crops. Yes, the ends would justify the means. Eva would become a patroness of the arts. She would create schools to help the needy. In time she could become the Eva of West Virginia, much like the Eva of Argentina.

The money that was coming in was laundered not only through real estate dealings but through Eva's "Killer B" strategy that involved buying, blight, and bulldozing. They targeted businesses that were struggling in areas hit hard by the opioid epidemic. Danny was the front man. All he had to do was dangle the words *economic redevelopment* to find plenty of takers in hard-hit cities and counties. He worked with government entities willing to condemn properties. It was no coincidence that Danny was often the only person bidding on the blighted property at auction. The bulldozing typically began before the ink dried; once the areas started to recover, the plan was to sell the properties for ten times what they'd paid. What was even better was that laundered money was paying for everything.

At Eva's urging, Danny was also branching out from skilled nursing facilities by setting up drug rehab treatment programs all over West Virginia. These facilities were often erected on the same sites Danny had purchased at condemnation auctions. Vast sums of individual, state, and federal money were being spent on expensive doses of Suboxone, Naltrexone, and methadone, and Danny's staff knew just how to maximize their billing. You were perceived as a good guy, and all the while you were making barrels of money.

Despite her frustrations with Danny, for the most part Eva knew that she and her husband made a good team. With her job as a public guardian, no one was looking over their shoulders, but she didn't want to be lulled into a false sense of security. On a daily basis Eva felt the need to warn Danny that loose lips sink ships. The man whose shortcuts had once almost ruined them financially seemed to have forgotten the past. Danny now strutted about like he was John D. Rockefeller. And even though he was running a rigged game, Danny still seemed to enjoy cutting corners. Whenever she caught him in one of his little schemes, Eva would always lecture him not to kill the golden goose. He acted contrite, but Eva wasn't sure he was listening.

Empire building wasn't easy, but Eva wanted to make her mark as the kind of person who turned dreams into reality, bringing museums and parks to West Virginia communities. One day there would be buildings named after her.

Mother Whistler could never accomplish that, but Eva Whistler could.

13

SPEAKER FOR THE DEAD

Nick "Deke" Deketomis was used to sitting on the plaintiff's side of the courtroom, but for this hearing he was working on the defendant's side. Seated next to Deke was Paul Vogel, and next to him was Jake Rutledge. Though the young lawyer was trying to hide his butterflies, Jake wasn't quite succeeding. For the third time in the last minute, Deke noticed him checking the time on his watch. Deke caught Jake's eye and gave him a confident smile, aiming for a look that said, "I've got this." Jake smiled back.

It wasn't that Deke didn't feel some of those same butterflies. This was a big day for their young case, and they were going up against heavy artillery. The attorneys general for the states of West Virginia and Ohio were trying to derail everything they'd done. It was going to be Deke's job to fight city hall—or state hall, as the case might be.

For Deke, this hearing was showtime. He didn't consider himself an actor, but he knew the importance of delivering lines so that his message was clearly heard and understood.

He casually stretched, and with one long tilt of his head took a measure of those assembled in the main courtroom of the Robert

C. Byrd Courthouse in Charleston, West Virginia. The gallery was almost full and included, he was glad to see, members of the media. Deke had wanted the Fourth Estate present; to his thinking, too many important cases were never reported to the public, resulting in the U.S. citizenry having no idea how their rights were gradually being eroded. On the other side of the courtroom, sitting directly behind the plaintiff's table, were Nathan Ailes and his legal team. Deke wished he was surprised by the sight, but he wasn't. There had been a time when influence peddling was confined to back rooms; nowadays the corporate shills saw no need to stay hidden from sight.

Sitting at the plaintiff's table were the two state attorneys general who were targeting Jake's case. Richard Monger—"Dick" to his friends—was the West Virginia AG. Next to him was Ralph Richards, Ohio's attorney general.

In private, Deke referred to them as the "two Dicks."

Monger was older and heavier and had less hair than the younger Richards, and yet there was something about the two men Deke found similar. It took him a few moments to figure out their common denominator: both men were smug. At the moment, each of them was scanning his phone for messages even though the bailiff had already requested that all electronic devices be turned off. By definition, attorneys general were supposed to be the "people's lawyers" for the citizens of their states. It wouldn't surprise him if Nathan Ailes and his team had prepared all the paperwork and done everything but file the pleadings on behalf of the two attorneys general.

Judge Willard Perry entered the courtroom, and even before the football player–size bailiff had a chance to call out "All rise," Deke and his team were on their feet. The two Dicks, who had to turn off their phones and put them away, were the last to stand. Deke was sure Judge Perry noticed their leisurely ways; the bailiff certainly did. Deke caught his askance look at Monger and guessed that the

AG was not highly regarded within this courtroom. Monger had a reputation as being strong on law and order, but Deke suspected that was more the result of his being strong on public relations than anything else.

After Judge Perry sat down, the bailiff called out, "You may be seated."

The two Dicks were among the first to sit.

Judge Perry wasn't one for wasting time. He lowered his black-rimmed glasses halfway down his nose, which made his dark eyes look as if they were being magnified, and stared at Monger. Deke was glad he wasn't the focus of those orbs.

"Mr. Monger," said the judge, "after reading the motion that you and Mr. Richards filed on behalf of the states of West Virginia and Ohio, I am left to believe your primary conclusion is that I have wasted hundreds of hours of my time paying attention to the opioid litigation that has been in front of me for months. That being the case, I'd like to hear a concise argument vis-à-vis this waste of tax-payer money."

The judge's sarcastic West Virginia French, combined with his baleful demeanor, seemed to throw off both Dicks. Monger started fumbling through some notes, as if hoping to find an answer there.

"Mr. Monger?" asked the judge, motioning for him to come up and speak at the podium. When he didn't immediately get a response, he turned to the man next to Monger. "Mr. Richards?" he asked hopefully.

Monger got to his feet and slowly approached the podium. Once there, he wiped away an imaginary wrinkle in his suit and made a point of standing up straight. Deke always had his researchers compile a profile of his opponents. Apparently, Monger's habit of hunching, combined with his bald head and aquiline nose, had caught the attention of the editorial cartoonist for the *Herald-Dispatch*, who liked to portray Monger as a hungry-looking vulture. Rumor had it that Monger hated the portrayal.

"Your Honor," Monger said, "I hope you were not under the misapprehension that either my office or that of the attorney general of the state of Ohio believes you've wasted your time on this case, or any case. That was certainly not our intent. As you can see in the paperwork you have been provided, the pleadings and arguments filed in each of our states are virtually identical. Because the legal grounds for dismissal is first being heard here in West Virginia pleadings, it was determined that I would be making arguments on behalf of both Ohio and West Virginia. It is our hope that by doing such, we will expedite this proceeding."

A clearly unimpressed Judge Perry said, "The court thanks you for that consideration, Mr. Monger."

Monger winced at the judge's address. Both state attorneys general had been in office long enough to have become accustomed to being addressed as "Mr. Attorney General." Stripping Monger of his title, thought Deke, was akin to removing his armor. When Deke had his chance, he would strip him down even further.

"And since you seem to be so worried about my wasting time," said the judge, "let's cut to the chase. I've carefully read all the pleadings, and there are only two arguments I would like you to elaborate upon.

"In your motion, you contended that this case should not be allowed to go forward, as some six years ago the states of both Ohio and West Virginia came to a settlement agreement with the *manufacturers* of opioids. It is your assertion that this settlement with those manufacturers also covered the *distribution* companies, all the way up to the present day. I'd like to hear the legal grounds for your position."

As the judge spoke, Deke watched Monger's straight posture lose some of its starch. The man's shoulders began hunching forward, and his head lowered; Deke wondered if he was the only one seeing the vulture transformation.

Judge Perry continued speaking: "The second argument I'd like you to address is your contention that your office and that of Mr. Richards have the exclusive right to bring actions such as this one on behalf of Ohio and West Virginia citizens. Some might say that smacks of Big Brother deciding what is best for everyone else. What is the basis of your assertion that no one besides the attorney general's office has the right to bring this kind of legal action?"

The judge's two questions, Deke noticed, seemed to have upset the hornet's nest in the form of Nathan Ailes, his team of three attorneys, and their two paralegals. It was almost as if the judge were presiding over a footrace and had shouted, "Go!" There were searches being conducted on laptops, and frenzied writing was taking place, with notes being hurriedly passed along to Ailes.

While all this was occurring, Monger was stalling for time. Making a pretense of establishing clarity, he was rephrasing the questions that had been asked of him.

Deke leaned in toward Jake and Paul and whispered, "The ventriloquist's dummy is waiting for the ventriloquist." His eyes slid from Monger to Ailes. Ailes finished what he was writing and surreptitiously passed Richards a note.

"Is that kind of communication allowed?" Jake whispered.

"Whether it is or isn't," said Deke, "I suspect Ailes wrote every word in the pleadings and argument, and I don't doubt the judge is now thinking the same thing."

Richards read the note, even as Monger began rehashing the terms of the settlement that had taken place between seven state attorneys general and a group of opioid manufacturers six years earlier.

"Judge," said Monger, "although some would have you believe that the state of West Virginia turned a blind eye to the opioid problem, nothing could be further from the truth. Years ago, the attorney general's office began studying the situation. We determined that the manufacturers and distributors of opioids recognized that, through no fault of their own, their products were being diverted from legitimate avenues of prescription and into so-called pill mills. These clinics, which popped up solely for the purpose of distributing narcotics and opioids, were prevalent not only in West Virginia and Ohio, but also in five other mostly southern states. Doctors saw as many as sixty patients a day, and—"

As Monger continued to speak, Judge Perry's glasses fell ever farther down his nose. Deke had been coached by Paul and Jake that the judge's displeasure could usually be read in his eyewear. Monger apparently didn't know that.

"You seem to have forgotten what I wanted you to elaborate upon, Mr. Monger," interrupted the judge. "I did not ask you to rehash the opioid epidemic."

While Judge Perry reiterated his questions, speaking slowly and simply, Monger was forced to stand there like a schoolboy being lectured by his teacher. When the judge concluded, Monger shot a look back toward his counsel table. Both Richards and Ailes nodded.

"Thank you, Your Honor," said Monger. "I'll answer your questions momentarily, but if it please the court, I'd like a quick consultation with Attorney General Richards."

The judge nodded, and Monger hurriedly made his way to his table. He was handed a set of notes that he quickly reviewed. After a rushed conversation with Richards and Ailes, he returned to the podium.

"Thank you, Your Honor," he said. "As you are aware, six years ago there was a consortium of seven state attorneys general that took action on the opioid problem. We brought the opioid manufacturers to the table, and they agreed to pay a fine of twenty-five million dollars. As part of that settlement, they also agreed to better monitor the distribution of their drugs."

"That twenty-five million dollars," said Judge Perry, "was split among seven state attorneys general. Isn't that correct?"

"Yes, Your Honor," said Monger. "And that's why we don't believe Mr. Rutledge's case can go forward. We engaged in a final settlement with the same people Mr. Rutledge is now suing. Mr. Rutledge's case purports to represent the interests of two counties, one in West Virginia and the other in Ohio. However, when we settled with the drug manufacturers, we agreed upon a release for the states, cities, and counties in each one of those seven states, including West Virginia and Ohio. It should also be noted that it was the position of all seven of the state attorneys general that we alone had the standing and authority to settle any and all claims on behalf of the counties and cities even without the signed releases of those entities. It is our contention that the precedent and case law in each one of those seven states clearly supports this position."

Ailes was standing and whispering in Richards's ear, all while his legal team continued to work feverishly at their laptops. Instead of ignoring what was going on, Deke made a point of incredulously staring at all the kibitzing taking place. Judge Perry joined suit and also stared down Ailes. After a few moments, the lawyer became aware of the scrutiny. He stopped talking, and under the judge's eye, slunk back to his seat.

"Mr. Ailes," said Judge Perry, "I was of the impression that this motion had been brought by Mr. Monger and Mr. Richards. Why is it, then, that I see you and your staff acting as if you are the ones who are conducting this hearing?"

Ailes stood. "I am sorry, Your Honor," he said. "Because I had pertinent and important information in regard to your questions,

I took it upon myself to try and pass on that information to the attorneys general."

"I suppose I should be grateful that you didn't choose to convey this information through the use of semaphore flags," the judge said.

"Once again," said Ailes, "my apologies."

The judge nodded but still looked skeptical. "In the interest of sparing this court any other theatrics, Mr. Ailes, you should know that I was just about to ask Mr. Monger if he could identify the counties and the cities in each one of those seven states where most of the opioids were sold. I will also be asking him to comment on the estimated loss of money experienced by each of those counties and cities because of increased costs for emergency medical services, law enforcement, and the resources necessary to operate county hospitals. In the hopes it will stave off any more note passing and conversations, I'm going to give you an opportunity right now to confer with Mr. Richards and Mr. Monger. Does that work for you?"

"It does, Your Honor," Ailes said, "and I thank you, but I must admit to being surprised by these particular inquiries, and I cannot help but wonder at their relevance."

"The relevance," said Judge Perry, "will depend upon the answers provided."

Ailes didn't seem reassured by the remarks from the bench. Still, he took the opportunity to confer with Monger and Richards. As the three men carried out their whispered conversation, Deke rose to his feet.

"What is it, Mr. Deketomis?" asked Judge Perry.

Even though his voice didn't sound welcoming, Deke was glad to see the judge reposition his glasses higher up on his nose.

"Permission to speak, Your Honor."

Perry nodded.

"If the plaintiffs have any problems answering your questions about those cities and counties where the most opioids were sold, my team would be glad to provide them to you. We would also be happy to discuss costs incurred by those cities and counties as a result of the opioid epidemic."

"Thank you, Mr. Deketomis," said the judge.

Deke sat down and pretended not to notice Ailes's dagger eyes directed his way.

"They're on the defensive," whispered an excited Jake.

Deke nodded. Truth to tell, though, he wasn't sure how he felt about the progression of the hearing so far. Judge Perry's questions had cut into some of the territory that Deke had planned on exploring. He hoped the judge hadn't prematurely exploded his side's ammunition; Deke liked to parcel out his bombshells for maximum effect. Then again, the judge's questions might be intended to get the state attorneys general to acknowledge the incredible insignificance of their settlement from six years before.

"You would think the lawyers at the top of the food chain in West Virginia and Ohio would look a little less like circus clowns," said Paul.

"I'm sure P. T. Barnum wouldn't like you disparaging circus clowns that way," said Deke.

The three-man conference broke up, and Ailes and Richards returned to their seats. From the podium, Monger cleared his throat. His shoulders were even more hunched now, and the vulture pose more pronounced.

"I regret to inform you, Judge," he said, "but at this time we will be unable to provide the court with the specific information you requested. Because we want to be sure of our facts, we'll be scheduling a conference call with all seven of the state attorneys general who participated in the settlement. That said, our contention remains that getting answers to your questions will be moot. As we have already argued in our briefs and pleadings, this court has very limited jurisdiction to take any action because the cities and counties that are claimants in this case have no standing to bring civil actions against these distributors. Doing such is the domain of the state attorneys general."

"I would tread very carefully, Mr. Monger," said the judge. "Are you saying that you will not be providing me with the answers that I have requested?"

"Not at all, Your Honor," Monger said. "As a courtesy to this court, we will meet with all relevant parties and do our best to provide as much statistical data as possible to Your Honor within the next few weeks."

"One week, Mr. Monger," said Perry. "In addition to fully addressing my questions, you will also provide me any and all emails, memos, briefings, or letters that you and the six other attorneys general created to communicate with the counties and cities about the settlement negotiations you were having with the opioid manufacturers before you signed your release."

If Monger had had a tail, Deke guessed it would be firmly planted between his butt cheeks. "Yes, sir," he said.

"Now," said Perry, "let's return to the subject at hand. I'd like you to be specific about the precedent and case law that supports your argument that cities and states have no legal standing to proceed."

Monger nodded and inhaled deeply. "Your Honor," he said, "I would direct you to page eight in our brief. There are six cases cited that all stand for the proposition that attorneys general are the only constitutional officers that can speak for counties and cities within their state. That's the law, and we believe it's very clear."

"Final answer, Mr. Monger?"

The attorney general nodded.

"Then for the time being," the judge said, "you may go and sit down."

As Monger walked away from the podium, Perry's gaze turned to Deke.

"Mr. Deketomis," he said, "I understand that you are arguing on behalf of your trial team. My strong advice to you is, do not spend your time rehashing what you have already outlined in your briefing. Instead, use this opportunity to put your case on record."

Deke understood what all good trial lawyers come to understand and to practice: never oversell your case when you believe you're winning. At the same time, though, Deke wanted to go on record. The right bullet points, he knew, would be picked up and circulated by the media. It was important that he connect the dots showing the cozy relationship between the cabal of the state attorneys general and the opioid distributors.

With measured steps, Deke made his way to the vacated podium. He carried with him carefully culled files that had been selected for these opening remarks.

"Thank you, Your Honor," he said. "There are several points I believe I must make to protect any record on appeal, as well as to provide the court a closer look at what this hearing is actually all about."

The microphone amplified Deke's words, although the device was unnecessary. He made sure his voice was heard in every corner of the room.

"I would like to submit a few items for the court's review in light of what we just heard from Mr. Monger, or should I say . . . Mr. Ailes?"

Deke held up a small stack of papers for the judge to see. "What you'll find in these cases, Judge, refutes Mr. Monger's assertion that state attorneys general have the exclusive right to bring cases on behalf of cities and counties within their state. I was hoping they would point these cases out to Your Honor at the hearing today, because for some reason none of them were included in the massive brief that they filed with this court. What you will notice as you review these cases is that there have been at least a half dozen cases that concluded just the opposite of what Mr. Monger represented to this court."

Deke stepped away from the podium. He wasn't going to be bound by its confines.

"Had Mr. Monger been more accurate in his argument to this court," he said, "he would have had to explain that there is almost a straight fifty-fifty split within the jurisdictions of Ohio and West Virginia as to whether or not a city or county has the right to proceed in a claim like this without involvement of the state attorney general."

He stopped in midstride. "Fifty-fifty," he repeated. Then he made his way back to the podium and said, "I leave it to you, Your Honor, to decide whether that omission was simply an oversight on the part of Mr. Monger and Mr. Richards."

"Objection, Your Honor." A red-faced Jazz Hands was on his feet.

"You are not an attorney on record here, Mr. Ailes," said the judge, "so I will not even deign to overrule you. Sit down, Mr. Ailes, and I don't expect to have to remind you of that again. Mr. Monger and Mr. Richards are both capable of mouthing their own objections, and I'm sure I'll hear from them at the appropriate time.

"Now, Mr. Deketomis, please proceed."

"Thank you, Judge," said Deke. "During his address to the court, Mr. Monger referenced how he and six other state attorneys general signed a gentleman's agreement barring cities and counties from proceeding against the opioid manufacturers."

Once again, Deke wasn't content to stand at the podium, but moved into a position directly in front of Monger.

"Let's agree to the fact that both of these *champions of the people* settled some claims in their twenty-five-million-dollar fire-sale giveaway six years ago. I'm sure I don't need to tell anyone in this courtroom that a lot can go on in six years. What Mr. Monger and Mr. Richards would have us believe is, 'That's just water under the bridge.' They would have us ignore all the opioid deaths, and all the economic devastation that mushroomed even after their dog-and-pony settlement. As we sit in this courtroom, we have not only the *right* to recover all the losses suffered by cities and counties between the time of that settlement and today, but we in fact have the *obligation* to do what the attorneys general didn't have the character or courage to do."

The more Deke talked, the more he could see from the corner of his eye that Nathan Ailes's face was changing colors. Monger was pretending to be color-blind, but Ailes finally made a strangled noise he couldn't ignore.

With some reluctance, he got to his feet and said, "Objection, Your Honor. Much of what Mr. Deketomis is saying is speculation, with statements more prejudicial than probative."

Judge Perry turned to Deke. "Mr. Deketomis?"

"If you would allow me a few minutes of the court's time, Your Honor, I would like to air a presentation created by our legal team that will provide you with incontrovertible facts and figures showing just what has happened in the six years since the attorneys general entered into their travesty of a settlement."

The judge considered Deke's request. "You may proceed, Mr. Deketomis."

"Thank you, Your Honor."

Deke nodded to an AV tech, and moments later the lights dimmed and a video screen lowered from the ceiling and settled to the right of the judge's bench.

A familiar face appeared on the screen—Monger's. He was identified by name and by his title. The interview had taken place six years before.

Monger's voice blared through the courtroom as the video played. "I would categorize our settlement with the drug manufacturers as a huge victory for the seven states that pursued this action. Through negotiations and sanctions, we have taken the important first step toward ending the opioid addiction crisis. I believe this is the beginning of the end of the opioid problem. This plague will soon vanish."

Deke had been tempted to follow up Monger's statement with black-and-white footage of Neville Chamberlain waving a peace treaty signed with Hitler, and proclaiming, "Peace for our time." Paul and Jake had talked him out of that, though. They had argued that the old footage of Monger was controversial enough.

On the screen, a graph materialized that showed statistics from the Centers for Disease Control. The numbers were clear for all to see, but Deke offered them with some oratory.

"In the six years since Mr. Monger's *victory*," said Deke, "between ninety and one hundred and fifty men, women, and children have died *every single day* from opioid overdoses."

Deke let that figure sink in, then tried to personalize those deaths. "Last Thursday one hundred and seventeen individuals died from opioid overdoses. Those individuals were sons, daughters, fathers, and mothers. Some lived right in this community. We collected as many of those one hundred and seventeen pictures of the dead as we could, and while we show you their faces, I will tell you how this terrible tragedy came to be, and how it continues to impact us."

One by one the faces of the dead came up on the screen as Deke spoke for them. But he wasn't yet finished. He concluded by putting up a map of the United States created by the National Center for Health Statistics showing drug poisoning mortality data in the country. The age-adjusted death rate went from dark blue to dark red, with dark blue signifying fewer than two deaths per one hundred thousand people, and dark red signifying more than thirty deaths per one hundred thousand people. The first map shown was from 1999; it was almost completely blue. With each passing year, the complexion of the map changed—the blues morphing into greens and yellows and reds. As twenty years passed, red blotches popped up everywhere. It was almost like the graphics were bleeding out for all to see. By the time the last of what Deke called the "death maps" were put on the screen, the courtroom was deathly silent.

14

THE HOMECOMING KING

Anna Fowler made sure it was Ruth Smith who answered the phone, and not her husband.

"Ruth?" she said, making her voice sound scratchy. "This is Anna. I'm afraid I caught that bug that's going around. Please tell Clint I won't be coming in today."

"I'm sorry to hear you're not feeling well again, dear," said Ruth. "I'll be sure to tell him."

Anna thanked her. When she'd left Clint's studio that awful day, she'd told herself that she would never be back. Her resolve hadn't lasted, though. There was no work to be found in Oakley, and little enough in the surrounding communities. Even though she had continued to model for Clint, their relationship was strained. Both tried to pretend that nothing had ever happened; at least they were studiously polite with each other. Still, Anna remembered her terror. Clint had never acted that way before. It was the dope he was taking, Anna thought, probably the same pills *she* was taking. An involuntary shudder came over her; she could pretend the thought wasn't disturbing, but it was.

Clint's near-assault had caused her to do a lot of thinking. She'd tried to rein in her own pill consumption, but it hadn't been as easy as she would have hoped. Ever since her abrupt departure from Clint's studio, she'd been vomiting several times a day. The moral victory, Anna supposed, was that her usage hadn't increased, but it hadn't decreased much either.

Now she was trying to surmount that mountain, but the pills were fighting back. Dry bread and water were about all she could hold down, and even that came up too often for her liking. Withdrawal was playing havoc on both her mind and body. Even sleep didn't bring her relief—what little sleep she'd been getting. Anxiety, cold sweats, and muscle aches didn't allow for much slumber. The only thing that helped was trying to stay busy. That staved off a little bit of the anxiety.

Still, at least once a day, Anna thought about how there was something she could do to relieve all her symptoms. All she had to do was take another pill or two. But doing that would be giving up, relinquishing control of her life, and she never again wanted to relinquish control the way she had when Clint had used her naked body to paint his nightmare.

Her nightmare, Anna amended. He'd drawn what she was becoming, and seeing that had scared her as much as Clint's rage. It was shock therapy, she supposed. There was probably nothing else that would have convinced her to try and get off the pills.

Anna finished up in the kitchen and brought her father a tray. "Some biscuits and ham, Daddy," she said, pretending to be cheery. The reality was, the smell of food was bringing her to the brink of nausea.

Her father merely nodded. "Skipping work today?" he asked.

He must have overheard her conversation with Ruth, thought Anna. "I've been under the weather," she admitted, "but it's more of a mental-health day than anything else. Besides, did you forget what day it is?"

"What are you talking about?" he said.

"It's May Day," said Anna.

Her father shrugged, the significance lost on him.

"Decoration Day, May the first. On May Day, Momma always went to the cemetery to pay her remembrances and do some sprucing up."

Decoration Day varied by community. In Appalachia and the south, it was usually celebrated in the spring or early summer. Some called it Cemetery Day. The national tradition of Memorial Day was thought to have resulted from Decoration Day.

Her father's face softened. Thinking about her mother always made him sentimental.

"You going to take some flowers to your momma?" he asked.

Anna nodded. "I'm going to put together a nice bouquet of wildflowers."

"That's a good thing," he said, and then coughed, trying to keep his emotions in check.

"Do you want to come with me, Papa?" she asked.

Because it was early in the day, Anna was confident she could cope with her withdrawal symptoms and still be able to care for her already mildly drunk father. Much to her relief, though, he didn't take her up on her offer.

He shook his head. "Too long of a walk to her gravestone," he said gruffly. "I'd probably fall."

"I'll tell her you wanted to be there," Anna promised. "I'll tell her you miss her."

He opened his mouth to offer his thanks, then seemed to reconsider when the words caught in his throat, causing him to nod instead and blink away the tears.

Anna tried to ignore the roiling of her stomach. Five minutes into her drive, she pulled over on the shoulder but resisted the urge to throw up. Taking deep breaths, she made her way out to an open field and began picking columbine, oxeye daisies, and larkspur. Her mother had loved wildflowers. When she would go out and collect them with Anna, she always quoted from Matthew, saying: "Consider the lilies of the field, how they grow. They don't toil, neither do they spin." The wildflowers were so abundant that Anna picked enough for three bouquets. She'd find the other two a proper home even if she didn't yet know where. It had been too long since her last visit to the graveyard. During her last visit there, she had run into Jake Rutledge. They had talked on the phone a few times since and had made vague plans to see each other, but Jake was busy with his case. It was just as well, she thought. Anna had her own problems she needed to resolve before considering having a social life.

Decoration Day had started in Oakley after the Civil War, with citizens tending to the graves of the many soldiers who had died. Central West Virginia had felt the pull of both the North and South, so the war had resulted in deep divisions in Oakley. There were families here that had had one sibling wearing blue, and the other, gray.

As Anna drove her father's truck into the cemetery, she was surprised to see so few vehicles there. Even in recent years, Decoration Day had been one of the Oakley's big civic activities. Remembering the dead, it appeared, was no longer a priority.

She picked a spot to park not far from where her mother had been buried. It was a sunny day, which was an excuse for Anna to put on a bonnet. As a little girl, she'd liked to wear her Easter bonnet on any occasion she could. Decoration Day had always been one of them. The old gardening basket she now toted had been used by her mother for many years. Together, they'd made a point of tending to unkempt graves. Anna had never imagined that one day she'd be tending to her mother's.

She placed one of her bouquets at the base of her mother's gravestone. The stone had her mother's name, and dates of birth and death. The inscription was simple: BELOVED WIFE AND MOTHER.

Look over me, God, Anna prayed, *so that one day I can live a life that earns just such an epitaph.*

She ran her hands across the lettering, dismayed to see that her fingers began to slightly tremble. The condition was affecting both of her hands. She was tired of the withdrawal manifesting itself in so many ways.

Anna emptied the contents of her gardening basket onto the ground. She took the kneeling pad, spread it out on the grass, and with the pruning shears, cleared grass and weeds from around the headstone.

While she worked, she chattered companionably. "Daddy gives you his best, Momma," she said. "But you know how he is. Nothing scares him more than shedding tears. That's why he's not here. The truth is, he misses you something terrible. And so do I, Momma. I'm in a bad place. I'd give anything if you were here to help me."

She took a cloth to the headstone, buffing it clean. Then she spent a few minutes of reflection before getting to her feet. If her mother were alive, she would be using her time to tend to the graves of others, so Anna tried to do as she would have done. She continued down the line of graves, spending a little time with each.

This part of the cemetery was for the newer arrivals. Many of the names were familiar to her, but even those that weren't got some sprucing up. What seemed wrong to Anna was the disproportionate number of young people buried in this section of the cemetery. Sometime in the future, Anna thought, a visitor might wonder if a war had occurred during this time and claimed all these young lives.

In a way, she supposed, it had.

Anna didn't spend as much time at the graveyard as she would have liked. She couldn't ignore the growing demands of her body. She finished her tidying and placed her third bouquet at Blake's grave. The homecoming king, she thought, being attended to by the homecoming queen.

"We're quite the royals, Blake," she whispered.

As Anna turned to leave, she noticed a handful of people spread out around the cemetery; one or two were tidying, as she had done. Decoration Day hadn't been completely forgotten.

After a brief stop at the store, Anna made it home from the cemetery and announced, "Daddy, I'm not feeling well. I'm going to go lie down."

Instead of expressing sympathy for her, he said, "Your boss called and left a message."

Anna wasn't up to dealing with Clint Smith. For the rest of the day—for the rest of the week—there was only one thing on her agenda. It was time to go cold turkey. The thought scared her, but seeing all those gravesites had cemented her resolve.

Already, Anna knew that the symptoms she'd been experiencing were a cakewalk in comparison to what was coming. She'd experienced the muscle aches, anxiety, sleeplessness, and running nose. Now her body was actively rebelling with abdominal cramps, nausea, and goose bumps. Soon enough, Anna knew, uncontrollable diarrhea and vomiting would lay her low. According to accounts of recovering addicts, you had to all but die to get better.

She went to her room and emptied her shopping bag of the items she'd bought. She had prepared as well as she could for what was coming. She had a bucket and bedpan handy; and her nightstand looked like a pharmacy—with antihistamines, electrolyte solutions, antidiarrheal medication, and ibuprofen. Anna had read up on what to expect, but there were some things that were difficult to plan for. As Mike Tyson once said, "Everyone has a plan until they get punched in the mouth."

She took an Advil and washed it down with Gatorade. The pain reliever wasn't the pill her system craved, and her body told her so. Would she be able to keep fighting when things got worse?

The doorbell rang. Anna suspected it was one of her father's drinking companions and ignored its summons. What she couldn't ignore was when her father started yelling her name.

"Anna, Anna, you got yourself a visitor!"

Hadn't she made it clear that she was sick? That was no lie either. But it wouldn't do to yell that to her father. By the sound of it, he'd left her visitor standing at the door.

She tried getting up, but dizziness won the first round. With her second try, she got to her feet. Her aching joints made her shuffle along like some old woman. She wondered who her caller was. She only had two friends in town, Tammy and Carol, and neither was in the habit of stopping by unannounced.

Clint Smith was not a face she expected to see, and she couldn't help but recoil both in surprise and fear. He'd never come to her house before and looked as uneasy as Anna felt.

"I'm sorry to bother you, Anna," he said, "especially when you're not feeling well."

"That's okay," she managed to say; still, she made a point of leaving a healthy distance between them. Just the thought of his Jekyll/Hyde transformation scared her even now.

What was reassuring, though, was seeing Ruth and two of the grown-up Smith children sitting in their car parked out on the street. The family waved at her, and Anna waved back. Then she turned to the artist, clearly wondering what was going on.

He met her eyes, and she was surprised to see him trying to blink back tears. He cleared his throat and then cleared it again.

"I came here to apologize to you, Anna," he said. "I had a whole speech ready for you this morning, but then you didn't come to the studio. I've forgotten just about everything I meant to say except for how sorry I am. I couldn't leave without telling you that."

"Leave?" asked Anna. "Where are you going?"

"The other day my family gathered for an . . . intervention," he said, looking sheepish. "They told me they loved me, said I had a problem, and encouraged me to go to rehab. I couldn't argue with anything they said, especially after how I had acted with you. There is no excuse for what happened that day, except for me to say it almost felt like I was possessed by some—thing—some force—I couldn't control." He looked away for a moment. "Anyway, I'm told I could be away for a month or more, and that's why I wanted to make sure you had this before I left."

His hands weren't as controlled as his voice. They were shaking as he handed her a manila envelope. Anna could feel her expression turning puzzled.

"It's a month's worth of pay," he said. "All cash. And it's also an inadequate apology."

"I can't take this, Mr. Smith—"

"You most certainly can. It's the least I can do. And the next time you see me, Anna, the hope is that I'll be my old self. No more of my phantasmagoria phase; I don't want that kind of darkness in my life. I'm going to get back to my portraits of West Virginia. That's who I am. I just hope you'll find it in your heart to forgive me in the meantime."

She gave him a wobbly smile. For a moment, she wanted to confide in him, to confess that she couldn't judge him because she, too, was struggling with darkness. But she found she couldn't say the words out loud. So she simply said, "I already have, Mr. Smith."

"That's a relief," he said.

"Good luck," Anna said, "and God bless you."

They shook hands, and then Clint made a slow retreat back to his waiting family. She felt a momentary pang of envy at his support system. Everything she'd read about going cold turkey had stressed that the best way to go about it was to have a caregiver helping with the process, not to mention medical supervision. In Anna's circumstances, that wasn't an option. She would have to go it alone.

Later, how much later she had no idea, Anna heard her father calling to her in the bedroom to say she had a visitor. It took her a few moments to distinguish that she was awake and not having another fevered vision.

Déjà vu, she thought. *Another visitor.*

"I'm sick!" she yelled, or at least attempted to yell. Her croaking voice almost felt as if it wasn't her own.

She grabbed the Gatorade bottle with a shaking hand and managed to get a few swallows down before she heard her father yell again.

What didn't he understand about her being sick? But at least for the moment her stomach wasn't trying to empty itself. Earlier she'd had to battle an hour or more of dry heaves. That had left her stomach feeling like it had been shredded.

Once more, she managed to get to her feet. She needed to make it clear to her father that she wasn't feeling well enough to talk to anyone in person or on the phone. Still, it was unusual for her to have two visitors in a day. She hoped it wasn't Shirley Wilson, the pastor's wife. She had been threatening to call on Anna for some time.

On unsteady legs, Anna made it to the door. Leave it to her father to not invite the person inside to wait. Anna opened the door and immediately regretted it. Standing there, looking impossibly handsome, was Jake Rutledge.

"Surprise," said Jake, "but the last time we talked, I did promise you that I'd stop by."

Despite her misery, Anna could see how nervous Jake looked. He was moving from side to side, and she knew it must have taken all his nerve to show up on her doorstep.

"I'm glad to see you," she said, "but your timing couldn't be worse. I'm afraid I'm sick."

"I hope I'm not the cause," said Jake.

"Of course not," said Anna.

"I won't keep you," he said, "but the reason I stopped by was to say thanks. I went to visit Blake's grave today, and I saw that you'd left him another beautiful bouquet."

"I was glad to do it," she said.

"I brought you something that might make you feel better," said Jake. He held up a paper bag. "We had talked about going out for coffee, and you told me you preferred tea, so I decided to bring you some. My mom used to always say that nothing settles the stomach like a cup of tea complete with honey."

Charmed, Anna raised one hand to try and fix her hair but then gave up. *I'm sure I look as bad as I feel,* she thought. As Jake extended the bag her way, a rolling wave of nausea seized her gut, forcing her to raise her hand to her mouth to try and stave off retching.

She was tempted to blame her condition on some virus or stomach flu. But her conversation with Clint flashed through her mind, and she felt like a hypocrite. It wouldn't do to pretend all was well. The time for lies was over. The deception had to stop, even at the cost of sending Jake running.

"You were sweet to bring tea, Jake. And more than anything I wish I could be pleasant and entertaining company, but it wouldn't be right for me to deceive you with what would just be an act. As hard as it is for me to believe, over time I've somehow became dependent on the same poison that killed your brother. Today is the day I began trying to regain control of my life."

Anna expected Jake's expression to change from one of concern to one of revulsion. She thought her revelation would kill any potential chance of romance between them. But he surprised her by setting the bag down, then reaching for her hand.

He doesn't even seem to notice how clammy it is, she thought.

"You're here at home going cold turkey?" he asked.

No more deceitful behavior, she thought. That was all part of getting clean. "I'm trying to," she said.

"Without anyone's help?"

"That's the plan."

"Change of plans," said Jake.

15
MEMORIES OF MOON PIES

As difficult as it was to await Judge Perry's decision on the attorney general's motion, a hiatus from the case was just what Jake needed. Trying to get Anna Fowler back on her feet would require a commitment on his part. Even under these conditions, though, he found himself enjoying the time he spent with Anna. If possible, Jake was even more enamored of her now than he had been in high school. She had been courageous throughout her recovery. The girl he had admired had grown into a strong and beautiful woman.

Jake knocked on the front door of the Fowler home and waited. He knew better than to knock again or ring the bell. He neither wanted to awaken Anna if she was asleep nor get on Mr. Fowler's bad side. Since his stroke, Gary Fowler moved slowly, if he attempted to move at all. He tolerated one summons to the door; a second directive got him hot and bothered.

Finally, Jake heard the sound of locks being unlocked. The door opened, and an unsmiling Mr. Fowler said, "You again?"

During Jake's frequent visits over the last few days, he had gotten used to Anna's gruff father. "Good morning, Mr. Fowler," he said. "Would you like a coffee or a doughnut?"

"What I'd like," Mr. Fowler said, "is a cold beer and a little peace and quiet."

But he pushed open the screen door as a signal for Jake to enter, then turned around and began shuffling toward the living room where his easy chair awaited.

Jake walked down the hallway. He softly knocked on Anna's door but didn't hear an answer. Jake had spent the day before in court and hadn't been able to be with Anna, although they'd talked for a few minutes last night. She'd told him everything was fine and pretended all was well, but she'd sounded on edge. Jake turned the knob and silently entered the room. Anna had her back turned to him and appeared to be sleeping. She was wearing a T-shirt; her perspiration was causing it to cling to her. The room wasn't hot, but since going cold turkey, her body's thermostat seemed to have a mind of its own, causing her to alternately boil and freeze.

As he did his best to quietly sit down on the one chair in the room, Anna turned around and opened one eye.

"Hey," she said.

"Hay is for horses," said Jake.

Her face scrunched up in thought, and she said, "True, but straw is cheaper, and grass is free; marry a farmer's daughter and you can have all three."

"I never heard that rhyme."

"You probably didn't say 'Hey' to your mother like I did," Anna said. "That was her way of trying to break me of the habit."

"I guess she didn't succeed," Jake said, smiling. "How are you feeling?"

Anna seemed to think about that. "I feel fluish," she said, "but I think less fluish than I did yesterday."

"You want something to eat or drink? I brought coffee, tea, and doughnuts."

Anna inhaled the aroma. "For now, I'm happy to sniff away, but I think I'll wait a few minutes before deciding if my body is up for the challenge."

Jake nodded and began to lower the bag of doughnuts and the coffee to the floor.

"Please don't wait on me to eat or drink," Anna said.

Her words were a relief to Jake. "Thanks. I could use my morning eye-opener. Last night I didn't sleep a wink for worrying about the outcome of the hearing."

He lifted the coffee to his lips and took a long sip. His satisfied sigh announced that the coffee had hit the spot.

"Yesterday I kept thinking about your case," said Anna. "It was a good distraction from my own situation. When do you think you'll know?"

"The judge asked both sides to supply him with some additional information within the week," he said, "which we did. He said his decision would be prompt, so we're hoping within the next ten days." Jake thought about something and began shaking his head.

"What is it?" asked Anna.

"It's nothing, really," he said. "I guess I'm still pissed off that our state attorney general was acting like a shill for the opioid distributors. I know it's naive of me, but you'd think if you entered into public service, you would want to help others and not just yourself."

"You think he's dirty or just an incompetent boob?"

"It's hard to know for sure," Jake said, "but it's clear that the opioid lobby might as well call his office their home away from home. The lawyer who represents the distributors, and who filed a motion to make my case go away, was actually advising the two state AGs in open court. I couldn't believe my eyes when I saw him whispering to them and passing notes. There should be a law against that."

"Maybe one day you'll write that law," Anna said.

"First, I'll have to survive this case."

"I'm proud of you."

"Then it's a mutual admiration society," he said. "I know what you've been going through to get that monkey off your back."

If only he'd been there to help Blake, Jake thought, like he was trying to help Anna. Strange how there seemed to be this connection between his dead brother, Jake, and Anna. It was almost as if Blake were coordinating their coming together from the grave.

"Don't congratulate me so fast," she said. "I'm still feeling . . . unsteady."

Jake nodded and said, "There's a reason for that. Your neurons have adapted to the drugs, and they're firing these electrical pulses. At the same time your receptors—those are the ends of your nerves—are craving an opiate high. That's why a lot of physicians recommend replacement drug therapy instead of going cold turkey."

"I didn't want to substitute one drug for another. To me, that was like choosing the lesser of two evils."

"I wouldn't look at it that way," Jake said. "It's more like choosing something other than poison, and that's never a bad choice. Opioids alter brain chemistry, which makes kicking the drugs hard. Even if it takes methadone to get off opioids, it's still better than the alternative."

"Intellectually I know you're right," said Anna, "but I hope it doesn't have to come to that. Still, I keep trying to convince myself the worst is over, but it really doesn't feel that way."

"It's likely you're depressed," Jake said matter-of-factly. That was probably why Blake had sounded so low-energy in the months before he had died. "That's another insidious aftereffect of opioid use. Your brain stops creating dopamine and endorphins—the drugs have essentially co-opted your brain into believing you can only experience feelings of pleasure through opiates."

"So I better get used to having the blues?"

"It might be some time before you feel like your old cheerful self," Jake admitted. "Your neurons have all been majorly trashed."

"I'm not sure if I have many of those little neurons left after these last few days," she said, then sighed. "I just need to put my boxing gloves on and fight through it. But thanks for being in my corner."

Jake lifted the bag from the floor. "Tea and doughnuts will help you over the potholes. If that's not in your rehab material, it should be."

Smiling, she asked, "So what kind of doughnuts did you bring?"

The hours passed. Anna apologized several times for not being better company and for feeling so lethargic. Several times she drifted off to sleep; that was fine with Jake. He knew recovery was a long process and hoped Anna had the patience and marathon mentality to successfully see it through.

Sometimes it was too much effort for her to hold her half of a conversation, so Jake simply carried on both sides. Anna looked happy to listen, and neither of them found the occasional silence uncomfortable.

Anna broke one of those silences by asking, "Do you still love Moon Pies?"

Jake began laughing.

"What is it?" she said, looking truly perplexed. "Once or twice a week you came by Daddy's service station to get a Moon Pie."

Fowler's Service Station had been a fixture in Oakley's downtown while he and Blake were growing up. It was a garage with two service bays, and next to it was a small convenience store whose scant merchandise had consisted mostly of candy and snacks. Anna had worked there since she was a girl.

"I've really never liked Moon Pies," Jake admitted.

Anna's brow wrinkled, and she did a small double take. "But that's what you always bought."

"The only reason I ever went into the Snack Shack was to see you," he said with a shrug.

She let out a disbelieving laugh, then said, "If you didn't like Moon Pies, then why did you keep buying them?"

"The first time I went in," he said, "I think my plan was to get a pop, even though my real hope was to engage you in a scintillating conversation that would open your eyes to what a wonderful young man I was. Of course, the reality was that after you said hello, I'm pretty sure I forgot my own name. I guess I must have been pretending to look for something in one particular area of the store when you asked, 'Do you want a Moon Pie, Jake?' That seemed to me a most wonderful suggestion, so I said, 'Yes, that's what I was looking for.' That probably would have been the end of it, except when I steeled up my nerve to come see you again, the first thing you said when I walked in was, 'I bet you want a Moon Pie.'"

"No!" said Anna.

"Oh, yes," he said, grinning. "For at least six years I stopped by on a weekly basis, except that month or two when it looked like you and Blake might become an item. I can tell you I wasn't coming in for Moon Pies; I visited to get a chance to talk to you. I think I loved the way you said 'Moon Pie.' It just sounded magical to me."

"What did you do with all those Moon Pies?" asked Anna.

"I gave them to my mother. They were a favorite treat of hers. She said as a girl her fondest memories of childhood were saving enough money to have a Moon Pie with a Royal Crown Cola, so it actually turned out to be a good thing. Mom was always so happy to get her Moon Pie, so I'm glad I ended up doing something for her, even though the truth of the matter is that for all that time, I was just trying to catch the eye of the cashier."

Jake was surprised to see Anna wiping away a tear. "That story was supposed to make you laugh, not cry."

"I feel stupid for forcing Moon Pies on you for all those years."

"Like I said, it all worked out."

"Would you believe me if I told you that your visits to the store were usually the highlight of my day?" asked Anna.

"I'd be surprised," Jake admitted. "I always assumed your friendliness was a pity thing on your part. My take on it was that you forever designated the Rutledge brothers as friend material, and nothing else."

She shook her head. "It was that way with me and Blake," Anna admitted, "but that wasn't how I felt about the other Rutledge brother."

Opening up to each other wasn't easy, but they were finding a way. "Being visited by the boy I knew would one day be the valedictorian," Anna said, "always made me feel special."

"You hid it well."

"Did I?" she said, sounding surprised. "One thing I can tell you is that I always made sure the vendor brought plenty of Moon Pies so that you would never be disappointed."

They both laughed at that.

"Daddy never really liked the idea of the convenience store," said Anna. "It came about out of necessity. People would be waiting for their cars and would want something to eat. I kept telling him we needed to expand that part of the business, but he resisted. He never seemed to understand that without the store, the garage would never have turned a profit. After I went away to become a dental hygienist, he tried to operate the store with a series of part-time cashiers, but none of them really worked out. And then when Momma got sick and Papa started working haphazardly, the business had no chance of surviving."

"End of an era when Fowler's Service Station closed down," Jake said. He thought about that and added, "Feels like the end of Oakley."

"It was supposed to be a temporary closing," Anna said. "It's only recently that Daddy finally realized he won't be going back to work. I guess all that blight-and-condemnation paperwork has finally killed his wishful thinking."

"I'm not following what you're saying," said Jake.

"The city says we're in arrears for violation notices they sent out. Daddy says he never received the notices, but I'm not sure whether to believe him or not. He's never been good about dealing with bad news; brushing it under the carpet has always been his way. I should have intervened, but I was dealing with my own problems."

"Tell me about the condemnation paperwork," Jake said, sitting forward in the chair.

"It surfaced about a month or two ago," she said. "A deputy came to the door hand-delivering paperwork that said *Final Notice*."

Jake frowned. "And this deputy told your father that previous notices had been sent out for violations at the business property?"

"That's right."

"Which deputy brought you this final notice?"

She thought for a moment: "The deputy everyone calls *Paint*."

And whom I call Whitewash, thought Jake. "Edward Dunn?" he asked.

Anna nodded.

"Something doesn't sound right," Jake said. "Condemnation proceedings, even in areas designated as blight, have to go through due process, which means a hearing has to take place. I'd like to look into this, if it's all right with you."

"I wouldn't presume to involve you in our family's business matters," said Anna.

"Why not? I'm a family friend, aren't I? And I'm a lawyer."

"It's not that I wouldn't be grateful, Jake." Then, in a voice not much louder than a whisper, she added, "It's just that we couldn't afford to pay you."

He raised one brow. "You haven't heard my payment plan."

She looked at him suspiciously. "What is it?"

"Put me on a Moon Pie payment program."

"But you just finished telling me you don't even like Moon Pies."

"I don't," he said, "but I'm beginning to think I'm a sucker for nostalgia if it involves you."

When Anna smiled, Jake felt a soaring in his chest. But then she shook her head and said, "I can't. You're already doing way too much for me."

"Quid pro quo, then," he said. "You can work off my legal bill."

"Doing what?"

"You'll see tomorrow."

Before leaving, Jake stopped in the living room to talk with Gary Fowler. Anna's father seemed to be in a more receptive mood than he had been earlier that day, but that might have had to do with the two or three beers that he'd already consumed.

"Have a beer with an old man?" Fowler asked.

"I'd rather have a few words with you, if you don't mind," said Jake.

Fowler motioned to the sofa, and Jake sat down. "I don't know if Anna mentioned to you that I'm a lawyer, Mr. Fowler."

"She said something about that."

Jake nodded. "Anna said there was a legal matter that had to do with your business. I might be able to offer some help."

Fowler tilted his Budweiser and took a gulp. "I told that sheriff he'd made a mistake," he said. "He told me he'd look into it."

"Did you sign anything he brought?"

Fowler nodded. "There was some legal gobbledygook that he said was to acknowledge receipt of his notice."

"Did he leave you a copy of what you signed?"

Fowler gestured with his beer. "He left some paperwork on the table over there." Then he took another gulp.

"Do you mind if I take a look?"

"Beat yourself up."

Jake walked over to the table and thumbed through the small pile. Among the pages were a notice of delinquency and a posted sales date. From what Jake could see, the Fowler business was to go to public auction in five days.

"Have you read this paperwork?" asked Jake.

"Like I said, I told that sheriff I never received no previous notices, and that I know I'm up to date with the taxes."

"Did Deputy Dunn mention a lien having been put on the property? Or an imminent public auction?"

"I don't recall him talking about nothing like that."

"If you don't mind, Mr. Fowler, I'd like to make copies of this paperwork. After that, if it's okay with you, I'd like to talk to Deputy Dunn."

"You trying to drum up some business?" Fowler asked, scowling.

"No, sir," said Jake. "As I told Anna, I won't be taking any payment for this, just acting as a family friend."

Fowler shrugged. "Fine with me, then."

"Since I'll be dealing with county authorities," Jake said, "do you mind if I write up something that says I'm acting as your legal representative?"

"You mean like a contract?"

"Technically, yes. But it will be short and sweet. Without it, county officials might refuse to discuss your business matters with me."

"Pretty soon you're going to need a contract to go take a leak," Fowler said. "What's the world come to?"

Jake couldn't help but grin at the old man's surliness. "I wish I knew," he said.

Fowler took a last swallow of his beer and then placed it next to the other empties.

"There's a pad of paper and a pen under the telephone in the kitchen," he said. "While you're doing your retrieving, you can get me a cold beer out of the icebox."

16
THE PINKIE PROMISE

One of the great things about being a lawyer, Jake was discovering, was that certain cases gave you the legal right to be nosy. You could ask questions on behalf of your client and shine light in those places where certain people preferred darkness. Jake knew what the typical knee-jerk response to lawyers was—it was an image that corporate propagandists had been portraying for years. Lawyers were depicted as parasites sucking the blood of hardworking individuals. What was rarely acknowledged was the unofficial oversight role that was increasingly filled by lawyers. Without the potential threat of legal action, important checks and balances wouldn't exist, especially in light of increasingly lax government oversight. It was often only the fear of a lawsuit that made individuals and businesses do the right thing.

Jake found Deputy Edward "Whitewash" Dunn sitting at his desk inside the cramped and worn county sheriff's office in Melton. In his hand was a hunting knife that he was using to peel an apple. The blade must have been honed to a fine sharpness; Dunn was having no problem skinning the apple.

Dunn's brown eyes narrowed at Jake's approach; they offered no welcome.

"Deputy Dunn?" Jake said. "I'm Jake Rutledge. The two of us talked after the death of my brother, Blake."

The deputy nodded his acknowledgment but continued his knife work without comment.

"Anyway," said Jake, "you might recall that I was graduating from law school at the time of my brother's death. Nowadays I'm a lawyer, and one of my clients has asked me to look into the potential condemnation of his business. In fact, after studying the paperwork you left him, it appears that my client is in imminent danger of losing that business. If I'm connecting the dots correctly, it seems that this coming weekend there is to be a public auction, and his business and the property it sits on will be up for sale."

Dunn took a bite of his apple, chewed it a few times, and swallowed. "Is that so?" he said.

"My client is Gary Fowler of Fowler's Service Station in Oakley," said Jake. "Do you remember serving him papers recently?"

"It's against department regulations to discuss the police business of our citizens," Dunn said. "That would violate our public trust."

Jake was glad he'd anticipated the deputy's stonewalling. "As I said, I represent Mr. Fowler, and I have a document stipulating such."

He extended the power-of-attorney memo, and Dunn reluctantly put down his apple and knife before taking it from him. After reading what was written, he asked, "Is it all right if I make a copy?"

"That's fine," said Jake.

Dunn took the document with him and disappeared behind a cubicle in the back of the room. When he returned, he handed Jake the original.

"Yes, I served Mr. Fowler papers," said Dunn.

"Mr. Fowler said that he told you there had to be some kind of a mistake," said Jake. "According to him, you were told he was up to date on his taxes."

"Lots of people say lots of things," said the deputy. "I have no idea if what they're saying is true or not. And I don't need you explaining the law to me, son. I've been doing this job since before you could walk on two legs."

Jake was unfazed by the man's commentary. "If that's the case," he said, "then you know that in order to condemn a property, or to have an area designated as blight, due process has to be observed. Mr. Fowler says he received no notices of condemnation prior to your visit. In accordance with the law, he should have received at least one registered letter, and there should be written confirmation that he received it."

"You took him at his word that he didn't get that letter?" asked the deputy.

"If the letter was sent," said Jake, "there should be a record of that. That burden of proof falls on the city or county, not Mr. Fowler. Of course, I know you were aware of that, Deputy, before I was even crawling, right?"

Dunn scoffed. "Consider the source," he said. "The man has had a stroke that slowed him physically, and I suspect mentally. From what I observed, he's not firing on all cylinders. In addition to that, when I went and visited him, it was obvious that he's in the habit of hitting the sauce long and hard."

"His stroke and drinking notwithstanding, Mr. Fowler told me that he made it clear to you that no one had contacted him about the proposed condemnation until you showed up. Did you look into his claim?"

"When people get squeezed, they start making up all sorts of stories."

"You haven't answered my question," said Jake.

The deputy didn't hide his displeasure at being forced into a corner. "No, I have not yet had the opportunity to see if Mr. Fowler was notified by local government in writing prior to my talking to him."

"You haven't had the opportunity? The auction is four days from now. Mr. Fowler told you that he is sure a mistake was made, and he was under the impression that you would be looking into that situation."

"I never promised him anything. He's lying if he claims that I did."

"Let's just say he assumed incorrectly, then," said Jake. "Still, I don't imagine it will take more than a phone call, or an email, to determine if a certified letter was ever sent to the Fowler residence."

The two men stared at each other. Deputy Dunn's jaw was set, and his teeth were clenched. He clearly didn't like anyone telling him his job.

"Okay," said Dunn.

"Okay, as in you'll look into it?" asked Jake.

The deputy nodded.

"Regardless of what you find," Jake said, "I'll be filing paperwork to remove the Fowler property from this week's auction listing."

"All you'll be doing is delaying the inevitable."

Jake's brows rose. "You seem pretty sure of that."

Dunn shrugged.

"While I'm checking out Mr. Fowler's situation, you think maybe I should take a look at the rest of the properties on the auction block to make sure that no additional mistakes have been made regarding their disposition?"

"You're welcome to waste your time," Dunn said. "Or is business that slow that you're just trying to stir up a little work?"

Instead of responding, Jake merely said, "Have yourself a nice day."

The deputy reached for his knife, and in one motion impaled his apple. "You, too."

Jake was surprised that it was Anna who answered his knock at the door, and not her father. That duty had fallen to her dad while she was recovering from "the flu." It was clear that she was feeling better. He'd gotten used to seeing her in flannel nightgowns. Now she had on jeans and a button-down shirt.

"I didn't expect you to be up and about," he said.

"I guess I got sick of being sick," she said. "I was even thinking of going outside to get a little sun. I know I'm about as pale as a zombie."

"I could use a little color myself," said Jake.

"Let's sit in the backyard, then," she said. "Spring has sprung."

It was a good summation for the day, thought Jake. The sun was out and infusing the afternoon with its gentle heat. The two of them walked through the living room. Gary Fowler had nodded off, even though his right hand was holding tightly to a beer can. He didn't stir as they walked past.

Once they were outside, Jake grabbed two Adirondack chairs from under an overhang and brought them out to the lawn. The Fowlers' backyard was good-sized, and it featured several large shade trees. A big garden bed that had lain fallow over winter circled much of the lawn.

"The garden used to be Momma's pride and joy," said Anna.

Jake situated the chairs so that they faced the sun, and he and Anna sat down. The rays touched their skin, and Anna sighed contentedly. "Light therapy," she said.

"There's actually something to that," Jake said. "Some doctors believe light stimulates the release of your own natural opioids. It stimulates your circadian rhythms and helps treat depression."

"I'm beginning to be afraid that you're going to spring a test on me covering all the information you've provided on drugs and addiction," she said.

"Blame my inner nerd. And my caring about you."

"In that event," she said, "it's all good."

"I guess I went a little overboard while preparing for my case," said Jake. "I learned way too much about drugs, including all the details about treating addiction."

"You should have mentioned OCD in your excuse," said Anna.

Jake's smile matched hers. "I should have," he agreed. "But while we're talking about treatment, have you thought about how you're going to stay clean?"

Anna shaded her eyes and looked up into the sky. "I hadn't really considered any long-term plan. I know there are some NA groups in the area."

"Support groups have their place," Jake said with a tentative nod.

"You don't sound very enthusiastic."

"The results are sketchy, I'm afraid."

She looked at him. "Then what's the answer?"

"There is no one answer," he said. "It's truly dependent on the individual. But you've already made it through the place that keeps the majority of people from even considering Naltrexone—you went through the necessary detox period. From this point forward, you could get a monthly injection."

"My little helper."

"There's no question that it will decrease your need for opioids. How is that a bad thing?"

"I guess I see it as a failure of willpower."

"Is taking a flu vaccine a failure of willpower? Or is it something you do to avoid getting the flu?"

His analogy made Anna smile. "I'll consider it," she said, "especially if relapse seems like a possibility."

"You should also be considering recovery housing. Some people find it helpful to live with roommates who are fighting the same battle."

Anna shook her head. "That cure sounds worse than the disease."

"Different strokes for different folks."

"I know me," said Anna. "The idea of talking about how I'm feeling, and spending every day listening to others discussing the same gives me the heebie-jeebies. Sitting around and yakking is not me. Even though I'm only a few days into recovery, I'm already feeling antsy not doing anything. It's better if I keep busy."

"Yesterday you said the same thing. That's why I brought you some work today."

"What kind of work?"

"It's sort of what a paralegal would do," Jake said, grinning, "but unfortunately, it's unpaid. Still, you'd be helping me, and doing your part in the war on opioids."

Anna smiled. "When do I start?"

"Not until the two of us get at least the start of a tan."

"The sun feels good, doesn't it?"

"Too good. I'm afraid I might fall asleep and wake up a lobster."

"I won't let that happen," Anna promised.

"Pinkie promise?"

They shook each other's pinkies. "While you're promising things," Jake said, "how about agreeing to long-term medical follow-up? A doctor really should be monitoring you."

Anna nodded. "I can live with that."

"Good," he said. "I know a good doctor I'd like to recommend to you."

"Since when did you become a professional angel?"

He held her eyes for a moment, hoping she'd see the sincerity there. "I wasn't there for Blake," he said. "I'm going to be there for you."

Anna nodded, then reached out toward him. This time she didn't extend a pinkie; she offered her hand. Jake took it into his, and they intertwined fingers. They sat there like that for a while, and Jake admitted to himself that he liked the feeling.

"I talked to Deputy Dunn this morning," he said after a while, "and then I went over to County Records. As far as I could determine, no condemnation notice was ever sent to your home address or the business address."

"That's good, isn't it?"

"It's good in that your family is not in imminent danger of losing the business."

"But?" she asked, squeezing his hand.

"But there's something about this whole process that doesn't pass the smell test."

"What do you mean?"

"All the businesses that were supposedly condemned and were supposed to be up for auction just happen to be in the center of downtown Oakley. Admittedly, values are depressed now, but when our town recovers from the opioid epidemic, and it will, those locations will be in demand."

"Isn't that the rule of business?" she said. "Buy low and sell high?"

Reluctantly, he released her hand and twisted in his seat to face her. "It is," he said, "but not if you manipulate the fair market value. I'm beginning to think that just the threat of condemnation is resulting in condemnation blight."

Anna shook her head. "What's that?"

"Let's say the government announces the need for eminent domain proceedings," said Jake. "That means they're going to be taking land for the public good and doing something with it like building a highway. When the government makes that announcement, it usually results in the devaluation of nearby property values because no one wants a highway running through their backyard. That's referred to as condemnation blight. For a business owner, that can be devastating. Values and rents can plummet. Often the only recourse for those affected is to go to court and fight to be paid at least fair market value for their devalued property."

"Where does that leave Dad's business?"

"Right now someone has their eye on getting your dad's property for almost no money. In West Virginia there are plenty of buildings that have been declared BAD—Blighted, Abandoned, and Dilapidated. For the good of the community, they're often subject to a wrecking ball. But the Oakley properties weren't like that. They weren't decrepit, and they were in a good location. There's no reason to condemn them except that in a condemnation proceeding, prices go way south. We're talking being worth pennies on the dollar."

"That sounds ugly," she said.

"It is ugly," he agreed. "And I'm sure there are other communities besides Oakley that have been targeted the same way. The case I'm working on is taking up all my time, but as soon as I have some free time, I'll be starting my own investigation into what's happened. In the meantime, though, because the county won't be able to prove they sent proper notice, your father doesn't have to worry about losing his business."

"Thank you for that," Anna said. "Now, didn't you say you were going to have me help you as payment for your work?"

"I could use your help," Jake admitted.

Anna took her index finger and touched the exposed flesh on her arm. In its wake was a patch of white. "It's time to go inside anyway," she said. "I'm already beginning to burn."

Jake returned from his car with two cardboard boxes full of documents. Anna directed him to put them down on the kitchen table.

"That's a lot of paperwork," she said.

"There are three more boxes out in my car. Nick Deketomis has a theme system he uses in depositions and trials that requires a special way of organizing every document we can put our hands on."

"And that's what we'll be doing?"

Jake nodded. "We'll be reviewing reams of emails, memos, and sales data that's being turned over to us from discovery requests that we filed. One area in particular that I want you to focus on is the mountain of material coming in from FOIA requests we've been filing almost every day."

"FOIA?" she asked.

"Freedom of Information Act."

"Show me what you want," said Anna, "and leave the rest to me."

For the most part, the two of them worked in silence. Jake had thought this particular work would be good for her. Anna had said she did better when busy, but in addition to keeping her occupied, doing the document review exposed the ugly and insidious side of opioids. Since this was rehab of sorts, Jake wasn't above using "scared straight" tactics.

The quiet was interrupted when Anna asked, "How will you use these files?"

"It's information," Jake said. "These documents tell stories that these drug pushers never believed would see the light of day. In court, they'll try to portray the average opioid abuser as some kind of lowlife. Our goal will be to explain how, at every step of the way, these companies understood the intricacies of how they would get people addicted, and how that would result in bigger sales. We want to expose what is called the 'oversaturation scheme.' In these documents we can see how they sold narcotic opioids by promoting their illegal street sale. Their key to success was to distribute multiple millions of narcotic drugs every year to cities and counties with populations between five hundred and one thousand people."

"You're saying they flooded small towns with millions of opioids?"

"It's right here in these documents," said Jake. "They knew the excess pills would move to the street market. As the street sales increased and profits soared, all the Big Pharma distributors internalized these black-market narcotic sales into their business plans. These documents will also help show that from day one, these monsters knew all the science about how it was almost impossible to rehab an oxy addict."

"I'm afraid I can attest to that," Anna said wryly.

They continued with their document reviews. Nothing was said for hours as they focused on their task; hearing Anna sniffling, Jake finally looked up and noticed the tears falling down her cheeks.

"Anna?" he whispered.

She shook her head, cleared her throat, but couldn't produce any words. Anna held up her index finger, asking for a moment. Finally, she was able to say, "One of the newspaper stories I just read got to me. It was right here in their company files, along with dozens of other stories, like they were keeping a record of all the people they'd hurt."

"Which one?"

"The nineteen-year-old who became a mother for the first time. She had to have an emergency C-section, and there were complications. Things went from bad to worse, and she had to get a hysterectomy. Her doctor gave her opioids for the pain."

Anna was forced to clear her throat for a second time. "She had never taken drugs before—not even aspirin, according to her husband. Eighteen months after giving birth, she overdosed and died."

Her tears were falling so fast the table was getting wet and threatening Jake's papers. He picked them up and said, "Why don't you take a break?"

Anna nodded. She wiped away the tears and walked to the sink to get a glass of water. After taking a few sips, she was able to speak, if not hide the pain in her voice.

"That poor little girl would have had her second birthday last week," she whispered. "I hope someone made her a cake."

17
RUSSIAN NESTING DOLLS

Eva Whistler looked at her husband, Danny, and sighed. He had come to her and confessed that there was a "little situation" in some Podunk town. Danny had apparently cut some corners. Would he ever learn?

"Play it again," said Eva.

"Thought you should know there's a lawyer sniffing around the properties. He's already been able to determine the county didn't send out any condemnation letters. I've been hearing from different people that he's sticking his nose in all kinds of areas we don't want him looking. This isn't what I signed up for. What are you going to do about this?"

Eva shook her head. The only encouraging thing about the voice mail was that the cop's voice hadn't betrayed any nervousness. She wished the same could be said for her husband. To use one of her mama's favorite quotes, Danny was looking as nervous as a whore in church.

"You want to explain why you didn't follow the plan?" she asked. "We were using the *family* money to buy properties on the cheap, but you decided you didn't want to go the legal route. You bypassed the city and county in order to pay nothing. You even made up some fictitious auction. Is that right?"

He averted his eyes, afraid to look at her. "I thought I'd expedite the whole process," he said, "especially when it looked like condemnation wasn't going to happen." In an even smaller voice, he added, "This was a perfect spot to put up one of our clinics."

"You've exposed our whole operation," she said, "for no good reason. You think saving a buck is worth going to jail over?"

Danny didn't answer. His silence, Eva was sure, spoke volumes.

"You've done this before, haven't you?" she asked. "You've stolen property and made it look as if the government was involved."

"There were no problems," he admitted, "until now."

"Jesus," said Eva, rolling her eyes and looking up to the heavens. Then she considered how to best deal with the situation. She was never going to be Mother Whistler again.

"How well do you know the cop?" Eva asked.

"He seems like a good ol' boy," said Danny. "We went out a few times and hit it off."

"Is he solid?" she asked. "Can he be trusted?"

"Hell, yes," he said.

"You need to call him back right now," she said. "We're going to come up with a story, and you're going to make sure he's got it down pat. When push comes to shove, he's going to have to stick to his story that he received a directive detailing the imminent condemnation of those properties. He can claim that paperwork is now somehow missing and that he has no idea why he was set up in such a way. Make sure he acts baffled as to why someone would have manipulated him. Have him say it makes no sense. Tell him if he does that, no one will be able to prove differently. And, of course, this week's pretend auction can't take place."

Eva could see that Danny was looking like a fish out of water. Remembering key details wasn't one of his strong suits.

"I'll bullet-point everything you need to say," she said, grabbing a notepad, and in precise print she jotted down her husband's talking points. Then she positioned herself next to Danny.

The cop picked up on the first ring. "Hey, Paint," said Danny, "I just got your message. Is the coast all clear?"

"I'm by myself," said the deputy.

"You got me curious. Who's the snoop?"

Eva put her ear right next to the phone to make sure she heard every word.

"The guy's name is Jake Rutledge," said the deputy. "He's this young lawyer who's a real pit bull. We go back a couple of years to when his twin brother died of an overdose. That set him off, and he started pressing me with all sorts of questions about drugs and opioids, stirring up trouble. Nowadays he's that fellow who's suing the opioid distributors in federal court."

Eva nodded. Danny didn't follow any current events other than sports—he was a big Mountaineers football booster even though he'd flunked out of West Virginia University as a sophomore—but Eva was well acquainted with Jake Rutledge and his lawsuit. The media had played it up and made him out to be this knight in shining armor. Hearing Rutledge's name made her even more uneasy about Danny's failed end run around the law.

As Dunn continued to speak, Eva wrote down questions for Danny to ask. She tapped her index finger on one of those questions.

"So," Danny said, "how is it that this Rutledge fellow became involved in the first place? I thought these properties were supposed to be slam dunks."

"They should have been," growled Dunn. "Until recently, the old guy who owned the business ran it as a service station and small store. Now his wife is dead, and he sits at home drunk and disabled from a stroke. What I didn't see coming was the old guy's daughter, and her having this lawyer for a friend. The daughter's a real looker, and I expect Romeo was trying to show off for her by helping out. This was just one of those flukes."

Eva tapped the page with her manicured fingernail, and Danny read something else she'd written.

"You're right, buddy," said Danny. "I guess we'll just have to pull the plug on this whole operation."

The silence on the other end suggested Dunn didn't like the sound of that. No doubt he'd been counting on a big payday.

"I'll make it up to you, Paint," said Danny. "I just need to do some regrouping."

Eva signaled to her husband that it was time to end the conversation.

"Paint," he said, "I'm sure I don't need to tell you not to say nothing to no one. Just to be safe, though, you need to keep me in the loop as to what this lawyer is up to."

Danny listened to Dunn's answer and then said, "That sounds good. You take care now."

He ended the conversation and turned to his wife, looking for approval. Eva, however, was preoccupied with the problem of this lawyer.

"The press coverage says this Rutledge is smart," she said. "And he's young and has a lot of energy. The word is that he's a straight arrow."

"Just our luck."

Eva nodded. With the right politician in their pay, an official blight designation could usually be obtained. A lawyer like Rutledge couldn't be bought, and it sure hadn't taken him long to sniff out Danny's scam.

"You're going to need to keep your head low," said Eva, "and not do anything else that's stupid. Since this lawyer's big case ought to keep him more than busy, maybe he'll lose interest in your redevelopment plans."

"The way you set up those shell corporations," said Danny, "they'd confuse even Sherlock Holmes. They're kind of like those Russian dolls. You know the ones I'm talking about? You pull a doll out of the box, and then you find a doll within a doll, and another doll and another one."

"Russian nesting dolls," said Eva.

"Yeah, that's it," he said.

Eva nodded, but she knew shell corporations weren't the impossible puzzles her husband seemed to think they were. A determined investigator would eventually figure out who was standing behind the curtain. She hated loose ends.

I will never again become Mother Goddamn Whistler, she vowed. That's why she'd made sure everything had been set up to make Danny the fall guy in case their operation went south.

"What are you thinking about?" Danny asked.

Eva could hear the hopeful tone in her husband's voice. They'd been married for more than a decade, but time hadn't cooled his ardor. Besides, it was better to keep him happy. That would make it easier to blindside him, if necessary.

Reaching for him, she said, "I was thinking about you."

18

NO ATHEISTS IN COURTROOMS

Deke's three-bedroom Huntington, West Virginia, apartment was serving them well as a work space. Jake, Paul, and Deke all had their own desks in the master bedroom; two paralegals and their office equipment took up the other bedrooms. Deke had also set up a residence in a Huntington apartment/hotel.

Half the week Deke spent in West Virginia, and the other half in Florida. Paul also divided his time between his office and Deke's work space. Since he didn't have his own office, Jake spent more time there than the other two men, though Deke had noticed how he now had a life other than this case. If Deke was any judge, he was betting Jake's outside interest was a girl. That would explain his upbeat mood and improved humor. It seemed to Deke that Jake had never gotten over the death of his twin. This woman was apparently just the tonic Jake needed.

On a Monday morning, Judge Perry's decision arrived in Deke's email.

"It's Perry's decision!" Deke yelled, quickly scanning what was written.

As he scrolled through the two pages, he shouted, "Thank God!"

Everyone began to high-five each other and crowd around Deke's desk. Their cheers brought in the two paralegals from the next room; Alison Stanley and Ron Beyer joined in the cheering.

"So," said Paul, "you're suddenly religious?"

"I understand that the Lord works in mysterious ways," Deke said, grinning, "but I'm glad that on this occasion, I don't have to second-guess my Maker."

"Amen," said Paul.

With the three men hovering around the computer monitor, Alison said, "We'll go make copies of the decision for everyone."

"Bless you," Jake said, drawing laughs and keeping with the religious theme.

While Alison and Ron were making copies, Deke continued to scroll through Judge Perry's decision.

"You sounded surprised by the verdict," Jake said. "Weren't you the one who told us we'd win?"

"I believed that the facts, and the truth, were on our side," said Deke. "But sometimes that isn't enough. Complex cases are always uphill climbs, and this is what I'd call an Everest kind of case. What I mean by that is you have to fight uphill until you get to a staging area. And then after catching your breath and doing some regrouping, you need to fight your way to the next staging area."

"So this is just a staging area?" said Jake.

"Afraid so," said Deke. "And that's both the good news and the bad news. We're halfway up the top of the mountain, and the ascent only gets tougher from here."

Jake nodded, and Paul added, "Don't let the clouds get in the way."

"What do you mean?" Jake said.

"The higher you go, the more clouds there are." Then Paul offered song lyrics with his analogy: 'So many things I would have done, but clouds got in the way.' Sage words from the immortal Joni Mitchell, a big talent you've probably never heard of."

Jake grinned. "I know Joni Mitchell. She was a favorite of my *grandmother's*."

Both Paul and Deke grabbed their chests, pretending they'd been mortally wounded.

"Our cub is growing teeth," said Paul.

"And claws," added Deke.

Paul leaned close to Jake, peering at something. "Does that explain what appears to be a hickey on the side of his neck?"

"Really?" Deke put on his reading glasses, but Jake had already pulled up his shirt collar.

"It's a shaving burn," Jake said, but his flush gave everything away.

Deke turned to Paul, who was shaking his head. "Strange place for a shaving burn," Paul said.

"And from the timing of its appearance," said Deke, "it appears our colleague must have been up late—*shaving*—last night. I hope he doesn't make a habit of that, especially with the work we need him to put into the case."

If it was possible, Jake flushed an even deeper shade of red. It made Deke think of when he'd been courting his wife, Teri. From the first she had put a spring in Deke's step. That had never changed.

"Don't worry about my—shaving," said Jake.

Alison and Ron returned with copies of Judge Willard's decision, and all three lawyers sat down and began to read what he'd written. Occasionally one of them would read aloud a section that they liked.

"I wish I was a fly on the wall listening to the two Dicks discussing this ruling," said Jake.

"If they're worth their salt as lawyers," Deke said, "they'll dissect the ruling and use it to figure out the strengths and weaknesses of their case and ours. That's what I'm going to want you to do, Jake."

"You want me to armchair-quarterback the judge's ruling?" he asked.

"Pretty much," said Deke. "We can use what he wrote here as a pretty good indicator of what jurors might think as they hear this case. In reading what Judge Perry said, it's clear I should have taken more time in showing that the DEA and the DOJ had a responsibility to the public to act earlier than they did in stemming the explosion of opioids. I should have tied that in as a preamble to the death charts, showing they turned a blind eye to the diversion of opioids. The judge seemed to like my analogy of where there was smoke, there had to be fire, but he would have preferred I made a better case for the fire. We need to more thoroughly develop that part of the story.

"The judge also agreed with me that it seems to be much more than a coincidence that four of West Virginia's highest-ranking DEA administrators left their positions to work at MHC and the two other largest drug distributors. We'll need to look for more smoking-gun documents on that Gang of Four, but Judge Perry seemed to understand how the distributors dangled big job opportunities in front of those particular agents every time they opened a new investigation. In the next round we need to hammer at all the conflicts of interest between the opioid distributors and the government, and how that allows them to circumvent the law.

"I want you to really focus on memos or directives that suggest the DEA purposely dragged its feet when it came to acting on specific investigations. I'd also like a timeline that shows how soon afterward those same agents went to work in the private sector, and at what salaries."

Jake was busy taking notes. "What about me?" Paul asked.

"If you're amenable," said Deke, "I'd like you to work out an opi-oid damages formula with the best forensic accountants available. You can pick sample cities and counties that best tell our story."

Paul nodded. "Even after all this time, I don't think there's been a true accounting of how much the opioid epidemic has economi-cally impacted cities and counties and states."

"You're right about that," said Deke. "For the most part, the gov-ernment has been trying to pretend the problem away, instead of defining that problem. In our damage model, you'll need to clearly define all the economic costs to governmental services before the opioid epidemic, and since its start."

"You mean as taxpayers we shouldn't be grateful that these dis-tributors made billions in profits," said Paul, "and left us holding the bag for billions in expenses?"

"That's exactly what we need to point out," said Deke, "although maybe we should be a tad less cynical. Anyway, I was glad Judge Perry saved his most scathing remarks for the twenty-five-million-dollar settlement entered into by the *cabal*—his word, not mine—of state attorneys general."

Deke picked up Judge Willard's ruling and began reading. "'There is no question that this settlement was woefully inappro-priate when first entered into; the passage of time reveals just how inadequate the settlement was, and how it did not meaningfully redress any wrongs. The end result wasn't so much a settlement as it was a Band-Aid applied to a gaping wound. The seven state AGs said that after settling, they would henceforth put the distributors' feet to the fire; that never occurred. Moreover, if I have correctly reviewed all the information submitted to this court, it does not appear that even one of those attorneys general did so much as take a basic fact-finding deposition before agreeing to a settlement. Also troubling to this court is the apparent intermingling of state and corporate interests. In such collaborations, the appearance of collusion is inevitable, not to mention the potential for abuse and conflicts."

Smiling, Deke stopped reading and said, "Ouch! I don't think I could have said it better myself."

"Maybe next time Jazz Hands won't be so flagrant about advising the state attorneys general while in court," said Jake.

"If you half closed your eyes," Paul said, "you might have thought he was Jeff Dunham, and Dick Monger was his puppet, Walter."

The three of them laughed, enjoying their victory, temporary though they knew it might be. For a few minutes they decompressed, chatting about anything other than the case. It was Deke who finally signaled that recess was over.

"I'm sure everyone knows it only gets more difficult from here on in," he said.

Paul and Jake nodded. All the smiles began to fade at the thought of the work that awaited them. Deke took a deep breath and turned his gaze to Jake.

"It's time to look beyond our short-term strategy," said Deke, "and consider the long game that we'll have to play. You started us on this road, Jake. You had the courage to challenge MHC, and now we're going up against the Big Three."

The lawyers were now referring to McQueen Health Corporation, Silicon Medical, and Sparrow Healthcare as the Big Three. There was a reason for that. The three Fortune 25 companies distributed more than 90 percent of pharmaceuticals around the country. They were the ones who had made huge profits from distributing opioids.

"I'm thrilled about the progress we've made," said Deke, "and I'd love to be able to proclaim, 'Damn the torpedoes, full speed ahead,' but the reality is that the Big Three does two hundred billion dollars in business every year. As far as they're concerned, litigation is merely the *price* of doing business. Trench warfare plays right into their hands. They can spend hundreds of millions of dollars fighting all the opioid claims, and then hundreds of millions of dollars or more on appeals. The opioid industry has more money than most nations do, and they're not afraid to spend it. If we try to battle them county by county, or state by state, we can't win even if the verdict goes our way."

This wasn't what Jake wanted to hear. "Why?" he asked.

Deke sighed. The young man was an idealist, and he wished he didn't have to rain on his parade. "They'll appeal," said Deke. "They'll buy influence, and find ways to hinder our litigation at every turn. Even if the top ten claimants' law firms in all of America combined forces, there is no way we could defeat the Big Three and their virtually unlimited resources. I'm not saying that we wouldn't have successes along the way, but those small-scale Pyrrhic victories would accomplish next to nothing."

"Pyrrhic victories?" Jake asked.

Deke nodded. "The Pyrrhic War was fought thousands of years ago between King Pyrrhus of Epirus and the Romans. Pyrrhus won two decisive battles, but his victories were costly. The enemy had the numbers to rebound from their defeats, but he did not. He said, 'If we are victorious in one more battle with the Romans, we shall be utterly ruined.' That, my friend, is a Pyrrhic victory."

"If you want a shorthand version," said Paul, "last year I took a defendant to court and was awarded a single dollar in damages. Now *that* was a Pyrrhic victory."

"What's the alternative?" asked Jake. "I'd rather have a Pyrrhic victory than wave a white flag."

"No one is talking about waving a white flag," said Deke. "I'm thrilled about the progress we've made. We had a critical win. But now that we've come to a new juncture, Paul and I are of the same mind that we have to look at the big picture."

Paul was nodding, showing his support for Deke's words.

"Obviously the next step," said Deke, "is to get possession of the ARCOS data."

ARCOS stood for the Automation of Reports and Consolidated Orders System, which the DEA used to keep track of drugs being distributed throughout the country. Manufacturers and distributors were required to report their controlled-substance transactions to the attorney general. That information was then passed on to the DEA, which was supposed to monitor the flow of the controlled substances from their point of being manufactured to wherever they ended up being commercially distributed. The information provided by ARCOS was supposed to be used by federal and state governmental agencies to identify if, and where, controlled substances were being diverted. Over the years, the reports should have raised plenty of red flags, but hadn't. The diversion of drugs had continued for years with virtually no repercussions. The drug distributors had not only been aware of the drug diversions, but had done everything they could to see to their continuance.

"It's not just a bunch of statistics," said Jake. "It's our road map to the epidemic."

"That's right," said Deke. "We'll have more than a smoking gun. By connecting all the dots, we can show who knew what, and when they knew it. And even more important, the ARCOS data will paint the picture of how the Big Three pinpointed areas in the U.S. as specific targets. They selected these areas because of economic despair. The data will show how areas with high job loss and increased poverty were an unbeatable combination to sell more narcotics."

"That kind of targeting is what killed Blake and so many others," Jake said. "The opioid trail is one of blood money."

"That's something we're going to show," said Deke. "But to have a national impact on the opioid epidemic, we need to think beyond the courtrooms of West Virginia and Ohio. You ever hear the phrase 'Think globally, act locally'? In our cases, we've acted locally. Now we have to look beyond the county and state courtrooms."

"I'm not following," said Jake.

"I don't want to put the horse in front of the cart," said Deke, "but at the same time we're fighting to get the ARCOS data, we need to be positioning ourselves for an MDL."

"Multidistrict Litigation," said Paul, translating Deke's shorthand.

"An MDL will put the opioid epidemic on the national stage," said Deke. "Our trench warfare in Ohio and West Virginia will only take us so far. Our goal will be to prevail in getting the ARCOS data, and then file a pleading requesting that a single judge be appointed to oversee all of the national opioid litigation—not just the cases we filed, but other cases filed in jurisdictions through the country."

"One judge, one jurisdiction, and one massive trial," said Jake.

"Ours isn't the only opioid case working its way through federal court," said Paul. "There are scores of other cases, most of them sharing common issues."

"Instead of one hundred circuses," said Deke, "with an MDL everything would be placed under one big top. Without such a setup in place, litigation would continue to be piecemeal, incredibly time consuming, and prohibitively expensive."

Deke was glad to see that the young lawyer was nodding. "I always had this fantasy of championing Blake's cause in the courtroom, but I'm beginning to understand that if your strategy succeeds, it would be that much bigger of a victory. *Not* a Pyrrhic victory," Jake added.

"That's how we see it," said Deke.

"It would streamline the process and save time, wouldn't it?" asked Jake.

"It should," said Deke.

"Then I'm all for it," said Jake. "I can't take any more of these delays, especially knowing more than four thousand opioid users die every month. For me, that's so difficult to accept."

Jake didn't have to invoke Blake's name. Both Deke and Paul could hear it in his voice.

"I couldn't agree with you more," said Deke. "And because of that, I propose we change our game plan. I want to go on a fast-break offense and push for our next hearing in no more than two months' time."

"Two months," said Paul. "I think we all better invest in some track shoes."

"Won't the Big Three fight the expedited hearing?" asked Jake.

"I suspect this will be one of those rare instances where they won't try and gum up the works," said Deke. "They know that with more information coming out every day showing their culpability, their case will only get weaker with time. My guess is they'll welcome an earlier date in court in the hope that they'll be able to close the doors on us getting the ARCOS data."

"I hope you're right," said Jake.

"I guess they didn't tell you in law school that 'the wheels of justice turn slowly,'" said Paul.

"If they did, I must not have been listening," said Jake.

"This week I'll get the ball rolling," said Deke, "and that means I'll be generating a lot of paperwork. You can be sure in the next hearing our opponents will try and improve on their arguments that all cities and counties must abide by any agreements made by their state attorney general. To try and preempt that, I'll have Alison and Ron help me build a wall with Judge Perry's words, supported by documents right out of the defendants' own file cabinets. My focus will be long, long hours of document review. It's the not-very-glamorous part of law, but nothing typically pays off more."

Deke looked to the other two men. "Anything else we need to talk about?"

When no one had anything to add, Deke said, "Today was a good day for our side. Let's use that momentum. I know we all have our particular roles in this case, but as a team we need to know what everyone is doing individually so that we can prepare in unison. Let's talk with each other on a daily basis. And how about we have another face-to-face a week from today at nine in the morning? That will be a good time to compare notes and strategize. I'm hoping we'll have been put on the docket by then, and we can define our game plan right up to the day of the hearing."

"Works for me," said Paul.

"Sounds good," said Jake.

19
MURDER FOR A JAR OF RED RUM

Eva was working on her laptop and only half listening to Danny when he said, "Eva, can I stab bats in a cave?"

She looked up to see her husband looking at her with that goofy smile of his. "What did you just say?"

"I said, 'Eva, can I stab bats in a cave?'"

Danny began laughing at her confused expression. "It's a palindrome. I saw your name in a sentence, and that's what got me reading this article on palindromes. A palindrome is a word that's spelled the same backward or forward."

"I know what a palindrome is," she said. Pointedly, she added, "It's a word like *boob* or *kook*."

Danny nodded, apparently unmindful of her disdain. He went back to the article and began reading aloud some of the palindrome phrases: "Do geese see God?" Then he added, "Was it a rat I saw?" And laughing, he concluded with, "Mr. Owl ate my metal worm."

"Murdrum," Eva whispered under her breath.

"What?" he asked.

"Nothing," she said. "I thought there was a problem you needed to discuss with me."

Danny made a little face. Eva wasn't fond of bad news, but Danny knew not to keep anything from her. "That deputy contacted me again," he said. "Even though that condemnation auction we had set up in Oakley never took place, that young lawyer is still nosing around."

"I see," she said. "Mr. Rutledge has been poking a lot of hornets' nests these days, including the DEA, the three biggest pharmaceutical distributors, and various other players in the black-market opioid trade. If you read between the lines, that means the Mountain Mafia. That means he has declared war against the government, three Fortune 25 companies, and the organized drug trade. It sounds to me like the man has a death wish."

Danny was nodding in agreement.

"In fact," Eva said, "it wouldn't surprise me if Jake Rutledge's propensity for upsetting apple carts resulted in his simply disappearing."

"That would solve our problem, wouldn't it?" said Danny.

Eva took his wishful thinking and ran with it. "Why, yes it would," she said. "And when you have so many enemies, the police wouldn't even know where to start their investigation."

A sudden realization came to Danny. "If this lawyer disappears, our interests might not even show up on the radar."

"I think you're right about that," Eva said.

"But I couldn't just . . ."

Her husband balked at even saying the word *murder*. "Of course not," Eva said.

Danny looked relieved.

"Still," she said, "it's a shame there's no way to get him out of our hair. That might save you a big headache."

"What do you mean?" asked Danny.

"I'm afraid if he finds out about some of those condemned properties you've managed to obtain, it wouldn't look good for you. I'm sure young and idealistic Jake Rutledge would develop a case that makes it sound like you were throwing widows and orphans out on the street. He'd probably make the argument that if you would throw your own sickly mother into a dirty broom closet, then you certainly would have no compassion for all those people you stole property from. Just imagine how that trial would play out."

Danny winced, and Eva started to reel him in.

"I wonder if this Jake Rutledge is as virtuous in real life as they say he is."

"I'm sure he's not," Danny muttered.

"You're probably right," said Eva. "Look at Congressman Roberts."

Rob Roberts was a three-term West Virginia congressman known mostly for his pro-life stance. During the past month he'd been facing the fallout from the public's learning not only about his twenty-two-year-old girlfriend (something his fifty-eight-year-old wife didn't know about), but also the fact that Roberts had paid for his girlfriend's abortion.

"I knew he was a hypocrite the first time we met him," said Danny.

"It wouldn't even surprise me," said Eva, "if our young lawyer abused opioids. After all, didn't his own brother die of an overdose?"

"I think I heard something about that," Danny said.

"For you," Eva said, "it would be a godsend if everyone believed he used opioids. He'd lose all his credibility, and no one would believe anything he had to say."

"Wait a second," Danny said. "I'm getting an idea."

It's about time, Eva thought. But her face didn't give away her impatience. She appeared attentive to her husband's every word.

"I could make arrangements for the lawyer to disappear," said Danny. "He wouldn't have to die. We could hold him somewhere while we get him strung out on opioids."

"Brilliant! There are so many people who want this lawyer out of their hair, the police will have to hand out numbers to all the suspects. Talk about muddying the waters. And, of course," she said, "you're going to use that deputy to help, aren't you? If down the road Rutledge tries to point the finger at the deputy for that real estate misunderstanding in Oakley, no one will pay any attention to anything he claims."

"Yes," Danny said, "that's right."

"Your deputy could even arrest a street dealer and get the dealer to claim that Rutledge was one of his longtime clients."

"And when it's shown that Rutledge is using," said Danny, "no one will ever believe anything that junkie lawyer has to say."

"No, they wouldn't," said Eva. "How clever of you." And under her breath, she whispered, "Murder for a jar of red rum."

It was a favorite palindrome of hers, but she didn't share that piece of knowledge with Danny.

20
HOG-TIED

Deke and Paul made small talk while waiting for Jake, who was already fifteen minutes late for their nine a.m. meeting. Neither man had said anything about his tardiness, as each expected him to walk in at any moment. Jake had never been late before. In fact, he was invariably the one who arrived early and stayed late. From the first, Jake had embraced the long hours. To all appearances he was a happy sponge, glad for the opportunity to soak up knowledge.

Finally, Deke addressed the elephant in the room. "When Master Jake does walk in," he said, "I think I'll take a long and hard look at his neck before I say word one."

"If he has another hickey," Paul said, "I'm going to pretend to be jealous. Or maybe I won't even have to pretend. It's probably been twenty-five years since my last hickey."

"I might join you in faking umbrage. We can say his being late is simply his way of showing off to the old guys."

"Speak for yourself. These days I find myself quoting Francis Bacon more and more: 'I will never be an old man. To me, old age is always fifteen years more than I am.'"

"I'm stealing that quote," said Deke.

When another five minutes had passed, each of them became concerned. Paul took out his cell phone and called Jake. After four rings, it went to voice mail, and he left a message.

Another five minutes passed. This time it was Deke who called Jake and left a message.

"It wouldn't surprise me if he had a flat," said Paul, "or if that beater of his broke down. I know the route he typically takes from Oakley. Why don't I drive along it? If I don't see him along the way, I'll just stop at his house. He's been working such long hours it's possible he slept through the alarm."

"I can't think of a better plan," said Deke. "While you're gone, I'll corral the paralegals just to see if they heard anything from him and forgot to pass the information our way. If they don't know anything, the three of us will start calling law enforcement to see if Jake might have been involved in an accident."

It was noon when Paul called Deke from the Rutledge house. "His car is here," he said, "but there's no sign of Jake. I knocked loudly, then looked in through the windows. Nothing appeared to be out of place."

Deke thrummed his fingers against the desktop. "I was afraid of that. That's why I already called Carol Morris, the security director of my firm. She's trying to track his location through his cell phone and is pulling his credit-card history. Depending on what she finds or doesn't find, she'll likely be flying to West Virginia today with a team. She's also put in a missing person's report to the state and city cops, but since Jake hasn't been missing for long, it was hard for her to get much traction with that. In the meantime, she's pulling what strings she can to make sure Jake gets on law enforcement's radar."

"What can I do from this end?" asked Paul.

"Carol has asked us to construct our best Jake timeline for the last forty-eight hours. That means I'll need you to reengineer Jake's movements. We need to know who he was seeing. Talking to Jake's new lady friend is a priority of Carol's."

"I have one or two numbers for contacts Jake has in Oakley," said Paul. "I'll start by calling them. If they can't tell me anything, I'll knock on the doors of his neighbors."

"Good luck with that," said Deke, trying not to sound worried.

In truth, he didn't have a good feeling about this. Jake was too committed to their case, and too conscientious of a kid, to have not contacted them by now.

Something was wrong.

Somewhere nearby in the darkness, someone was in a lot of pain. Their groans and moans and cries of pain were just short of screams. Jake wished they would stop, because his head was pounding, but the cries continued for several minutes. He tried to open his mouth to say something before realizing the source of the noises. *He* was the one who was groaning.

Jake opened an eye. The light was like a stab to his optic nerve. He shut his eyes tight, and then to block out all light, he cupped a hand over them. He found that it didn't hurt quite as much if he held himself steady. Still, his head continued to throb. What the hell had happened?

He remembered leaving Anna's house at about nine the night before. The two of them had been doing work on the case, but it hadn't been all toil. They'd set aside time to play two games of cribbage; Anna had won both games. Jake had pretended to pout, and Anna's "sympathizing" with him had included a kiss.

Right after her kiss, Jake had said, "Now you see why I threw those games."

"Revisionist history," she'd shot back. "You fought tooth and nail to win."

"I was playing for the consolation prize," he said. "That's my story and I'm sticking to it."

Jake might have smiled at the memory, except he was afraid any movement would bring on even more pain. One of the many things he liked about Anna was her competitiveness. Growing up, he and Blake had always vied with each other over gin rummy, chess, backgammon, Scrabble, and cribbage. Since Blake's death, Jake had rarely played any of those games. But Anna was a gamester and had reinvigorated his latent interest in gaming. As he'd been leaving the Fowler house, she'd challenged him to a Scrabble contest the very next night, taunting him by adding, "If you dare."

Jake thought hard, following his memories through the rest of the night. He'd arrived home around nine fifteen. Instead of being vigilant, he'd been distracted, thinking about Anna. It was only when he was inserting his key into the door that he heard movement behind him. He'd turned, but had gotten only a glimpse of the two men. They were dressed in black and wearing ski masks. He'd tried to brandish his key as a weapon, but he'd been far too slow. One of the men was already swinging some kind of club. When it connected with Jake's head, his world went black.

I'm lucky to be alive, he thought.

He opened an eye once more and had to fight off nausea, which meant he'd likely suffered a concussion. He knew it was important now that he stay awake long enough to take in his circumstances. Even though it hurt to move, he forced himself to gradually turn his head. He was in some kind of cage or pen, with fabric draped all around it, blocking most of the outside from view. The cage was rectangular, probably four feet high and eight feet long. There was something familiar about the heavy iron bars. *It's one of those boar traps,* Jake thought suddenly, *designed to take in a passel of pigs.* But this trap had been modified. The spring door was secured with a chain lock so that it couldn't be opened. T-posts had been driven deep into the dirt below to anchor the trap. The cage had few comforts or amenities other than some mats and blankets that lined the floor. Food had been left in an old metal galvanized feed bucket—jerky, pepperoni rolls, and hush puppies—and there were two one-gallon jugs of bug juice—water that looked to be flavored with red Kool-Aid.

Jake knew West Virginia had more than its share of "hogzillas," huge feral pigs, some weighing north of three hundred pounds. The cages that corralled such behemoths were designed to withstand lots of punishment.

He continued his slow-motion surveillance. Even though he moved as gingerly as possible, it took all his willpower not to retch. As far as he could tell, he was sitting in the middle of a small forest clearing. He could see trees, but there were no houses nearby, nor were there any roads. His view, however, was limited because of the draping around the cage. It took him a few seconds to realize that the draping was camouflage, meant to disguise the cage in the event of an air search—almost like a hunting blind.

He strained to hear anything but couldn't pick up any sounds of cars, or any voices.

No people, no houses, and no roads, Jake thought. It seemed as if he'd been left in the middle of nowhere. Normally he might have screamed for help, but just the thought of raising his voice caused his head to throb that much more.

They hadn't killed him outright. He supposed that was a good thing, even if it didn't feel like it at the moment. But who was *they*? And what did they want?

Suddenly conscious of how dehydrated he was, Jake steadied himself with his hands and moved forward on his knees, half walking, half crawling over to where the two jugs were. Flipping off one of the caps, Jake raised the jug up above his lips, and in so doing scraped the bottle against the top of the cage. Even though he used both hands to steady the jug, the strain made his arms tremble. He gulped the red liquid once, twice, and then a third time, and lowered the jug to the ground. Then he replaced the cap on the jug and sank into one of the mats lining the cage, exhausted by his efforts.

As he lay there, Jake realized that although the bug juice had been cloyingly sweet, it had a bitter aftertaste. The thought crossed his mind that someone might have poisoned it, but that seemed unlikely. If his captors' goal was to do him harm, there had been no shortage of opportunities. Still, the aftertaste made him suspect the water might have been drugged. What better way to keep him compliant than to make him sleep away his captivity instead of spending his time plotting an escape? Maybe that's why he was suddenly feeling so tired.

The buzzing around his head grew louder. Jake wasn't sure if the noise was being caused by insects, or from the beating that had left him senseless. At the moment, though, he was too tired to care. Cradling his aching head in his arms, he stretched out on the mat and fell asleep.

21
PRAYERS CAN'T HURT ANY

It had been four days since Jake had been a no-show for his nine a.m. meeting with Deke and Paul. For most of that time, Carol Morris had been coordinating the overall campaign to find out what had happened to him.

There were seven main members of what Deke was referring to as "Team Jake." Under the auspices of those seven, volunteers and temporary help had been brought in to help alert the public to Jake's disappearance.

Carol brought the meeting of Team Jake, all of whom had assembled at Deke's apartment, to order. Those unfamiliar with her might have assumed from her appearance that she was some suburban grandmother. Her comforting smile and amiable demeanor often helped her obtain information that otherwise would have eluded others. But Carol had spent most of her career in law enforcement, and her many sources and resources had made her invaluable at heading up security at Bergman/Deketomis.

"Let me say at the onset of this meeting that Jake's whereabouts are still unknown," she said. "However, I am now confident that we have an accurate timeline for the thirty-six hours prior to the time he went missing. This timeline was formulated by accessing his cell phone records during the time he had it in his possession. From what we can determine, though, it appears likely that Jake's phone was taken from him and destroyed on the night we believe he went missing.

"Before Jake disappeared, he was in the company of Anna Fowler at her father's house in Oakley. Jake was with Anna on Tuesday evening from approximately six in the evening until nine o'clock. Bennie and I have already had a chance to talk to Anna, as has Paul. She provided us with good leads, a few of which we are continuing to follow up on. Since some of you hadn't met Anna, I thought this would be a good opportunity for you to do that, as well as to ask her any questions you might have."

Anna looked around to those in the room and offered a few nods. She had already been part of two Team Jake conference calls, but this was the first time she'd had a chance to physically meet with Deke, Ron, and Alison.

In Deke's career he had deposed hundreds of individuals. It didn't surprise anyone that he was the first to ask a question. "Was Jake your boyfriend, Anna?" he asked.

Anna blinked away tears as a sad smile came over her face. "I'd like to think he was on the way to being so," she said, "but it would be presumptuous of me to say that he was. I can say we were friends, and becoming friendlier, although we were cautious about getting involved too quickly because of my circumstances."

"And what circumstances are those?" asked Deke.

"Earlier this month I went cold turkey. I had become dependent on opioids, and Jake was helping me kick that habit. In fact, I'm sure I wouldn't have been able to get this far without him."

"How long have the two of you been going out?"

"It's been recent," she said. "As odd as it might sound, we reacquainted at the Oakley graveyard. We had been friendly all during our school years, and for a time I sort of dated his brother, although that was more of a friend thing than anything else. Jake and I lost touch when he went away to school. We stumbled upon one another when we got back into town and then recently reconnected again. As it happened, Jake came over to my house unannounced on the very day I'd decided to go cold turkey. He reentered my life at what I would have thought was the worst possible time, but turned out to be the best."

"Tell me about your last night together," said Deke.

"I wish there was more to tell," she said. "I'd made a chicken casserole for my father—he likes to eat early—and Jake came over after work. The two of us sat down to eat at around six thirty. Most of our conversation was about the case. I hope you don't think Jake was talking out of shop; it was more like he was using me as his sounding board. You see, I had been helping him with some of the case paperwork in return for his doing legal work on a family matter. But you need to understand that Jake was aboveboard even in what he referred to as our 'quid pro quo arrangement,' and had me sign a nondisclosure agreement."

Deke offered a reassuring smile to the nervous young woman. He liked the way she was being protective of Jake. "Rest assured, Anna, that Jake had already told us that he was utilizing your services."

At the time, Deke and Paul had assumed Jake's mysterious helper was his girlfriend, but they hadn't pressed him on the matter. Anna looked relieved, and maybe a little pleased, that Jake had mentioned that she was providing help, and gave Deke a grateful smile.

"During our talk that night," she said, "it was clear that Jake was excited about some of the discoveries he'd made that day concerning the DEA. I wish he'd offered up specifics, but he didn't. What I most remember is that he said that what he found out would help expose the Gang of Four."

There was head nodding from those in the room, and Carol said, "Deke and Paul, in case you haven't had time to read your email this morning, you'll find a file from me referencing Jake's notes pertaining to the aforementioned Gang of Four, as well as our own supplemental findings. It appears that Jake was able to determine that between bonuses and salary incentives, those former DEA agents were making well over seventy thousand dollars more than others with the same titles already working at the Big Three pharmaceutical distributors. Bennie and I were able to verify that on the day we believe Jake went missing, he had talked to two very cooperative DEA employees who confirmed that their former bosses had dragged their feet on investigations into opioid distributors."

Deke shook his head. "Leave it to Jake to go where angels fear to tread. Do we think his asking those questions can be linked to his disappearance?"

"We don't know," said Carol. "What we know for certain is that these four agents look and smell dirty, like they had been paid off by the Big Three to look the other way when it came to any opioid investigations. Bennie has talked in person with three of the four individuals in question."

All eyes turned to Bennie. He dwarfed the chair that was holding his huge 275-pound frame.

"It would probably be more accurate to say that I've tried to talk to them," he said. "Unfortunately, I haven't been able to get anyone to speak with me for more than a few seconds."

"What's your gut feeling tell you?" asked Deke.

Bennie thought about it for a moment, then shook his head. "These guys are freaked out to be in our headlights, but if I had to hazard a guess, I doubt that they had anything to do with Jake's disappearance."

"Have you gotten anywhere with anyone at MHC?" asked Paul. "We know for a fact that two of their goons offered Jake a substantial bribe after the motion to dismiss his case was put aside. After refusing their offer, the two of them baited him, and after he took a swing, they beat him up."

Carol answered that question. "Based on the descriptions you provided, we believe we've identified those two individuals as employees of a security company that MHC has on retainer. Unfortunately, Jake's assailants were in Texas on the night he disappeared."

"That doesn't mean MHC, or one of the other Big Three, didn't hire out the job to other goons," said Deke.

"No, it doesn't," Carol said.

"It was for that reason I called Nathan Ailes the day before yesterday," said Paul. "In as nice a way as I could muster, I asked him if his clients might have had anything to do with Jake's disappearance."

"And how did Jazz Hands respond to that?" asked Deke.

"He pretended great umbrage, and said only an idiot could come up with such a ridiculous notion. Then he ended the conversation by asking if we would be continuing Jake's case in his absence, or if we were considering abandoning it."

"He really asked that?" said Deke.

"I'm afraid so."

"I can just hear that prick asking Mary Todd Lincoln, 'Aside from that, Mrs. Lincoln, how'd you enjoy the play?'"

Despite everyone's somber mood, laughter filled the room. Deke had known they needed the comic relief.

"Anything else we should be talking about?" he asked.

Deke scanned the room. When no one said anything, Deke turned to Anna. "Earlier you said that Jake was helping you on a family matter, and that the two of you had a quid pro quo arrangement. Would you mind telling us what Jake was doing on your family's behalf?"

"No problem," she said. "I was told there was some sort of bureaucratic mix-up surrounding my father's former business, a service station in Oakley. Earlier this month a sheriff's deputy showed up at the house and gave my father paperwork saying the county would be auctioning off his downtown property because he had failed to make some kind of payments to the county. Jake went to the station house to talk to that deputy and told him that the sheriff's department and the county hadn't followed state and local law. From there he determined that there was no paperwork to document the county's claim. Needless to say, the auction never took place, but Jake was still trying to get to the bottom of what had happened, and wasn't satisfied with the answers he was getting."

"That explains a file Bennie and I were looking at yesterday," said Carol. "It was labeled 'Fowler's.' Now Jake's notations make sense. Apparently, he was searching for any patterns of abuse or fraud in nearby counties similar to what your father experienced."

"I'd like you to forward Jake's file to me," said Paul. "I think his instincts were good. Where there's smoke, there's fire. I'd like to continue his search to see what I can find."

Deke turned to Anna and shook his head. "I'm sure that must have been disturbing to you and your father. Why is it that people have to go to war these days over damn near everything just to protect themselves?"

When his rhetorical question went unanswered, he looked at the faces around the room. "Any other toes Jake was stepping on that might have gotten him into trouble?"

Heads swiveled toward one another, but no one said anything.

Deke returned his gaze to Anna. "Ms. Fowler, there's no ex-boyfriend who might have been jealous?"

Anna shook her head.

With a nod of her head to the two paralegals, Carol said, "This week Ron and Alison have been training the new hires who will be working our twenty-four-hour toll-free hotline. They've also been overseeing the distribution of reward posters with Jake's picture on it. By tomorrow, those posters will be on display throughout the state, and we need to prepare for a tsunami of crazy."

Bergman/Deketomis was offering a $100,000 reward for any information leading to Jake's whereabouts.

"Do we have anyone working with the media besides Ron and Alison?" asked Deke.

"I brought in Molly Gold," said Carol. Molly was the head of PR at the firm. "She made sure every television station in the state played up Jake's disappearance. And she's continued to beat the drums to make sure that the offer of reward money will generate a second news cycle. If that doesn't result in Jake's being found, Molly suggests that in two or three days we organize a candlelight vigil. Doing that will help keep Jake in the public eye."

Deke sighed. "Let's hope so," he said. "The more eyes we get on this, the better. Have you had any better luck motivating law enforcement to make Jake's disappearance their biggest priority?"

"Two detectives have been assigned to the case," she said. "They seem professional, and they're putting in the time and legwork, but haven't uncovered anything we don't already know."

"Assure them we'll provide any resources they need," said Deke.

Once more, he looked around the room before asking, "Any other suggestions as to what we might be doing to bring our boy home?"

The room was quiet. It was clear that everything that could be done to help locate Jake was being done.

"Prayers can't hurt any," whispered Anna.

"Amen," said Paul.

22
A DIET OF BUG JUICE

"**S**crew you!" Jake shouted, then raised his middle finger as high as the cage allowed.

Other than a few birds that momentarily stopped singing, nothing in the woods seemed to notice Jake's outburst. He hoped someone was monitoring him and that he wasn't wasting his time merely cursing the universe. His sharp eyes had picked out what he thought was a camera positioned in a sugar maple some twenty yards away from his prison. The camera seemed to have been angled to look in through the fabric's narrow opening. If not for the occasional reflection of light off its lens, he doubted he would have noticed it.

What he didn't know was whether his captivity was being livestreamed to some other location. It was also possible that there was no camera and it was only wishful thinking making him see things. But surely whoever was holding him captive would have him under surveillance. Just in case they'd missed his first commentary, Jake flipped the bird at the camera for a second time.

For at least a week, he'd been cooped up in the cage. He couldn't be any more specific than that because there were holes in his memory. Most of the time he'd slept. The sleep wasn't only to while away the time; Jake knew his food and water were drugged. To date, he'd had no contact with his captors, or none that he could remember. On three occasions he'd awakened to find that his waste bucket had been emptied and food had been left. That he'd slept through the visits suggested he'd been drugged. He suspected even more potent drugs had been introduced into his system while he slept—those would explain the sore red lesions he'd found in the area of his hip. It would also explain his fugue states, the way he wasn't even aware of the passage of time.

The food that had been left for him was stick-to-your-ribs fare: a pie tin of homemade cornbread along with helpings of boiled potatoes, hush puppies, boiled eggs, hot dogs, sausages, and bologna. Fruit seemed to be an afterthought, but he had gotten a few apples and bananas, as well as carrots.

At the moment, Jake was down to a hush puppy and the last few inches of his drink. He wondered if his diminished larder was a psychological ploy by those holding him. Maybe they wanted him on edge and off balance. If so, he had to admit it was working; he was increasingly anxious to be resupplied.

He reached for his bottle of bug juice. That's what he and Blake and their friends had all called it when they were kids. How sweetened water had come to be called bug juice by all of them, he didn't know. The flavored sugar water was poor-man's soda pop.

Jake lifted the bottle, bemused that his captivity had reacquainted him with the drink of his youth. He started out taking a circumspect sip but found himself downing a big gulp. It had gotten so that he was now craving the bug juice.

The drink left him feeling more relaxed. It also focused him on the need to escape. As he did several times a day, he began doing what he thought of as his escape exercises. Positioned on his back, he kicked at the cage, probing for weak spots. It must have looked like a supine version of vigorous bicycling. He put all his weight into leg strikes. Each kick made a clang like a bell being rung. Certain noises traveled long distances; he hoped his clarion call might make someone curious enough to investigate.

All his banging, though, didn't seem to have any effect on the cage; if there was a weak spot, he had yet to find it. The compact space restricted his movements; he couldn't gather enough momentum to throw himself at the cage. After what he imagined was about ten minutes of kicking the metal, Jake was forced to take a break. He didn't want to overheat and face the night with damp clothes. It was already cold enough even with the blankets. But it wasn't only the sweating that made him stop. He hated to admit it, but his captivity already had him out of shape. That's what happened when you couldn't stand up straight and walk around. He had tried to keep fit with push-ups and sit-ups, but those weren't aerobic exercises.

For the umpteenth time, Jake considered how he might escape his cage. *What would MacGyver do?* he wondered. Would it be possible to make some kind of fulcrum using his shoelaces and the old galvanized pail? Or maybe he could remove the pail's handle and strop its ends against the metal until they were sharp. But even if he managed to hone the edges to razor sharpness, it would require a whole lot of filing to cut through the bars.

The opening of the cage was probably where it was weakest. Or it would have been its weakest spot had it not been secured with a fabric-covered chain lock. Even if Jake was able to get through that material, he was fairly sure there wasn't a weak link in that chain.

Tonight, it's important that I stay awake, he thought. *I'll ask questions of my captor and learn who's behind my abduction and find out why I've been taken.* Maybe he could get his unknown jailer to sympathize with his plight. Jake could talk about Anna. All he had to do was speak from his heart and voice his real concerns. He felt bad about not being there for her when she was at her most vulnerable. He hoped she hadn't relapsed.

"Everything was going so well," he whispered.

It had felt like he, Deke, and Paul were the legal dream team. It didn't matter what the opposition threw against them. They had tried high-powered attorneys, and even the almighty attorneys freaking general from not one, but two states. But their side had never blinked, nor would they. The truth would make their case for them.

He thought about Paul and Deke. Every day he had gone into work like an excited kid. They had been teaching him so much. And what he missed most was the laughter when the three of them got together. They were all committed to their cause, but the other two men liked laughing as much as Jake did.

It had been fun to laugh again. He thought about how Blake's death had changed him and made him more somber. It wasn't until he'd made these new friends that he'd felt it was okay to be happy.

"I miss them," Jake whispered, "and I miss Anna." He found himself fighting off tears, aware that his emotions were becoming more difficult to control. The enforced solitude was taking its toll on him. It was easy—too easy—to wallow in loneliness.

That kind of pity party, he realized, threatened to be debilitating.

Prison or not, he thought, *I need to use my time. It's important that I stay sharp, no matter what.*

Finding that inner resolve bolstered him. "What I need to do," Jake said aloud, "is prepare my case for when I get out."

There were lots of excuses not to do that. Jake knew he looked like hell. His scratchy beard itched like anything. The clothes he was wearing were dirty, and his hygiene was limited to a gum-sized sliver of soap that his captor had left, along with a few small bottles of water, which were enough for a sponge bath. His sleep was fitful, as drugged sleep often is. The mats he'd been left to sleep on diminished the hard ridges of the bottom of the cage, and the rocky earth under that, but even a lumpy mattress would have been better. All that was bad enough, but the biggest obstacle of all was his state of mind. The doctored bug juice muddled his thinking, made it feel like he was slogging through an unremitting fog. But he couldn't let that stop him.

"Failure is not an option," he said.

It was his favorite line from his favorite movie. The Apollo 13 astronauts had found a way to surmount what must have seemed like the insurmountable, and so would he.

Jake turned his head and looked toward the nearby stand of trees. He thought about a piece of advice Deke had given him. "You need to tell your story to the jury in a way that resonates with them. They need to know why *you're* there, and why *they're* there."

Jake thought about his story, and then he began to talk to the trees, recognizing that a jury would never actually hear the words he spoke. But today he would speak the words that came from his heart even if it was just a conversation with a grove.

"Ladies and gentlemen of the jury," he said, "my name is Jake Rutledge. My twin brother, Blake, died of an opiate overdose. That's why I'm here. Since his passing, I have tried to make sense of why Jake died. Finding those answers has not been easy. But the truth is that Blake did not have to die, just as so many thousands of other individuals didn't have to die. As this trial progresses, you will hear about my long journey to discovery. For now, though, I just want to tell you a little bit about my brother. Blake was my best friend in the world, and I guarantee that you would have liked him."

Jake's voice cracked, but he didn't stop talking. And it seemed to him that the trees leaned a little closer to hear what he had to say.

23
MR. SANDMAN

Willpower, and a sharp rock, kept Jake awake, but as the night grew later, it became increasingly more difficult to stay alert. Not being able to move much made his task harder. In the event he was being monitored with an infrared camera, he didn't want his captors to know what he was up to. Even so, he was forced to jab the sharp rock into his flesh over and over again so as to not nod off. As the night wore on, he wondered if his unknown jailers were actually planning on visiting him. Maybe they no longer had any use for him. Maybe they would just let him starve to death.

Jake played mental games to try and occupy himself. He came up with his fifty greatest basketball and baseball players of all time, followed up by his version of the ten greatest quarterbacks. Most of the all-time greats he knew only through old game footage, but he did his best to be fair.

Gauging the time was difficult, but Jake figured it was around midnight when he heard what he believed to be an engine. The sound came closer but then seemed to fade away again. Still, if he was right about having heard the engine, there had to be a road not too far away. And maybe, just maybe, someone was coming to see him.

Jake waited expectantly. As the minutes passed, he listened closely for sounds in the night and was surprised by the difficulty of the task. He'd become accustomed to the noises of the wind and the rubbing trees and the rustling leaves. But they were deafening, masking any sounds that might be related to human activities.

Keeping completely still, not even moving his head, Jake stared through the opening in the fabric that camouflaged his cage. Even though his heart was pounding, he took shallow breaths to keep his chest from rising and falling. He knew anyone approaching him would have to go through the woods. Maybe there was a path among the trees, or a game trail. Minutes passed. Jake had almost given up hope when he spotted a flashlight moving amid the foliage. The swaying branches seemed to cast the light about so that it looked like a dancing will-o'-the-wisp.

The light went out as whoever was approaching drew near. His visitor didn't advance undetected, however; dry leaves crackled, and twigs snapped.

Jake continued to play possum. If his jailer thought he was asleep, he might not take his usual precautions. Jake pretended to be deep in dreamland, but even his snoring sounds weren't enough to lull the other man into complacency.

With one eye cracked open, Jake tried to see what his captor was doing. He could tell from the person's size and shape that it was a man. He slung what looked to be a large backpack from his shoulder and began unzipping its compartments. The aroma of chicken made Jake salivate. And there were potatoes as well, his nose told him. He hoped his stomach wouldn't start growling and give him away.

Through slitted eyes, he watched, hoping that his visitor would pull back the opening in the fabric and then unlock the cage, giving Jake the opportunity to charge. Unfortunately, that didn't happen.

Keeping his distance from the cage, the man unscrewed what looked to be a pole, or maybe a telescoping fishing rod. The pole extended out, doubling in length, and then the man began screwing something onto its end.

There was enough moonlight for Jake to see the syringe being affixed to the end of the pole. It was a device typically used on bulls or unruly cattle, and Jake realized it must have already been used on him at least twice.

As the man lifted up the fabric, Jake changed the pattern of his breathing and made waking noises. Then he raised his head and looked toward where his visitor was standing.

"What . . . what?" Jake pretended surprise. He shook his head violently, almost as if trying to escape from the grip of a nightmare. Then he sat up and said, "Who are you? And what do you want?"

The man didn't answer at first. He looked to be about Jake's age, with a long brown mustache. Even though it was night, he was wearing a worn baseball cap. Black lettering stood out on a yellow rectangle, a capital *A* atop a *T*. Jake had seen the letters before: they signified the Appalachian Trail.

"What the hell is going on here?" Jake demanded.

"This ain't good, Jesus," screeched the man. "Not good at all, Lord." His Appalachian twang bespoke the mountains and cloistered hollows.

"Don't just stand there," said Jake. "Get me the hell out of this cage." He pretended not to notice the man's inaction. "I've been locked up for a week," he said, "or maybe longer. I don't know for sure."

"Y'all be still," the man whispered. "What if they watchin' us now? You better pray that ain't so."

He turned around as if afraid, peering at the tree where Jake had suspected a camera was positioned.

"But they partyin' now," Screech said, "so we's probably safe. You only alive cuz of me, you know. And Jesus. Can't forget Jesus. His goodness wash away my sins. You'd've been kilt, but I told them, 'Thou shall not kill.' And I reminded them that you be good with the solution with a little time. They was okay with givin' it a go. Time and the low toss, that's all he needs, I tell 'em. Course it wouldn't hurt to have Jesus as well."

Even though Jake had been born and bred in West Virginia, the hillbilly's accent was still hard for him to interpret, so he tried a different tack.

"You brought me lettuce?" he asked.

Screech looked confused. "I got you food and drink. And I got-cha solution. I knew you'd be hawngree. Seven percent, some calls it. I say it wun-hunderd percent. You take it, you all in, right?"

Jake wondered if it was his tiredness that made it difficult to follow Screech. "Why am I being held captive?" he asked.

"Don't know your particulars. Make it right with Jesus. That's my advice. We was told to make you disappear for *a while*. There was some talk about those two words. What is *a while*? That there is why you alive. Course some think we already past *a while*—'specially since those that told us to putcha away *a while* haven't been calling to see how you doin'. To some, that's a sign. If they don't care, we don't care. It's almost like you already disappeared permanent. But I say for now, for *a while*, we let you be Sleeping Beauty."

"Sleeping Beauty?" said Jake. "What do you mean?"

"You eat the apple and you sleep, right? You only supposed to wake for Prince Charming. You not supposed to get up from that sleep. You not supposed to talk to no one. It's lucky you boring. Watchin' you is like watchin' paint dry. But anyone see you now, they might say ya gotta be kilt. Dontcha make that mistake again with no one else. I'm okay, though, cuz you already with the solution. Soon, maybe already, you're not agin us. You with us with the low toss. Life is mighty fine, is it not? I can see it in you, cuz I stopped by to see what condition your condition is in. You already got the thirst, dontcha? Only one thing for the thirst, and that's all the something you need. That and Jesus. Can't forget Jesus."

It was surreal, thought Jake. This man with the screechy voice was jumping from threats to old music lyrics to strange and untethered observations. In the space of a few seconds, he had gone from euphoria to paranoia.

"If you let me out," said Jake, "I'll make sure you get a large reward. Besides, you don't want to keep me penned up. Kidnapping is a capital crime."

"You hear one word I say? I got my reward on earth. And you getting yours. And one day with Jesus, I get my reward in heaven. I go from one club to another. If you lucky, you do the same. When you one of us, you one of us. But that take *a while*. In a month or so, there's only one way to go. Until then, if you want to stay aboveground, you stay put."

"What do you want from me?" asked Jake.

"Only one thing: turn around and drop your drawers."

"The hell I will!" said Jake. "I'm not going to let myself be speared."

"Ain't no spear," said Screech. "It's your salvation. I calls it the Sandman. You work a cattle ranch in Romney, like I done, the Sandman becomes your best friend around livestock with bad attitude. I don't tolerate no bad attitude."

"Stick your Sandman up your ass," said Jake.

"Suit yo' self. Between me and Jesus, he knows I tried. You dyin' means I don't got to worry about no more midnight runs."

Screech began filling his backpack. The man's movements made Jake's throat tighten. He tried to tamp down his panic but couldn't.

"Don't," he said.

Screech nodded. "I can see you scared. Nothing scarier than the end of good vibrations. Earthly salvation lots better than ashes and dust."

"I'll do whatever you say," Jake said, "but I'm not keen on shots. How about I put my arms through the bars and face away from you? You won't need to give me a shot that way."

"This ain't no negotiation. You decidin' on life or death. What's your choice?"

Jake took a deep breath. If he hoped to fight another day, there was nothing he could do but capitulate. He turned his back on Screech, loosened his belt, and then lowered his pants.

"Won't hurt much," Screech promised. "I know just how and where to do the shooting. The Sandman makes it easy."

Screech stuck the syringe pole through an opening of the cage and positioned it near the fatty area of Jake's hip. As promised, the injection was relatively painless. The hillbilly injected him with a push of his thumb, then withdrew the syringe.

"Next time I say grace first," promised Screech. "Give thanks before the meal."

After a few moments, Jake began to feel warm and a little bit woozy.

"When you sees me next," said Screech, "I betcha you welcome me with open arms. You be happy to see me, that I know. Patience might be a virtue, but like the song says, let's get that party started. Hell, you probably have your drawers off just waiting for Mr. Sandman."

"Mr. Sandman, bring me a dream," sang Jake, and then started laughing. It shouldn't have been funny, but it was. "Bung, bung, bung, bung," he continued, offering up the song's refrain.

"That's right," said Screech, laughing along with him.

Jake sang another verse. "Sandman, I'm so alone, don't have nobody to call my own."

"No more walking alone," said Screech.

But he wasn't alone, thought Jake. He had Anna. How had he forgotten about her? Jake conjured up her image and tried to hold on to it, but it wasn't long before she was lost behind a veil of sand.

24

AN INTERRUPTED VIGIL

Three weeks after Jake's disappearance, the Friends of Jake organized a candlelight vigil at the West Virginia capital of Charleston. The purpose of the event was to keep the citizenry of West Virginia thinking about Jake. As it turned out, the mystery of Jake's disappearance was the lead story for the night, but not for the reasons the Friends of Jake had intended.

The crowd gathered for the vigil a little before dusk—and more important for their purposes, before the start of the five o'clock news. It was a good turnout, especially for someone who'd been missing for as long as Jake had been. Participants were given unlit candles and Jake's picture. The plan was for the candlelit walk to take place after music and speeches.

The event opened with a local band playing John Denver's "Take Me Home, Country Roads." Just about everyone in the crowd knew the lyrics, and when the more than hundred voices sang the song's refrain, it was clearly heartfelt, for they were singing not only for their beloved West Virginia, but also the missing Jake Rutledge.

The poignant moment normally would have been a perfect media lead-in to a story about the mysterious disappearance of attorney Jake

Rutledge, a West Virginia native son, but in the midst of the singing, Deke noticed that none of the cameras were filming live shots.

He turned his head to Paul and whispered, "Something's wrong."

Paul did his best to keep up the pretense of singing. "What?" he said.

"I'm going to find out," said Deke, and made his escape still singing along with the others: "'I should have been home yesterday, yesterday.'"

The media was situated on the outskirts of the crowd. Deke found a platinum-blonde reporter carefully scrutinizing her makeup in a compact mirror while touching up her ruby-red lipstick.

"Excuse me," he said.

Instead of lowering the mirror, she merely changed its angle so that she was looking at Deke.

"We were told that there would be live coverage of our event," he said. "From what I can see, that's not happening."

"We were preempted," the reporter said, turning the mirror back on herself. She smacked her lips together to blot the newly applied lipstick.

"What preempted us?"

The reporter finally turned Deke's way, and he noticed a change coming over her. Suddenly she was smiling and accommodating. Apparently, she had recognized him and was probably angling for an interview. Deke played her game and smiled back. They had to keep Jake's name out there, even if most people seemed to believe he was already dead. Deke couldn't, or wouldn't, accept that.

"I'm Katie King," she said, extending a hand.

He could tell she was struggling to remember his name. Deketomis, he knew, was a mouthful. "Nick Deketomis," he said.

"The famous lawyer," she said.

Deke pretended to be flattered. Because he was usually in a David-versus-Goliath position, it was always important to curry favor with the media, especially when his opponents had the money to buy advertisements. And often to buy people.

"It's so nice to meet you, Ms. King," Deke added.

"The pleasure is mine," she said, batting her eyelashes.

Holding his smile, Deke said, "I'm wondering if you can tell me, Ms. King, why this story was preempted."

"The news director in our studio made the decision to go with another live shot," she said.

"Do you know what that other story is?"

"All I know is some sheriff scheduled a press conference that had to do with your missing friend," Katie said. "The news director said the cop's statement would make for better TV than everyone singing 'Kumbaya.'"

Too late, she realized how that sounded. "Not that singing is a bad thing . . ."

Deke wasn't interested in her apology. He wanted to know what the police had to say about his friend. "Is there some breaking news about Jake?"

"That's what I understand," she said, "but I don't know the particulars."

"Who would know?"

"I'm sure Carl does." Katie looked around and then pointed out a thirtysomething man with a headset who was smoking a cigarette.

"Carl is our field producer," she said.

"Excuse me," said Deke, taking his leave of Katie.

"I'm told we'll still be doing a spot here," she called to his retreating back. "Are you available to be interviewed in about ten minutes?"

Deke offered up a noncommittal backward wave. He was trying not to show the alarm he felt. A deputy holding a news conference about Jake was worrisome. Three weeks was a long time to be missing, although Team Jake had done their best to remain upbeat.

The field producer was taking a last puff on his cigarette as Deke approached him. He dropped the butt, grinding it into the asphalt.

"Carl?" Deke asked, extending his hand.

The producer also recognized Deke. That wasn't surprising, given all the public pleas for help Deke had been making. "Mr. Deketomis," Carl said, shaking the offered hand.

"I was just talking with Katie," Deke said, "and she tells me that our live spot got bumped because of a law enforcement announcement regarding Jake."

"Afraid so. The studio decided on the other live spot. But that doesn't mean we won't still be doing something here. In fact—"

Deke interrupted him. "What I need to know is what the deputy had to say about Jake."

Carl shrugged. "I couldn't tell you. I haven't been listening to their feed. But if it's important to you, I can make a call and find out."

Deke did his best to hide his impatience: "Please."

The producer took a few steps away, turned his back to Deke, and then made a call. From what Deke could gather, Carl was talking to another field producer. The two men exchanged some small talk, and then Carl asked his question.

"Really?" Deke heard him say.

Whatever the man on the other line was saying evoked some incredulous laughter. "No," Carl said, and was treated to more details. That prompted him to laugh and say, "Tell me, why is it that those who try to come off as Boy Scouts always end up being scumbags?"

Carl would have talked longer, save for Deke's sharp cough. "Hey, I got to run," he said. Clicking off, he turned back to Deke.

"Long story short," he said, "they arrested a drug dealer today, a Mexican national named Guillermo Flores. Anyway, this dealer decided to make a full confession, and said for the past year he's been supplying drugs to your friend."

"What?" In Deke's one word there was more than skepticism; there was complete disbelief. "This drug dealer identified Jake as a client?"

Carl nodded. "He said that he's been supplying Jake with opioids and black tar heroin for almost the entire time he's been in the U.S."

"That's a lie."

Carl shrugged. "Law enforcement evidently doesn't think so. Their theory is that the pressure got to Jake, and that he was so worried about his secret coming out that he fled the area."

Deke cursed under his breath before saying, "The dealer is probably trying to cut a deal by making up a story."

"From what I was told, law enforcement was adamant about no deal having been made." Carl shrugged again. "I guess it makes sense, when you think about it. It's always the closeted politician going on about the sins of homosexuality, and the sanctimonious preacher preying on the underage girls in his flock."

"You don't know Jake," Deke said angrily.

Carl narrowed his eyes. "Do you? During the press conference they said Jake's twin brother died of an opioid overdose. They also said his new girlfriend is an addict. I didn't know about that."

"She's in recovery," said Deke. "She credited Jake for helping to get her clean."

"Is she here?"

He sounded hopeful, which prompted Deke to lie. "No, she's not."

Deke was fuming. This assassination of Jake's character would likely throw a huge monkey wrench into their efforts. By tomorrow morning, most West Virginians would believe that the reason Jake Rutledge had gone missing was because he was a drug addict. No one would care about finding him.

"Your reporter said you'd be doing a story from here," said Deke. "I'd like to be interviewed for that story. I want to talk about the Jake Rutledge I know, an honorable young man who took on a crusade against opioids because he knew firsthand how devastating they were, having had to bury his own twin brother. Jake saw the consequences of opioids; there's no way he became victim to them."

Carl looked unimpressed, but he said, "That sounds good. Why don't you give us two minutes to prepare?"

Deke nodded. He would use the time to consider how to best refute whatever claims this drug dealer had made about Jake being an addict. Realistically, though, the damage had already been done. It hadn't been that long ago when Deke's own enemies had set him up. Even though he'd proved his innocence in court, he knew there were plenty of people who still believed he was a cold-blooded criminal. Even now, he heard the ugly whispers. "You know that Deketomis? He got away with murder." It was easier to think the worst about someone than the best. Why that was, Deke didn't know. Maybe it was human nature. Maybe most people knew it was easier to capitulate than to take a stand.

Jake wasn't around to defend himself, but Deke was, and he sure as hell wasn't going to let the slings that were now being unleashed upon his friend and comrade go unanswered.

25
THE LOTUS-EATER

In the time since his lone encounter with Screech, Jake had kept revisiting the episode. Sometimes it felt like a dream. The whole thing had certainly been strange enough.

It was possible that Screech had been playing him—with that thick accent and his cryptic remarks—but it hadn't felt that way. Strange as it seemed, the man had acted as if he were looking after Jake's best interests. Screech had referenced orders to have Jake put away "a while." It was unclear who'd given those orders, but it was helpful information. Screech and his group weren't running the show, and communication with whoever had hired them had broken down, leaving Jake in a strange state of limbo. Luckily, Screech had continued to see to his care. Jake hadn't even been aware of his last two visits. He only knew Screech had been there because his waste bucket had been empty and there were new supplies.

Jake had heard there were more churches per capita in West Virginia than anywhere else in the country. He didn't know if that was true, but having grown up in the Mountain State, he did know that faith was a bedrock for most citizens. Screech seemed to be a believer—Jake recalled him saying something about having his reward on earth. But he'd also kept saying the solution was the solution. And hadn't he said something about a seven-percent solution?

That jarred a distant memory. Jake had once seen a Sherlock Holmes movie called *The Seven Percent Solution*. Through various stratagems, Watson had managed to get Holmes to see Sigmund Freud so that the psychiatrist could treat his friend's cocaine addiction. Even the great Sherlock Holmes was no match for cocaine; addiction had made him experience debilitating hallucinations.

Screech had told Jake he was already "with the solution," but he hadn't seemed to be referring to only what was in the syringe. He'd also referenced Jake's "thirst." All these connections were making everything clearer in Jake's mind, but that didn't mean he was feeling any better.

If anything, he was feeling worse.

Confessions of an English Opium-Eater, Jake thought. The book was a first-person account written in the early nineteenth century by Thomas De Quincey. Jake had read the book, and scores of others like it, as preparation for the trial. He had wanted to know about addiction.

But he hadn't wanted to live it. Now, Jake realized, that was what he was doing.

That sudden awareness—*I'm an addict*—caused an alarmed intake of breath. He felt like a secondary observer making notes on his own symptomology: the dry mouth and dry nose, his constipation, his sometimes-blurry vision, and the shortness of breath he occasionally experienced. There was a part of him that was shocked, that reacted with numb disbelief, but there was another internal measurement that said this was no revelation at all. His subconscious had been well aware of what he was doing every time he reached for the bug juice: feeding his dependency.

Jake let out the pent-up air. Physically and mentally, it felt as if the floodgates had opened. Screech had referenced the low toss several times during their conversation. But he hadn't been talking about baseball. Low toss didn't mean an error or a passed ball or a throw down at the shoestrings. Someone in Appalachia had remembered their Homer. *Low toss* was the hill pronunciation of *lotus*: another nickname for Hillbilly Heroin.

Jake did his best to recall what Homer had written in *The Odyssey* about the lotus-eaters. In their own way, they'd posed a bigger threat to Odysseus than the Sirens or the Cyclops or even the storm sent by Poseidon. After several of his men ate the lotus leaves, a blissful forgetfulness came over them. They didn't want to go back to the ship, nor did they have any desire to return home. Odysseus had been forced to chain to the ship those who'd eaten of the lotus; given any opportunity, the lotus-eaters would have returned to their idylls of pleasure.

Screech had recognized Jake's panic at being separated from the drugs; his jailer, clearly an addict himself, was voicing his own anxiety at that prospect. Jake had long suspected that the bug juice, with its sickly sweet flavor and astringent aftertaste, was drugged, but he'd assumed it was just sleeping pills meant to keep him compliant. Now he saw how naive he'd been. The juice had been filled with crushed opioids. They'd intended to turn him into an addict.

No one can blame me, Jake thought, tamping down panic. His very survival had required him to drink. And he hadn't known for sure his drink was drugged, even though he might have had his suspicions.

But was that just denial? The justification of an addict?

"But I'm the victim here," Jake whispered.

The irony wasn't lost on him. He had imagined himself a great reformer, ridding the world of the opioid scourge. Now he was just another junkie. Whoever had wanted to ruin him, destroy his case, couldn't have plotted better. If he'd been murdered, his memory would have only helped the cause. Junkie Jake would be of no use to anyone—of no credibility to anyone—even himself.

For a moment, Jake contemplated simply giving up, proclaiming that nothing could be done, sinking back into the haze that a part of him had welcomed during these past weeks. Blissful forgetfulness. His choice was to either stay in the land of the lotus-eaters, or to try and get away. He thought of Anna and the agony he'd watched her go through. He didn't know if he had her strength. Few people succeeded at going cold turkey. Jake wondered if Blake had tried to kick his habit. His brother must have felt as alone as Jake was feeling at that moment.

Something caught his eye from between the folds of fabric concealing his cage. It was just the wind moving through the trees that he'd practiced his opening arguments to earlier. But above the droning of the wind and the rustling of leaves, Jake heard a voice speak as clearly as though it were there in the cage with him.

"I've got your back, brother," it said.

26
LET ME COUNT THE WAYS

Deke knew the fix was in, or more likely, multiple fixes. The damage to Jake Rutledge's reputation was immense. Over the course of a day, he'd gone from being thought of as a courageous crusader to what many now believed was just another drug addict. The life and death of his brother was being rehashed; Anna, Jake's "addict" girlfriend, was being subjected to character assassination.

From experience, Deke knew the wisdom of the old adage that a lie can travel halfway around the world while the truth is putting on its shoes. Despite that, he had taken it on himself to try and set the record straight, giving as many electronic and print interviews as possible. While the lie was circulating, Deke was trying to put the shoes of truth on his friend's feet. Sometimes the race didn't always go to the swift, so Deke would focus on being relentless.

The conspiracy against Jake's name hadn't spontaneously occurred. What had proved the most damning was the statement issued by Guillermo Flores that he'd been supplying the young lawyer drugs. From the first, Deke had asked, "Who the hell is this Guillermo Flores? And who the hell set him up to say what he did about Jake?"

It was fortunate that Carol Morris and Bennie Stokes were already beating the bushes in West Virginia working on Jake's disappearance. The two of them had been making calls most of the night trying to get answers to Deke's questions.

The three of them huddled over coffee a day and a half after the vigil. "Guillermo Flores is what they call a Jalisco boy," said Carol. "You know what that is?"

Deke nodded. "The cartels take clean-cut farm boys from the middle of Mexico, and they set them up all over the U.S. to sell their product."

"The Jalisco boys came in and filled the void left when the opioid pill mills closed shop and left town," said Bennie. "The pill mills got out while the going was good, avoiding oversight and potential prosecution. What's that old line about nature abhorring a vacuum? Into that vacuum came the Jalisco boys and black tar heroin, which users seem to feel is most comparable to the opioid pills they were used to taking."

"Opium by any other name," said Deke, "but still kills the same."

"Guillermo Flores has been in West Virginia for the last thirteen months," said Carol. "We've determined that he has lots of clientele in Oakley. If Jake were going through a dealer, the odds are that it would be Flores."

"Has one credible person surfaced who claims Jake was using drugs?" asked Deke.

Carol and Bennie both shook their heads.

"Is there any truth to the rumor that Flores was also Blake Rutledge's dealer?" asked Deke.

"No truth whatsoever," said Carol. "Blake's dealer was widely fingered as a man named Derek Parsons. He died of an overdose just a week after Blake did."

"The Jalisco boys have put many of the local dealers out of business," said Bennie. "They operate like a pizza-delivery chain. Call comes in and the drugs go out. The dealers don't consume their own product. They stay clean, don't sport any ink, and they do everything they can to stay out of the limelight."

"If that's the case," asked Deke, "then why did Guillermo Flores volunteer to drop a dime on Jake Rutledge?"

Carol gave him a significant look. "The deputy sheriff who made the arrest claims that Flores tried to bargain down his charges with the information on Jake."

Deke could tell she wasn't buying it. "So," he asked, "what's wrong with that story?"

"Let me count the ways," she said, but not in an Elizabeth Barrett Browning manner. "Everything about this case is hinky. The Jalisco boys know the cartel insists they keep a low profile. All the time they're in the U.S., they pretty much work and sleep. They make about ten times what they would working on the farms they come from, but the cartels use their families back home as leverage to ensure they never get out of line. If they're arrested, they know the cartel will supply them with a lawyer. If they have to spend any time in jail, the cartel will make sure their family back home gets rewarded. Because of that, they know to never talk, and that if they do talk, serious harm will come to their families. So why didn't Guillermo Flores follow the usual script?"

"Why?" asked Deke.

Carol and Bennie exchanged glances, and then he spoke for them: "Sheriff's deputy Edward Dunn."

Deke furrowed his eyebrows. "Like Dunn-Edwards paint?" he asked.

"*Paint* happens to be one of his nicknames," said Bennie. "Anna said Jake called him *Whitewash*."

"Whitewash as in a covered-up investigation?"

"Bingo," said Bennie. "We found it interesting that Flores, as well as the other Jalisco boys, essentially operated with impunity in Dunn's jurisdiction until his recent arrest. And then, lo and behold, Flores confessed to being Jake's dealer."

"What Bennie didn't mention," said Carol, "is that our friend Whitewash happens to be the same deputy who paid an official visit to Anna Fowler's father telling him his property was going to auction."

"Curious and curiouser," said Deke.

"It's clear the cartel must have some arrangement with Dunn," said Carol, "or whoever Dunn answers to, or both. For all of Flores's cooperation, the charges against him were not reduced. In fact, they've accelerated his extradition—he's scheduled to be returned to Mexico tomorrow."

"You're kidding me," Deke said.

"I wish I was."

He ran a hand through his hair. "That's convenient for a whole lot of people, but not for Jake." He pursed his lips, giving some thought as to what he should do. "You know where Flores is being held?" he asked.

"They've processed him locally," said Bennie. "He's in a cell in the town of Melton."

"I think the three of us need to take a drive," said Deke. "I'll be behind the wheel, while the two of you find out anything else you can about Guillermo Flores."

"And what do we do once we get to Melton?" asked Carol.

"At that time," said Deke, "Mr. Flores will meet his new legal counsel."

27

LOST AND FOUND IN TRANSLATION

Carol and Bennie divided up their duties and worked their phones all during the drive to Melton. Getting information on a Mexican national, especially one who had avoided being included in any data banks, wasn't easy. Luckily for them, Carol had contacts high up in the PF, the Policia Federal, better known by their nickname: the *Federales*.

They determined early on that Flores had no criminal record. In first-world countries, you can find lots of information on the citizenry; at the Flores farm, there was apparently no home phone, nor had Guillermo ever received a Mexico driver's license.

Carol's contacts at the Secretariat of the Interior, the agency that governed the Federales, put in calls to police officers with jurisdiction over where Flores lived. Those cops weren't personally familiar with Flores, but they made their own calls and talked to a few people who knew the family.

Guillermo—or "Guillo," as he was known—had grown up on a small corn farm. By all accounts, he was a hard worker and a good man. Like so many of his countrymen, he'd made the trip north in order to make money. There was no stigma attached to his livelihood; if anything, what he did was considered his familial duty. By working for the cartel in a foreign land, he could ease his family's financial burdens.

It took Carol a good part of their drive before answers started coming in. After finishing with one call, she said, "Guillo has a fiancée. She's named Isabella, but he calls her 'Bella,' which you probably know in Spanish means 'beautiful.'"

"Bella," said Deke. "I like it."

"According to Bella, Guillermo wants to build her an *arco iris* farm after they get married. That translates to 'rainbow.'"

"What does he mean by that?" asked Deke.

"Guillo doesn't want to work another corn farm once he's done with the cartel," said Carol. "His dream is to grow flowers."

"Flowers the color of a rainbow."

"That's the visual," said Carol.

"Our boy is a romantic," said Deke.

"It takes one to know one."

Deke couldn't help but smile.

"By all accounts," said Bennie, "this Guillo is a good kid."

"That's all I've been hearing as well," Carol agreed.

While Carol had been working the international front, Bennie had concentrated on the local scene.

"The problem is, no one in West Virginia seems to know much about Guillo. He kept to himself. He was professionally polite to his customers, but there was little in the way of personal interaction. Most describe him as being shy. He apparently came to the States speaking very little English, but he managed to pick up the language even though he's reticent about speaking it."

"So you're saying he understands English just fine," mused Deke.

"That's right," said Bennie.

"That's useful to know," said Deke. "I'm pretty much the same way when it comes to Spanish. I can *comprende* pretty good, but because my accent is pure Panhandle cracker, I'm reluctant to speak it."

"Whenever you visited the rez," said Bennie, "my brother and I were always convinced that you spoke Mikasuki better than we did. You always seemed to know what we were saying when we were trying to pull one over on you."

Bennie had grown to know Deke during one of the lawyer's many visits to the Big Cypress Reservation when Deke was representing the tribal nation against polluters who had used the reservation as a toxic chemical dumping site. It was Bennie's mother, a true force of nature, who'd hired Deke to represent the Seminole tribe even while she herself was dying from cancer likely caused by the illegal chemical dumping. After her death, Deke had taken a personal interest in Bennie and the Stokes family.

"How are you so sure I don't speak Mikasuki?" Deke asked, smiling.

Bennie shook his head and rattled off a few words in his tribe's language. At first Deke nodded and pretended to understand, but then he started laughing. "I guess I can't bluff you anymore."

"The Florida Seminole nation was always wise to the white man's bluff," said Bennie, "Let me remind you that we're the only Native People who never signed a treaty with the white man."

"Speaking of bluffing, Deke," Carol said, "what's your plan for getting in to see Guillo? It seems to me that some mighty big strings have been pulled to make sure he doesn't have a chance to talk with anyone before being extradited to Mexico."

"I've always been a big believer in righteous indignation," said Deke. "Add to that some thinly veiled threats, and my ability to nimbly navigate through whatever kind of chaos comes my way."

"In other words," Carol said, "you're going to wing it."

"That's pretty much the plan."

Deke walked into the Melton sheriff's deputy station and strode up to the reception desk.

"May I help you?" asked the middle-aged receptionist.

"Has the interpreter arrived yet?" asked Deke. He'd adopted the body language of being harried, and his speech was overloud.

"Interpreter?" asked the woman.

Deke looked at the nameplate on her desk, which identified her as Joanne Potts. "Yes, Ms. Potts," he said, speaking as if she were hearing impaired, "there was supposed to be a Spanish interpreter waiting here for me."

A smiling Carol and a frowning Bennie had positioned themselves behind Deke. Good cop, bad cop. The receptionist was looking more uncertain by the moment.

"My name is Nick Deketomis," he said. "I'm a lawyer here to see my client."

Deke raised a piece of paper he was holding and appeared to examine what was written on it. "His name is Guillermo Flores."

By that time, Deke's volume had drawn the attention of two sheriff's deputies seated at their desks. One of the men got to his feet and walked over to Joanne's side. She looked more than happy to leave him to deal with Deke and company.

"May I help you?" the deputy asked.

Deke pretended to squint while trying to read the man's badge. "Deputy Dunn," he said, as if trying to place the name.

"That's right."

Once again Deke consulted the paper he was holding, stabbed at the page with his finger, and said, "You're the arresting officer."

"And who are you?" asked Dunn.

"Nick Deketomis, attorney," he said. "Has the interpreter arrived yet?"

"What interpreter is that?"

"The interpreter for Guillermo Flores. He doesn't speak English, right? And since I don't speak Spanish, we obviously need an interpreter."

"Whoa," Dunn said, raising a hand. "Flores has not asked to speak to a lawyer."

Deke shook his head. "That's where you're mistaken, my friend. I have in my possession a phone message showing that Mr. Flores, or someone representing him, called my office and requested that I represent him."

"Our prisoner hasn't made a phone call," Dunn said.

"Really?" said Deke, looking baffled. "How do you know that?"

"We took away his phone."

Deke let the words float there for a moment, wondering if Dunn would realize what he'd just admitted. "Let me see if I understand what you're saying: you took Mr. Flores's phone away and never allowed him to call a lawyer or anyone else for help. Is that what you're saying, Deputy Dunn?"

Dunn's expression grew stony. "Like I told you, he didn't make any call."

"Then he made the call to us before you confiscated his phone. Either that, or he had a friend request our representation on his behalf."

"None of that sounds likely."

"What doesn't sound likely is you reading him his rights."

"I Mirandized him," Dunn said stubbornly.

Deke rolled his eyes. Carol looked at the cop skeptically; Bennie just stood there looking damned intimidating.

"I assume you read him those rights in Spanish?" asked Deke.

The deputy looked uncertain as to how to answer. Finally, he said, "He understood what I was telling him."

"And how do you know that?" Deke said.

"I asked him."

"In English?"

"The arrest was by the book," Dunn said.

"And while you were speaking Spanish to him," Deke said, "I'm thinking you might have left out that part about his right to immediately speak to a lawyer. Which, by the way, would be me. I'm that lawyer, Deputy Dunn. I'm that guy you didn't want him speaking to. But as much as you didn't want that, it would be an even bigger mistake to turn me away right now. You know why? Because if I can't talk to my client, I'm going to direct all my attention to you. And the first question I'd like to ask you is, 'How did you come to arrest my client?'"

"He's not your client."

Deke raised his brows. "At a future date, I'll be happy to debate that in a federal courtroom, where I will sue you personally, and sue this entire sheriff's department, for at least a dozen civil rights violations. But that's for later. What I am asking you right now is, why did you arrest my client?"

Dunn crossed his arms. "Read the report. He had a broken taillight. When I pulled him over, it was clear he was nervous about something. That's when I saw the baggie on the floor of the passenger seat."

"And according to you, this baggie contained heroin?"

"It did."

"And was this your first interaction with my client?"

"Yeah," said Dunn, who was looking increasingly sullen.

Deke decided it was time to up the ante.

"Let me get this right, Deputy. For more than a year Mr. Flores, a Mexican national, has been dealing drugs within your jurisdiction.

He's been doing this seven days a week, twelve hours a day. And yet you never met him. I'm sure had you asked any of the many addicts in Seneca County who their dealer was, they would have offered up my client's name. Why didn't you do that?"

"Look," said Dunn, "I'm tired of this bullshit, and I don't have to answer your questions."

"In lieu of my not being able to talk to my client," said Deke, "I intend to depose you. There are a number of questions that I look forward to asking."

Deke paused long enough to take a breath and to take a read of Dunn. The deputy, he was sure, was on the ropes.

"What I find so very coincidental in this matter is the timing of my client's arrest," said Deke. "And that arrest only becomes more suspicious when this office starts making public statements speculating on the disappearance of Jake Rutledge."

"Mr. Flores was trying to plea bargain," said Dunn. "That happens all the time. There's nothing suspicious or preposterous about that."

Deke raised his index finger to his lips and then started tapping as if in deep thought. "Deputy Dunn," he said, offering up the name as if it was a question of sorts, "I've seen or heard that name before. Oh, yes, now I remember. Didn't you have some kind of run-in with Jake Rutledge?"

The question made the deputy look distinctly uncomfortable. "There was no run-in," he said.

"Must be my mistake," said Deke.

The deputy did his best to offer up a conciliatory smile, but the effort just made him look as if he were ill. "I'm sorry your interpreter was a no-show," he said, "but I have work that I need to attend to."

"Does anyone in this office speak Spanish?" asked Deke.

Dunn spoke for Joanne and the other deputy. "Afraid not," he said.

Deke sighed. "In that case, I think the best we can accomplish here is to agree that we can't agree about my right to have a lengthy sit-down interview with my client. At a minimum, though, shouldn't I be allowed to say hello? Even without an interpreter, I'd like my client to know that I'm his lawyer."

Turning to Carol and Bennie, Deke said, "Either of you know the word for 'attorney' in Spanish?"

"Is it *tiburon*?" Only those who knew Bennie well would have been able to discern his smile.

"That doesn't sound right," said Deke.

"I think that means 'fish,'" Carol offered.

"No," said Bennie, "now that I think about it, I'm pretty sure it means 'shark.'"

"Well, I can't have my client be told that his shark is here," said Deke.

The deputy saw his chance to get out of Deke's crosshairs, while at the same time marginally fulfilling the attorney's request to see his client. "As a courtesy," he said, "if you want to talk to Mr. Flores, I'll allow you five minutes, but no more."

"Five minutes?" said Deke. "That's not enough time to say howdy do."

"You want to see him or don't you?"

Carol and Bennie weren't allowed to accompany Deke, but they were seated close enough to the holding cell to hear Deke say, *"No hablo español."*

Deputy Dunn was seated much closer to the cell. In fact, he seemed positioned to hear every word of what was supposed to be a private conversation. After Deke said that he *no hablo español,"* he added something else in what seemed to be pidgin Spanish;

Carol heard Deke say something about Bella this and Bella that.

As Deke had no doubt intended, the conversation between the two men sounded stilted and incomprehensible—Deke only able to communicate with his pidgin Spanish, and Flores in his supposedly almost-nonexistent English. Over the course of the five minutes, Carol watched Deputy Dunn's face gradually relax; by the end, he was practically smiling.

Dunn walked over to the holding cell and announced that their time was up.

Carol could hear the indignation lacing Deke's voice. "I really need to come back and speak to my client with an interpreter. As it is, we weren't able to talk."

"Sounded like the two of you talked the whole time," Dunn said.

As the two men came out of the cell, Deke said, "I did learn that my client's last name means 'flowers' in Spanish."

Now Dunn couldn't even hide his smile. He even grinned when Deke added sternly, "Be advised that the sheriff will be hearing from me." Given that Flores was supposed to be extradited to Mexico tomorrow, he no doubt assumed he was off the hook.

"Let's get the hell out of here," Deke said, pausing by Carol's and Bennie's seats. "This has been a huge waste of time."

"Have a good day," Dunn called after them.

Carol waited to speak until they got into their rental car. "Well?" she asked.

"Guillermo told me he never heard of Jake Rutledge," Deke said. "In fact, he said he feels sorry for him. But since the cops and the cartel are forcing him to play ball, he's going along with their script."

"I guess he really doesn't have a choice in the matter," she said.

Deke nodded. "At least I was able to get the straight story out of him. And one day soon, he'll be able to recant. I promised Guillo that I'd have a good lawyer waiting for him the moment his plane sets down in Mexico."

He started the car and then seemed to remember something. "Guess what? I'm pretty sure I just agreed to invest in a flower farm in Mexico."

"I know for a fact how much Teri loves flowers," Carol said. For much of the year, Deke's work kept him away from home and his wife, Teri. Everyone in the office knew that he invariably presented Teri with a bouquet of flowers each time he returned.

"She and Guillermo's Bella have that in common," Deke said. "Both of us hope to be able to give the women we love a rainbow."

"Ah," said Carol, "I can see Teri has trained you well."

She was sitting in the passenger seat and reached over to give Deke an attaboy tap on his shoulder.

From the back seat, where he had spread out his massive frame, Bennie said, "You're setting the bar awfully high for the rest of us guys."

"I think I'll sell shares to my flower farm," said Deke. "Bergman/Deketomis can run on flower power."

Bennie lifted his forefinger to his lips and said, "Shh." Then he spoke into his cell phone. Deke and Carol listened while he ordered a dozen roses for his wife.

When he finished his call, Bennie shrugged. "I never imagined we'd be in West Virginia for as long as we've been."

"When your team finds Jake," said Deke, "the time away will be worth it."

"Do you think he's still alive?" asked Carol.

"I do," said Deke. "I asked that same question of Flores. He thinks Jake is alive as well."

"Did he tell you why?" asked Bennie.

"He pressed the limits of my Spanish," Deke admitted, "but I'm pretty sure he told me that the authorities wouldn't have bothered extorting a confession out of him if Jake wasn't alive. Of course, I couldn't ask him to elaborate since I knew Dunn was listening, and Guillo could only stick out his neck out so far."

"I came to that same conclusion," said Carol, "although I've been hoping it's not just wishful thinking."

"Jake's alive," Deke said. "We all need to operate under that assumption."

28
"I LOVE LIARS!"

The sun had set three hours earlier in Huntington, West Virginia, but Deke and Paul continued to work at their desks. For them, it was another fourteen-hour workday.

Deke got up from his chair and stretched. His back ached, and he gently moved from side to side, and then up and down, in an effort to loosen it.

"Want some ibuprofen?" asked Paul.

"I took two an hour ago," Deke said.

What Team Jake was calling "the ARCOS hearing" was scheduled to be heard in Columbus in four weeks. The team had pushed hard for the expedited hearing, but that was before Jake's disappearance.

Because of Jake's absence, the two lawyers were placing even additional pressure on themselves. They couldn't do anything to directly help find their missing comrade, but they could honor the cases he'd set into motion by doing everything in their power to win. Deke's reminder of Jake's will could be seen in a piece of paper he'd taped to a wall. Using a black Sharpie, he'd written *What Would Jake Do?* That was the WWJD reminder everyone on Team Jake was living by.

"'One game away from the Super Bowl,'" said Paul.

Deke had to smile. Paul was quoting Jake. "The one conversation I never had with our young warrior was what would happen if we failed to win this ARCOS hearing."

Obtaining the DEA's ARCOS data was a necessary stepping-stone to national litigation. The same kind of opioid tragedy that had plagued the tiny counties in West Virginia and Ohio that Jake represented also existed throughout the U.S. With the ARCOS data, Deke intended to show that there was a well-defined pattern to the way the drug corporations had perpetuated their own terrible epidemic.

"He's one hell of a recruiter," said Deke. "And since we can't win one for the Gipper, how about we win for Jake?"

"That sounds like a good locker-room speech to me," said Paul.

"At least we'll have an even playing field in that we'll be arguing the ARCOS hearing in front of one of the most respected federal judges in the country."

"What's your take on Judge Sargent?" asked Paul.

"His background checks every professional box. He came out of private practice, and then became one of the most respected prosecutors in the U.S. Attorney's office, before moving on to being chief judge of his district. Back when he worked in private practice, Sargent represented the city council for three years, and because of that, he understands city and county government, which might be critically important. Few jurists have his real-world experience."

"He's set some pretty stringent ground rules for the hearing," Paul said.

Sargent had informed the lawyers that the ARCOS hearing would be conducted over the course of one day. Both sides would be allowed two witnesses; those witnesses couldn't be questioned or cross-examined for more than forty-five minutes.

"I like our odds when it comes to brevity," said Deke. "Nathan Ailes likes the sound of his voice too much to ever be brief. I also like it that we'll be arguing our case in Ohio, which is pretty much where the opioid epidemic began."

"Have you decided on which other witness you'll want on the stand?"

"I'm reviewing every video of every deposition we've taken," Deke said. "What I want is someone who will help us make our ARCOS case, as well as show the need for an MDL. Right now, I'm leaning toward calling one of the retired DEA investigators."

They'd already decided that Paul should interview Carol Morris on the stand. Her law enforcement experience and her familiarity with opioid trafficking would make her an expert witness. Carol's testimony would be important in detailing the workings of the "Oxy-Express"—the route of illegal opioid distribution that extended from New York to Florida. Through questioning, she would demonstrate to the court that the opioid epidemic extended far beyond Ohio and West Virginia. That would justify the need for an MDL and make their case for getting possession of opioid distribution figures from ARCOS.

"I'll focus on identifying what we need to hammer on during the cross-examination," said Paul. "It's too bad we don't know who Jazz Hands will be calling as witnesses."

"He'll probably want to put his best liars on the stand," Deke said. "Right now, I have three likely candidates for the prize of best liar."

"I'm glad we took so many depositions," said Paul.

Deke offered up a few nods. He was a great believer in taking depositions during every stage of litigation. Time and again, people's stories changed from one deposition to the next depending on what kinds of rulings were coming from various judges—a clear sign that the opposition was coaching its witnesses to say whatever they thought would have the most sway with the court.

"It's too bad we couldn't put up a graphic showing the spoon-fed verbatim responses of every drug distributor employee we deposed," said Paul.

"Yeah," said Deke, "the only time you hear that kind of uniformity in talking points is when everyone has read the same memo. For our purposes, though, that couldn't be better. The more Ailes's witnesses spout the company line, the easier time I'll have predicting what they'll say and how to best respond."

Deke found himself smiling.

"What?" Paul asked.

"I love liars," Deke said. "In a strange way, they make my job fun."

29
THE SHADOW JURY

Ever since thinking that he'd heard Blake's voice, Jake had gained a newfound determination to escape. He'd tried to be more mindful of Screech's comings and goings in the hope of anticipating his movements. Although Jake hadn't been awake to witness the delivery, three days ago he'd been left a change of clothes, some hand towels, baby wipes, an additional sleeping mat, DEET, and two gallons of bug juice along with some food that was nearly gone. Screech's visits seemed to be defined by how long the food and drink lasted, which meant that Jake was being monitored.

Jake had always prided himself on having iron willpower. In college and law school he'd thought nothing about pulling all-nighters. In high school he'd been an undersized and underweight defensive end on the football team, giving up as many as fifty pounds to those he lined up against. He'd never been a star player, but his brains and his will had often found ways to prevail against the opposing team's brawn.

Odysseus's lotus-eaters had lost all their free will to the plant's overwhelming charms. Jake was still trying to hold out from complete capitulation. That's why at this moment his lips were parched;

he was trying to resist drinking from the drugged jugs unless absolutely necessary.

It was his stubbornness, more than anything else, that sustained him. And the sensation of his brother being there encouraged him. That gave him the will to fight, even after his long captivity. Finally, he'd come up with a plan that he hoped was viable. Over the last few days, he'd been making preparations that had required some privations on his part. Based on his almost exhausted supplies, Jake was betting that Screech would be showing up tonight. Only then would Jake find out if his sacrifices had been worth it.

But as exciting as the prospect of escape was, Jake also felt a tug of fear. Getting free might require him to be without any bug juice for a time.

From inside his cage, Jake did a set of exercises. He needed to maintain as much strength as possible. After his workout, he started in on his daily mental exercise: he imagined he was presenting his opioid case alongside Paul and Deke. Work made him focus, sharpening his fuzzy mind. He knew that if he ever had the chance to participate in a trial, he would need to allow his anger and his sadness and his true sense of compassion for addicts like Blake to be tangible for the judge and jury.

At least his opioid usage hadn't completely dulled his passions, Jake thought. Deke had once suggested that, depending upon the case, it might be good for Jake to open by telling the story of his involvement in the lawsuit and why it was so important to him.

Of course, he also remembered Deke lecturing him that there were evidentiary limitations on what he could and couldn't say about his personal experiences, but for now Jake didn't have to worry about that.

"Ultimately it doesn't matter if the case will be heard by a judge or by a jury," Deke had said. "Neither wants smoke and mirrors.

They want substance, and they want the truth. What they'll want is a story they can relate to, and that's what you have. When the time comes, we'll try to push the limits on what's actually allowable in your opening statement, but you'll see that the simpler your talk is, the better it will be received, warts and all. I know you feel guilty for not being there for Blake. Go ahead and admit that. And it will be all right for you to be mad at Blake as well. He shouldn't have died like he did. You'll be representing thousands and thousands of people who experienced the same heartbreak and anger and outrage for so many injustices inherent in this epidemic."

In Jake's long solitude, Deke's words were making more and more sense. Jake looked around and took stock of his imaginary courtroom. Intellectually, he knew that Deke was right to say the case was about the economic devastation of counties and cities caused by the opioid epidemic. It had nothing to do with making the Big Three admit that their actions had ultimately killed Blake, even if that's the message Jake would take from a victory. In court the entire trial would need to focus on the analysis of lost money rather than the loss of so many human lives. But this was his cage . . . and his soapbox. He was alone in a forest, and he needed to speak words that comforted him at this moment. Later he could worry about the realities of a courtroom—and what was allowed and what wasn't.

Because his prison was too small for him to stand, he turned his shoulder and head, pausing here and there to make eye contact with his imaginary assemblage of people.

After acknowledging the judge with a nod, Jake took a measured breath and said, "One week before I was due to graduate from the West Virginia University School of Law, my twin brother, Blake, died of an opiate overdose. I'm told a doctor called me with this news, but to this day I don't remember anything about that call. It was like someone just turned off the lights in my head and left me in darkness.

"What you need to understand is that all my early memories involve Blake. It wasn't *my* childhood, it was *our* childhood. The two of us did everything together, from eating birthday cake to riding tricycles. Blake was always there at my side. We grew up as womb-mates, we used to tell people. I never had to go find a best friend; Blake was my best friend from the day we were born. And, yes, he was the older brother. How he loved to lord those twenty minutes over me. 'Little brother,' he would often call me, or, 'Young Jake.' I'm smiling now just thinking about it. That was Blake. From the first, he staked out his position as class clown. Since I knew I couldn't compete in that arena, I pretended to be the class brain. I'm confident, had he wanted, that Blake could have staked his claim to that title as well. Everything always came intuitively to him.

"When I went off to college, Blake held down the homestead. By then our parents had died. My family had lived in West Virginia for generations, and that was something Blake held on to. So, when I was told the person that I was closest to in this world was dead, I couldn't comprehend that loss. And when I learned how he died, it seemed that much more incomprehensible. I was sure Blake was too smart to do drugs. After all, he was an athlete and strong and only twenty-five years old.

"I needed answers as to what had happened, because Blake's death made absolutely no sense to me. That's when I started asking questions. But each question I asked was like pulling at a loose thread on your sweater, and then pulling another, and before you know it, ending up with a pile of yarn. There were always more questions. How is it that pill mills seemed to spring up overnight all over West Virginia? How is it that drugs that were supposed to be carefully controlled were handed out like candy there? How did

Big Pharma mastermind the lie that opioids were not addictive? And how is it that over the course of time the treatment of pain management changed in such a way that so-called normal prescriptions all but guaranteed addiction?

"The poet Sir Walter Scott wrote these lines: *Oh what a tangled web we weave, when first we practice to deceive.* This country's three major drug distributors are responsible for the distribution of more than ninety percent of the opioids. Over the course of this trial, you will see all the tangled webs woven by these drug distributors. You will see how these Fortune 25 companies conspired and plotted and are responsible for hundreds of thousands of deaths. They unleashed poison upon the land, and that poison was such a contagion that hometowns all over West Virginia are now swaths of wasteland.

"This case was always personal for me. This case was always about my brother, Blake. His death—no, his murder—is why I am here. I don't hide the fact that I am here for revenge. When I speak, I hope you hear more than my own voice. I hope you also hear Blake, and the thousands who no longer have voices. My journey has brought me to this place to speak to you. Blake's story can finally be heard."

As Jake finished with his imaginary opening remarks, it was as if he could hear Deke offering up his critique. "There was great power in that statement, Jake, but ninety percent of what you just argued would not be admissible in the case we are actually trying."

Still, he wished he had a tape recorder so that he could practice delivering the words that gave him so much comfort. To hell with the economic losses to the cities of West Virginia. He wanted his words to go to the thousands of mothers, fathers, sisters, and brothers who had lived through real pain that could never be measured by dollars and cents.

There, thought Jake. He wished that could have been the real focus of his lawsuit.

Later, Jake chewed on an apple and then took a measured swallow of the doctored bug juice. All his talking had been thirsty work, and he was feeling more tired than he would have wished. *That's what happens when you become an addict,* he thought. *It eats away your reserves and takes a toll on your body.* If he wanted to continue working, he needed a boost. Raising a jug of bug juice, Jake swallowed a large gulp.

"Short-term coping," he said, rationalizing to an unseen audience. "This is what happens when you have to deal with increased dopamine neuronal activity."

The bad thing about having studied addiction was that Jake was aware of his own symptomology as it was developing. He knew the depressing realities of opioid addiction. Even after he quit the opioids, it took the average addict up to three years before their dopamine levels returned to normal.

"And those that suffer from low dopamine levels," Jake said to his unseen jury, "have to deal with mood swings, depression, and chronic fatigue, as well as the inability to concentrate."

What he refused to consider, at least for the moment, were the long-term consequences of recovery. How would he be able to do trial work if he was depressed, tired, and unable to concentrate?

To stave off sleep while he waited for darkness to fall, Jake thought about the things that were important in his life. On the personal front, Anna dominated his thoughts. He'd been pretty sure, even before his abduction, that he was falling in love with her. In her presence he felt helpless, and not in control; he felt captive to her moods and what she said. All these feelings were unique in his experience; he had never felt them with anyone before. Truth to tell, he hadn't even known such feelings were possible.

It was a terrible time to fall in love. He was supposed to be there for Anna's recovery. That in itself was reason enough to avoid becoming

237 / Mike Papantonio

involved. Addiction muddied thinking and emotions. As complicated as their love had been, the dynamics were even crazier now. Even if Jake escaped his jail, he would return home an addict himself.

Over the course of history, he wondered, how many other couples had found love amid the ruins? There was always some calamity going on, or some plague or some war, and yet love found a way. Jake didn't know if it would this time, but he offered up a silent prayer for the two of them to be able to navigate all the travails that came their way.

By now the sun had fully set, so once again Jake went over his preparations. There were any number of ways his plan could go wrong. Success would need more than its share of luck.

At least it was a cloudy night. That was a start. The less visible he was to Screech, the better.

It was important that he position his body just so. Screech always injected him around his hip. During previous injections, Screech had taken into account that Jake was wearing clothing. His pole syringe allowed him the safety of injecting from a distance. That was one of its advantages.

Jake was counting on its disadvantages.

Afraid of being monitored, he had positioned the tarp so that he could work on his preparations without being seen. He had rationed much of the food that Screech had brought, and now used it for a purpose other than eating.

The bread he'd chewed up, making it into a paste. He applied the doughy material to his backside and hip, and then ripped off strips from one of his layered shirts. Jake tied the shirting around his backside and hips and then stuffed boiled russet potatoes inside the cloth. Between the paste, potatoes, and strips of fabric, he had more than an inch of padding. He camouflaged the lumps by covering up with a blanket, and then settled into a supine position where he did his best not to move. Jake didn't know if a boiled russet potato had the same kind of consistency as piercing through flesh, but if he was lucky, Screech would plunge his pole syringe into one of the potatoes and not notice the difference.

All this time in captivity, thought Jake, *and that's the best plan I can come up with.* If it didn't work, he would sink further into addiction. There'd probably come the point not too far down the road when he would stop even caring about escape.

But he wasn't at that point yet.

Jake put the focus of all his five senses into one. He didn't move as he monitored the sounds of the night. Finally, he made out what he believed to be the coughing motor of a distant vehicle. If he was right, Screech was only about a ten-minute walk away.

Don't think about the plan, he told himself. *Don't think about anything.* He was probably just being superstitious, but he was afraid of putting any vibe out there for Screech to glom onto. He did his best to keep totally still and think only benign thoughts.

Finally, Jake heard Screech's approach. His captor was quiet, but not silent, revealing himself with muffled footsteps. Not far from his cage, Jake could hear a bag being placed on the ground. Then he listened to the faint tread of footsteps circling the cage.

That wasn't the only thing Jake heard. In the nearby woods, he could hear the unmistakable sound of a shovel digging into the earth.

Someone other than Screech was there. And that someone was digging a hole.

Jake's heart was pounding. It took all his willpower to keep his breath steady. He could think of only one reason for midnight spadework. His grave was being dug.

He heard a can being moved; its contents were unmistakable, filling the night air with the unmistakable scent of benzene. Before

Jake's burial, they were planning on a cremation. *Out of the frying pan into the fire,* thought Jake. He prayed that they weren't planning to burn him alive. Jake continued playing possum, keeping his breathing regular and steady. He wanted it to appear that he was experiencing a deep slumber.

"Jeezus," whispered a voice. "This ain't right. I'm like Punch-us Pilot. I said it wasn't no fault of his. But they said he had to be kilt. I tol' them there'd be no blood unto my hands. Jeezus knows that to be true."

Screech stopped talking long enough for Jake to hear a muted clang. Was he readying the pole syringe? Out in the woods the shovel work continued. Closer to Jake, there was a slight rustling sound, and he felt one of the potatoes being pushed into his hip. Jake was glad the potatoes had been slightly underboiled. The pressure on his hip continued until he heard the click of the plunger, and then the needle and pole were withdrawn.

Jake held his breath. If his plot was going to be discovered, now was the likely time. He was afraid the syringe was now coated in a starchy substance and that Screech might notice that.

Don't shine your flashlight, thought Jake. *Everything is fine. All is well.*

For now, wishful thinking was all he had. When he'd formulated this plan, he hadn't known his life would depend upon it.

He kept his eyes closed and continued to offer up deep, steady breaths. It was still too early to think his ruse had succeeded, but Screech no longer seemed to be trying to hide his movements. He was whispering to himself again. "I'm here to make sure he don't suffer none, Jeezus. I'm here to pray for his soul. Ain't no one else going to be witness to him. Ashes to ashes and dust to dust."

The whispering stopped, and Jake had the sensation of Screech looking at him in the darkness. He remained still, not even daring to breathe. It was likely Screech had upped the potency of his injection. He would have wanted to make sure that Jake didn't awake before the coup de grâce was administered.

Screech's whispering started up again, and Jake heard him walking toward where the shoveling was going on. When Jake had been planning his escape, he'd only taken into account having to deal with Screech. Now there was a second person to contend with.

He offered up a silent prayer. His best opportunity to get away would occur only if the second man continued shoveling while Screech came back and unlocked the cage. Jake would have to act as soon as the lock was removed. Surprise would certainly be on his side, but it had been more than an hour since he'd moved. His body would be stiff and might not be able to react as quickly as he'd like. If so, that would eliminate the element of surprise. Screech might even have time enough to get out and relock the cage.

And what if Screech returned with the second man? If that occurred, Jake would have no choice but to try and fight his way to freedom. Given his physical condition, he knew the odds of his surviving wouldn't be great.

I'll go out fighting, though, he vowed.

He waited, the passing minutes seeming impossibly long. In the distance he could hear Screech and the other man talking as the sound of shoveling continued. The forest soil would have a lot of roots, or at least that's what Jake hoped. That would make the digging go more slowly. Anything that bought him more time was welcome.

The approach of footsteps curbed Jake's thoughts and fears. He was relieved to hear the sound of shoveling continuing. Screech was returning on his own.

That's when Jake heard another voice, a familiar voice. "Don't worry, Jake," Blake said. "I got your back, brother."

In his mind, Jake answered, "I got your back, brother."

Feeling that Blake was there with him brought a peace to Jake that he hadn't felt since his abduction. The calm couldn't have come at a better time. Nearby he heard a key turning in a lock, and the chain around the cage door coming free. The chain clanked as it struck the ground. Then Jake heard the door open.

"Hey, you!" Screech shouted.

Jake didn't stir. The sensation of Blake being with him was the only thing that saved him from reacting to Screech's sudden shout. Though his eyes were closed, Jake was able to make out a light shining on his face. Screech was using a flashlight to study him.

That wasn't enough. "Whatcha doin'?" yelled Screech.

Jake continued his steady breathing.

Satisfied that his prisoner was passed out, Screech made his way into the cage.

In his head, Jake heard Blake say, "Not yet."

Screech was getting closer. "Like Mary Magdalene done your feet, Jeezus, I be seein' to the anointin'. My hands got no part in this here killin.'"

"Wait," Blake advised.

Screech's breath was ragged. It sounded like he was crawling now. The two of them would be on the same level.

"Get ready," said Blake.

In his mind's eye, Jake imagined Screech reaching for him. He would be bent over in the confines of the cage, trying to figure the best way to drag him out.

"Now," said Blake.

Jake felt a hand make contact with his ankle. His leg was bent at an angle, just waiting for the opportunity to react. Jake kicked out, his foot catching Screech's neck and snapping his head back against the metal cage. The surprise attack left Screech gasping for air.

"Run!" said Blake.

Jake began crawling over Screech, who struggled to breathe. His captor wasn't totally incapacitated, though. He grabbed at Jake's leg as he passed by. With a backward kick, Jake struck out again, smashing his foot into Screech's rib cage.

Because most of his wind had been knocked out of him, Screech's scream was muted. Jake got to his feet and quickly shuffled out of the cage. He closed the door, chained it shut, and listened for the sound of the other man approaching. Luck was with him. The second man was still busy shoveling.

Jake tried to straighten up but found himself unable to. His captivity had left him bent over. Still, he had to put distance between himself and the man digging his grave. The darkness was Jake's friend. The man with the shovel was about fifty yards away and had his back to him.

Without thinking about it, Jake grabbed the gas can and began running. He was only able to get a few steps before Screech regained his wind and began shouting. Jake raced toward the woods, hoping the night and the trees would offer enough cover for him to escape. He could hear someone crashing through the ground cover behind him.

The woods were five steps away. Four. Jake was running as fast as he could, but his imprisonment had taken its toll. There was no way he could outrun them. He was just too weak.

"I got your back, brother."

Blake was talking to him again.

"It's time to play hide and go seek," said Blake. "There's a good tree now."

Jake saw the tree. It was larger than most of the surrounding trees. The trunk was thick enough that he could hide his frame behind it. Jake gave his all in a final sprint, and then slammed his back against the tree. Had he made it there undetected? Jake wasn't sure. He sucked in a lungful of air and tried to quiet his heavy breathing.

He didn't have to wait long. The crunch of leaves announced the man's approach. Jake heard the clang of metal on a rock and realized the man had brought the shovel with him.

The footsteps slowed. The man was listening, trying to pick up any sounds of Jake's escape. The stillness made him more cautious. He made a careful approach. Jake tracked the sounds, inching his body around the tree, away from his pursuer. The shadows of the forest canopy cloaked him.

"You got this, little bro," said Blake. "Warm," he said, "warmer, hot . . ."

The glint of raised metal showed itself. The shovel was held out, ready to be swung. Jake stepped toward the inside of the shovel, and with a backhand swing smashed the gas can into the man's face. There was the crack of breaking bones, and the metal can split.

Screaming, the man dropped to the ground. The gasoline spilled out onto his face, burning the man's eyes. Jake tossed the can down and made his way into the night.

30
TAKE A KNEE

Adrenaline pushed Jake at a good pace, its effects giving him a boost for at least a mile. But the rush that had accompanied his escape abandoned him and left him feeling shaky. He wished he'd downed more of the doctored bug juice before escaping. He tried to ignore the feeling of cramps, even though with each step he became aware of an increased gravity. An opioid user would describe his symptoms as jonesing.

As Jake walked, he began trembling, but he couldn't blame the cold. It was the frigid touch of drug withdrawal.

He tried to be methodical in his movements. He traveled in the direction he believed would take him to a road, and civilization, but even with the light of the moon, it wasn't easy navigating the terrain. He found himself following a game trail, although he couldn't find anything to suggest it was ever traveled by those with two legs. He began to pause more frequently, and he took to marking trees to make sure he wasn't wandering around in circles.

The woods started to thin out, allowing him to see more easily, but no road presented itself, nor did he spot any distant lights. Judging from a few things Screech had said, Jake suspected he was in the southeastern part of the state near the Kentucky border. It was a sparsely populated part of West Virginia, an area he didn't know very well.

The sound of slow-running water drew him to a creek, and he drank deeply. Normally he would have feared contracting giardia, or some other waterborne illness, but he couldn't afford to get dehydrated. Already his stomach felt hollow, as if it were missing something. Before the cramping grew too bad and he became too debilitated to move, he needed to find help.

He followed the stream as it wended downstream. He'd heard that if you were lost, following a source of water was usually a good way to locate civilization. He hoped that would prove true.

His confinement in the cage, along with being drugged, had left him weak. Hours after his escape, he still found it difficult to stand up straight. The vertiginous feeling impeded his walking, and despite trying to move forward carefully, he kept stumbling. The branches and stones along the creek bed seemed positioned just so as to trip him up. Although he'd so far avoided falling, his plodding pace made him impatient.

There had to be a damn house around here. And where was that road? Every few minutes he would stop and listen, hoping to hear something. It was possible a road was close by, but because of the hour, no one was out driving.

The fear of making his situation worse finally brought Jake to a stop. Once daylight arrived, people would be up and about. He'd have a much better chance of finding someone. Besides, he was tired of stumbling around.

Once more he filled his stomach with water from the creek. His hope was to stave off the cramping he was beginning to feel, but it didn't seem to help. He curled up on the ground.

Dawn felt as if it would never arrive. His roiling stomach and pounding head seemed to slow time, filling him with only the awareness of his ailing body. Finally, though, the day broke, and Jake continued with his marathon. He felt like one of those runners who had hit the wall. Of course, in his case that wasn't it exactly. He was dealing with opioid deprivation, not low blood sugar and a buildup of lactic acid. Still, like one of those runners, he'd reached the crossover point where he was fatigued and disoriented. There was a part of him that wasn't there.

He could die, he realized, and it might be a long time before his body was even found.

Got to keep moving. Got to stay alive.

Step by step he followed the creek. One foot and then another. That was all he could do.

When the path along the stream widened, Jake didn't notice at first. It was all he could do to keep moving. He almost walked by the dirt pullout before it registered with him. Raising his head, he saw that beyond the pullout was the broken asphalt of a country road.

He made his way to the road. Tears began to fall from his eyes.

Early in his escape, Jake had been unsure of what he'd do when he found a road. He'd been afraid that Screech and his friends might be driving the roads searching for him. Now, that didn't matter. What he needed most was his fix of opioids. Jake dropped to a knee.

"Take a knee, boys," he remembered Coach Rockwell, his high school football coach, saying. Everyone had called him Coach Rock.

The coach had said those words on those rare occasions during practice when he'd allowed the players to rest. Even then, though, the coach had used that quiet time to explain something. Somehow, like magnets that attracted one to the other, Jake and Blake had always taken a knee right next to each other.

From one knee, Jake was waiting for whatever Coach Rock had to say. But it wasn't Coach Rock who was speaking. Jake looked up to see a pickup truck coming his way.

He managed to raise a hand and wave.

31

THE RETURN OF THE NATIVE

Anna looked at the name and number displayed on her cell phone screen. Caller ID showed the call was coming from Williamson Memorial Hospital. In the time Jake had been gone, Anna had received calls from a lot of individuals she would have preferred not talking to. She was fairly sure she didn't know anyone in Williamson, and for a moment considered letting the call go to voice mail, but that was something she still found herself unable to do. *Maybe it's Jake on the other line,* she thought. It was the same thing she thought every time an unusual number came up, even though she'd been disappointed time and again.

This time, though, her hope was justified. When she heard Jake's familiar voice on the other line, Anna asked, "Is it really you?"

And then she found herself wiping away tears, repeating "Thank God" over and over, and talking to the man she loved.

Four members of the media, three men and one woman, were situated on the steps below the landing at Williamson Memorial Hospital. A microphone stand had been positioned above them so that everyone could hear what the Good Samaritan had to say. Earlier in the morning, Ethan Carter had been traveling on a country road in eastern Mingo County when missing lawyer Jake Rutledge had flagged him down.

Cameras were trained on Carter, who seemed to enjoy being the center of attention. He came across as a good ol' boy. He was fortyish, had a two-day beard, and was wearing jeans and a T-shirt. A pack of smokes could be seen in his shirt pocket. According to Carter, he worked as a "jack of all trades."

"When I first seen him," he said, "I thought he was a ghost." Then he added, "A dirty ghost."

The media laughed.

"When did you realize your passenger was Jake Rutledge?" asked one of the reporters.

"It was a few minutes," said Ethan. "At first all he kept saying was that he was sickly."

"Sickly?" called a woman. "Did he elaborate?"

"Not right off," he said. "But I surely believed what he was telling me. He smelled something awful. I even thought about having him ride in the cargo bed."

Another reporter spoke up. "Did he ask you to take him to this hospital?"

"What he told me was that he needed to get to the nearest emergency room," said Ethan.

"Did he say what ailed him?" asked the reporter.

"Yes, he did," said Carter. "He told me he was going through withdrawals."

At those words, the four reporters all straightened up. They had their lead.

With Bennie driving, Deke and Carol were both able to work their phones. Deke sat in the back seat with Anna, and between calls tried to comfort her with reassuring smiles and a few supportive pats on her hands. According to what Anna had told them, Jake was in a bad way. He'd said his captors had turned him into an addict. Despite Anna assuring him that all would be well now that he was free, Jake believed that he had somehow let her down, as well as his friends.

While Carol was working with law enforcement trying to locate where Jake had been held as prisoner, Deke was on the phone with the hospital, making arrangements on Jake's behalf. He was able to get Jake a private suite, and he persuaded the hospital administration to agree to his bringing in specialists to treat Jake. Deke made it clear that he would accept nothing less than the best when it came to Jake's treatment.

Even though Team Jake had gotten a head start on the media announcement, news of the lawyer's return was now circulating around the state. To keep the media, as well as other unwanted visitors, from bothering Jake during his recovery, Deke hired a security team to control access to Jake.

Between making her own calls, Carol was also monitoring the radio news, flipping between the stations.

"The news seems to be following a familiar script," she said. "After they announce when and where Jake turned up, the next thing they mention is that he was hospitalized as a consequence of his drug addiction."

"What they should be saying," said Anna, "is that he was hospitalized to deal with the aftereffects of barbaric captivity. Anyone confined in a pen for a month would have been hospitalized, even if they hadn't become drug dependent during their ordeal."

"We'll be addressing that," Deke promised. "We'll also be putting out a more complete narrative. We won't question the state of his return, but we will stress our delight at his making it out alive. And we'll be very vocal about the need to find those who abducted him."

"We should also talk about how he escaped," said Anna. "He'd still be locked up in a pen if he hadn't figured a way out. He's a hero, not a villain."

"That's the way I see it as well," said Deke. "And that's what we'll be telling the world."

Anna nodded. Her cheeks were red. It was understandable that she wasn't thrilled about the character assassination of her boyfriend.

"We need to get the word out that his captors made Jake an addict," she said. "Jake told me his only source of water was infused with opioids. His choice was either to die of thirst or to become an addict."

"In a month's time he became an addict?" asked Bennie.

"That's all it takes," said Deke. "The Big Three claim they didn't know how addictive opioids are, but we've uncovered documents that show they did. Regardless, they advised doctors to prescribe three months of pills for pain, which was typically ninety pills. As it turned out, patients taking opioids can become addicted in just one month."

"This is so unfair," said Anna. "Jake was deliberately poisoned by someone."

"Don't worry," said Deke. "We're going to help Jake, and we're going to get the true story out there. For now, though, you have to be strong for him. A few years ago, I was accused of murder. At the time it seemed as if I was deemed guilty by virtually everyone in Florida. I was able to get through that terrible time because of my wife, Teri. She provided me unconditional love, along with the supportive safe haven I desperately needed."

"I'll do the same for Jake," Anna said. "And that's a promise."

If there still was a heart of coal country in West Virginia, it could be found in Mingo County. Fewer than five hours after Jake had been picked up on a backwoods road, Bennie pulled into the parking lot at Williamson Hospital.

An enterprising camera team was waiting for Jake's friends to arrive. They tried to waylay Deke and company, but the visitors didn't even slow down.

"I promise I'll talk to you later," Deke said, waving them off. "But right now we need to see our friend."

Security cleared their entry into the hospital, and the four of them were guided to Jake's private suite. As Deke entered the room, he saw the IV lines that fed into Jake's arm. The young lawyer had shaved and showered but still looked as if he'd been through an awful ordeal. Red insect bites, some of them infected, stood out on his exposed flesh. Still, Jake tried to be brave, calling out greetings to his visitors. Anna was the last to enter his room. When he saw her, Jake's veneer broke, and tears began falling down his face. Anna hurried over to his side, where she took his hand.

As he squeezed her fingers, Jake said, "I wanted to go cold turkey, but I'm not as strong as you are, Anna. And the doctors strongly advised me against even attempting that. They said I'm so weak it could kill me."

She wiped a tear from his cheek and said, "Weren't you the one who told me treating addiction wasn't a matter of strength or weakness?"

He took a deep, unsteady breath, and finally nodded. "It feels like I said that in another lifetime," he said.

A tall dark-haired woman standing at the foot of Jake's bed said to Anna, "I used pretty much those same words on a fiercely argumentative young lawyer I was attempting to treat." Her white coat with blue stitching identified her as *Jane Locklear, M.D.,* and she introduced herself as the attending physician.

"Good lawyers are invariably stubborn," said Deke. He offered his hand to Dr. Locklear. "Nick Deketomis."

As she shook it, she asked, "Are you bragging or confessing?"

"A little bit of both," said Deke.

"Dr. Locklear's logic wore me down," Jake said. "Of course, it didn't help that I was having seizures at the time."

In a smaller voice, he added, "The Naltrexone stopped those."

"As I told Jake," Dr. Locklear said, "that course of treatment could well have made the difference between life and death. It's clear his captors kept him on a high dose of opioids."

"Bastards," said Bennie. His growl was as fierce as his scowl.

Another figure walked into the already crowded suite. "Paul!" said Jake.

"Did you leave any room for us in there?" asked a woman's voice.

From behind Paul, Alison Stanley waved to Jake. Next to her was Ron Beyer, the other paralegal, who gave Jake a thumbs-up.

"There's not even room enough for Bennie," said Paul, "but that's not going to stop me from getting a hug."

He swooped down on Jake and threw his arms around him. Directly behind him a line formed, everyone wanting to give Jake a squeeze.

"Hurry it up," joked Deke. "I want to get my turn. And then I want to hear Jake's story."

"I'll vacate the area so as to give everyone a little more room," said Dr. Locklear. "But I'm afraid this reunion must be short-lived. In ten minutes I'll be clearing everyone out of here. Jake needs his rest."

32

MORE DEALING THAN HEALING
ALONG THE OXY-EXPRESS

Three weeks after his escape, Jake wondered if a part of him would always be imprisoned. That's how it was with addiction . . . and recovery. He didn't yet feel free of the drugs. Anna understood. To a large degree, she was in the same position.

Still, Anna was doing her best to be supportive. They'd spent the morning together, and she'd made breakfast. Jake had feigned enthusiasm upon seeing the biscuits, eggs, bacon, and fresh juice, but she could tell his happiness was tempered.

"Are you excited about the ARCOS hearing tomorrow?" she asked.

Jake had to think about his answer. It bothered him that his responses now seemed more plodding than before. His days of quick replies and reactions seemed to have deserted him.

"Yes and no," he said.

Anna looked disappointed by his answer, and Jake had half a mind to say, "I'm an addict who's taking a drug to deal with my addiction. What do you expect from me?"

"It's *your* case," she said. "If not for you, it would never have happened. And whatever's decided by tomorrow's proceeding might be monumental."

"It *was* my case," Jake said. "Now I'm window dressing. While I was imprisoned, a lot of decisions were made about the direction of this hearing, and what comes next. I was left out of that whole process."

"You're still one of three plaintiff lawyers," said Anna, "working on a case you initiated that now possibly has nationwide consequences. You need to quit feeling sorry for yourself, Jake."

"What I need is for people not to tell me what I should be feeling," he said.

The hurt look on Anna's face made Jake wish he could take back his words. "I'm sorry," he said. "I know you're trying to help. And I know you want the best for me. The truth of the matter is that I'm no longer capable of contributing to this ARCOS hearing. Whether it's the Naltrexone I'm taking or what the opioids did to me, my thoughts these days are cumbersome. In the past I could always count on my memory not failing me, but now my own mind feels like a stranger to me."

"I've been there," said Anna. "I *am* there. But trust me, things do get better with time."

"I hope you're right," he said, "but things won't get better by tomorrow."

"This is still your case whether you participate in the hearing or not," she said. "And Paul and Deke know that. They also know what you've sacrificed. You *deserve* to feel like you belong, because you *do* belong. And besides, didn't you always say that you were only doing this for one reason?"

Jake nodded. That reason had been his one constant. "I took it up to try and get justice for Blake."

"So how has that changed?"

"It hasn't," he said.

"Remember that when you're in the courtroom tomorrow," Anna said. "I wish I could be there to see you."

"I wish you could, too," Jake said. "You can blame the defendants for the closed courtroom. They told Judge Sargent that they'll be presenting sensitive information that needs to be kept private. We suspect it's another ploy to buy time, but the judge decided to honor their wishes."

"I'm surprised that you're not already on your way to Columbus," she said.

"I didn't want to leave without having a morning together with you. Deke offered me a spot on his firm's private jet, but I said I would rather drive."

"You're kidding. You turned down a chance to fly in a private jet?"

"I like driving," Jake said, grinning.

"No one likes driving more than flying on a private jet."

He shrugged. "The truth of the matter is that I've never flown before, and I didn't want to admit that to Deke."

"Poor-kid pride?" she asked.

"Something like that," he said. "And I was also worried about my stomach acting up. It hasn't been right since my captivity, and I didn't want to ruin the flight for others by getting sick in midair."

"Promise me that next time you're offered a ride in a private plane, you'll agree to go," she said.

"Why is it so important to you?"

"Because you need to be willing to take a chance and do what you want, instead of always worrying about the consequences."

"I promise," he said.

And as if to show that he meant what he said, and that he wasn't going to avoid taking chances in the future, Jake leaned over and gave Anna a kiss.

❖❖❖

It took Jake only two and a half hours to reach Ohio's capital. Using the GPS on his cell phone, he was able to navigate through the downtown-Columbus business district. Deke's firm had booked Jake a room at the Leveque Tower, a storied downtown hotel. Even though he was wearing his best suit, when he checked in he felt like an impostor, an intruder in a world where he didn't belong. *What am I doing here?* he thought. And that was even before he opened the door to his room.

The suite was about as big as the Rutledge family home in Oakley. When Jake looked in at the cavernous space, his first thought was that he had been given the key to the wrong room. As a precaution, he wiped his shoes on the hallway carpeting before stepping inside. After taking half a dozen uncertain steps forward, he saw that a gift basket had been set up on a table with plates and a champagne flute.

I'm definitely in the wrong room, he thought, but that's when he saw that the basket had a card with his name on it. The message inside was short: *Enjoy!* Next to it was Deke's name.

Jake walked over to the sheer curtains and pulled them open. From seven stories up, he looked out over downtown Columbus and the Scioto River. The sun was in the process of setting and was casting a golden glow on the water.

Using his cell phone camera, Jake took a few pictures. The results didn't do justice to what he was seeing, but he forwarded the best shot to Anna, along with his love.

That night Jake begged off meeting the others for dinner, claiming he didn't feel 100 percent. Deke didn't push him very hard; since Jake's return everyone had understood that he was still recovering from his ordeal.

Though Jake knew his bill was being charged to Deke's firm, after seeing the prices on the room-service menu, he felt too guilty to put in an order. He decided to get a little exercise while seeing what food choices were available near the hotel instead. Besides, it would be his chance to explore a little bit of Columbus. Three blocks from the hotel, he found an open sub shop. The turkey sub was just his speed—he was a West Virginia boy, and more comfortable in the absence of pretense.

Still, it wasn't like he pined for sackcloth and ashes. Later that night he couldn't help but enjoy his splendidly appointed room. In particular, he loved the mattress. It was firm yet gentle. Goldilocks would certainly have approved. Within ten minutes of settling into bed, Jake fell into a deep sleep.

The next morning Jake made a breakfast out of the cheese and fruit in his gift basket, and then grabbed a coffee on the way to the Joseph P. Kinneary U.S. Courthouse. It was only a half-mile walk from the Leveque, and when he arrived, there was still an hour before the hearing was due to start. He had nervous energy needing to be burned off, so he decided to play tourist. He walked around the five-story building, taking in its neoclassical design, including a massive colonnade and elaborate iron grill encasements.

The interior of the building was no less ornate. At another time he would have enjoyed touring the building, but with all the adrenaline pumping through his veins, he decided it was best to find the courtroom where the ARCOS hearing was scheduled to take place. Even though he would be playing third fiddle for the hearing, it was nice to feel so energized. *I actually feel alive,* he thought. Since his captivity, he hadn't felt that way often.

The courtroom was empty save for security. Before being allowed admittance, Jake had to provide identification. After his name was checked off, he made his way inside. In the quietude, it almost felt like being in a shrine. There would be no spectators today, and no one sitting in the jury box. Jake's eyes scanned where the bailiff and court reporter would be sitting. He studied the witness box and the judge's bench.

Footsteps and familiar voices made him turn. The two paralegals, Ron and Alison, were waving at him. "Jake the snake," said Ron.

Even though the paralegals would only be indirectly involved in the hearing, they seemed to be as nervous as Jake. Everyone shook hands. Jake was glad his wasn't the only sweaty palm.

Carol and Bennie made their entrance next. The two of them were working up until the last minute, with Bennie consulting an index card and posing questions to Carol. Though they were too far away for Jake to hear what either was saying, he could guess what Bennie was asking. Paul was going to put Carol on the stand and question her about the massive diversion of opioids from legitimate hospitals and pharmacies to pill mills, focusing on the area along Interstate 75 known as the Oxy-Express.

Carol's testimony would be used as a springboard to help the judge understand how relevant the DEA's ARCOS system was to their case, as well as to the entire opioid epidemic. By using the data from ARCOS, Paul would contend that they could show how and where the controlled substances had been diverted while at the same time illustrating the criminal conduct by the opioid distributors. He was confident the figures would show that the distributors in conjunction with the manufacturers had been running a sophisticated government-sanctioned drug cartel on American soil.

"Getting that data," Deke had said to Paul and Jake, "will virtually assure us the chance to centralize a national case in an MDL."

The quiet courtroom suddenly became noisy as Nathan Ailes and his army of lawyers and staff began filing into the courtroom. Jake couldn't help but be reminded of briefcase drill teams he'd seen marching at the Doo Dah Parade in Pasadena, California, and the Macy's Thanksgiving Parade in New York City. Dressed in identical suits, sporting the same conservative briefcases, they operated much like an army drill team, but they wielded briefcases instead of rifles.

"All Ailes is missing is cadence calls for his team," Jake murmured.

The eyes of the two men met, but neither acknowledged the other. Jake remembered how Ailes had tried to intimidate him at the first motion to dismiss. Since then he hadn't allowed Ailes to have that kind of power over him. In the back of his mind, though, he wondered if it was Ailes who had arranged for his abduction. Law enforcement, as well as Carol and Bennie, were continuing to look into that, but as of yet, there were more questions than answers.

Deke and Paul entered the courtroom together and made their way over to the plaintiff's side. They greeted Jake with a hug and a pat on the back. Both men, he was happy to see, were pumped, and by appearances more than ready to go. Luckily, they didn't have to wait long.

Judge Edward "Sarge" Sargent entered his courtroom, and everyone rose. He gave a smile and a nod to those assembled, and then he took a seat. The bailiff instructed everyone to sit. Jake sat at the table with Paul and Deke, but he'd chosen the seat farthest from the aisle so as to not impede their movements. As he surveyed the courtroom, he felt his heart pounding. It had been a long journey getting here and being given this opportunity. Even if this case was about the money to most of those in the courtroom, to him it was about the people who'd been affected. They were the ones who mattered.

Though the judge had set strict ground rules for the hearing, he had an easy manner that extended to the way he spoke. He was one of those understated and confident individuals who knew exactly what he was doing. Judge Sargent explained how the proceeding would work, and then asked if there were any questions. Deke had agreed to allow Ailes to begin with his witnesses, as he saw an advantage in being able to be the first to cross-examine.

Jake was an insider to what was going on, but at the same time he felt like an outsider. Still, because his involvement was limited, he was able to watch the proceedings more closely than he might otherwise have been able to. Perhaps because Ailes knew the clock was running, he curtailed most of his grandstanding and poetics when he called Dan Abernathy to the stand. The only thing he didn't forsake were his dramatic hand gestures. Still, as the examination began, Jake had to begrudgingly admit that Ailes was on his game.

As security director at MHC, Abernathy was able to speak knowledgeably about how the ARCOS drug reporting system worked. Abernathy came off as credible; he didn't speak like a bureaucrat, but more like the street cop he'd once been. Burly, and with a ruddy face with a five o'clock shadow, he also looked more like a cop than a DC insider. As Ailes's questioning continued, it became apparent that Abernathy was the perfect shill, offering up reasons real and imagined why the ARCOS data should not be released.

"The less the public knows about the location of the DEA drug distribution warehouses," said Abernathy, "the better it is for everyone concerned. Can you imagine the risks associated with these warehouses if they were targeted by some of the more sophisticated gangs? Or worse, if organized crime were to try and compromise their security? We work diligently to keep all the details about our warehouses as secret as possible."

Jake wasn't surprised to hear Abernathy's plea for what he called "the continued anonymity of the warehouses." He knew that Deke and Paul had been certain that card would be played, and they planned to respond to it.

"Thank you, Mr. Abernathy," said Ailes. "You are certainly not alone in that opinion. In fact, I talked to Andrew Jeffords, the head of the DEA, and he said much the same thing. I asked Mr. Jeffords to write an affidavit to this court, which I have included in my pleadings. Mr. Jeffords also said that if the ARCOS data was released, he hoped that it would be put under seal and not released to the public for at least six months."

"I will review the affidavit carefully," said Judge Sargent. "Six months seems a long time."

"The release of all the ARCOS data would certainly create fallout within the DEA," said Ailes, "and like any bureaucracy, they would need time to prepare."

"I will take that under consideration," the judge said. "Do you have any more questions for your witness?"

"No, Your Honor."

Deke was already out of his seat and approaching the witness stand to cross-examine Abernathy. Ailes had done his best to throw Abernathy as many softballs as possible. Deke, Jake knew, would come in with the heat.

Jake was not disappointed.

"Mr. Abernathy, you claim releasing the ARCOS data is—and let me use your words—a 'huge danger' because it would reveal the locations of the twenty-eight DEA drug distribution warehouses in this country. Is that true?"

"Yes," said Abernathy.

"Would it surprise you to know, Mr. Abernathy," said Deke, "that I was personally curious as to the locations of those twenty-eight warehouses. So, what do you suppose I did?"

"I have no idea." By his tone, Jake thought, it was clear he didn't care either.

"I simply Googled the information. Would you be surprised to hear that it took me less than twenty minutes to get all twenty-eight locations?"

"Am I supposed to be impressed?" asked Abernathy.

"I don't really care whether you're impressed or not," said Deke. "What I do care about is your sitting on that witness stand and uttering total nonsense, like you just did."

Ailes jumped to his feet, with, as Jake thought, ten fingers blazing. "Objection, Your Honor. Counsel is badgering this witness for no reason."

"Let's see where this goes first," said Judge Sargent, "and then I can decide if any badgering is going on."

With a nod to Deke, he said, "Continue."

"Twenty minutes, Mr. Abernathy. These warehouses are not top-secret installations, as you and Mr. Ailes would have us believe. And yet you just now said if the public knew how many drugs were going in and out of these warehouses, that would pose a terrible risk to those working at those facilities. Did you not tell the judge that while you were under oath?"

"Yes, I said that. And it is my belief that the locations and the details about those distribution warehouses should not be publicized. The vast quantity of drugs being moved could attract the wrong attention."

"But isn't that like saying we shouldn't mention there's gold located in Fort Knox?"

"I don't think that's a fair analogy, sir," he said.

"Well, how is this analogy, Mr. Abernathy? There are hundreds of nuclear missile silos spread throughout the United States, and right on Google Earth there are detailed maps that show the location of every one of those silos."

"I think we're talking about apples and oranges," said Abernathy.

"In that case," said Deke, "why don't you please tell me if this is an apple or an orange, Mr. Abernathy?"

At his signal, a large video screen descended from the ceiling. Moments later a map with location coordinates materialized.

"This is one of your warehouses, Mr. Abernathy. If you'd like, I can show you twenty-seven more, each with its exact location."

"Do whatever you want."

"I'll spare you the repetition," said Deke, "but instead let me show you another graphic."

On the screen the map was replaced by a list of names. "It took me an hour to get a list of every employee working at the warehouse we just saw on the screen. You still think there's anything secret about these warehouses?"

"I don't see any reason to tempt fate," said Abernathy, now looking considerably less composed.

"Mr. Abernathy, I know that Mr. Ailes questioned you in your role as director of security for MHC, but you didn't always have that position, did you?"

"Not always."

"In fact, for fifteen years you were an investigator for the DEA, were you not?"

"I was."

"During your tenure at the DEA," said Deke, "you led two investigations that looked into the business practices of MHC, your current employer. The results of each investigation determined that MHC was supplying pill mills with amounts of Oxy that were twenty times higher than the guidelines clearly established by the DEA and all regulatory norms."

"All that is public record," said Abernathy.

"That's correct," said Deke, "but what isn't public record, sir, is that you, as head of those investigations, recommended no fines and no sanctions against MHC."

"I didn't think they were warranted," he said.

"You didn't think they were warranted? If my facts are correct, Mr. Abernathy, and I am quite sure they are, both of those pill mills you investigated were located in the same city in West Virginia. Where the population was ten thousand, yet around *seven million* pills were shipped into that city per year. Did I get that right, Mr. Abernathy?"

Ailes stood up. "Objection, Your Honor. I don't see the relevance of this to any ruling on the ARCOS data."

Jake held his breath, waiting for the judge's answer. Luckily, he didn't have to wait long. And what he heard made him happy.

"Then I suggest you listen more carefully, Mr. Ailes," said the judge. "Objection overruled."

Judge Sargent nodded at Deke to continue.

"There was one matter that wasn't on the public record, Mr. Abernathy," said Deke. "And I could find no mention of it in the media either. At the conclusion of your second investigation of MHC, you left the DEA, isn't that true?"

"Yes," he said.

"And you took a job at MHC," said Deke, "that paid fifty percent more than what you were getting with the DEA. Isn't that also true?"

Ailes was on his feet again. His agonized expression was mirrored by those on his team. "Objection," he said.

Judge Sargent had already heard enough. "Please sit, Mr. Ailes. And please answer the question, Mr. Abernathy."

Abernathy sighed. "That sounds right," he said.

"No more questions, Your Honor," said Deke.

"Thank you, Mr. Abernathy. You are excused," said the judge. "Mr. Ailes, you may call your next witness."

Suzanne "Suzie" Stone was an attractive fortysomething blonde who was wearing an expensive if revealing outfit. Her skirt ran a little high, displaying her tanned and shapely legs, and her blouse ran a little low, showcasing her ample cleavage. Suzie had bleached teeth and bleached hair. She didn't appear to believe in stinting, either on her makeup or her jewelry.

Deke would have been surprised if Suzie hadn't been a cheerleader during high school and a sorority girl in college. She was quick to smile, and unconsciously seemed to flirt with every male she came into contact with. Based on her sales figures, it was apparent that during her office calls, doctors—at least the male doctors—were quick to pull out their order pads.

When Suzie was shown to the witness stand, she patted the bailiff's arm and flashed a smile. Both Deke and Paul had anticipated a witness like Suzie. Her goal would be to explain why the plaintiffs did not need the ARCOS data because the same information was arguably available within the individual records of every pharmacy or medical clinic the distributors did business with. Ailes would emphasize that what Deke and his team wanted was "overkill" and "unnecessary." Smiling Suzie would agree with his assessment, putting in her two cents under the guise of her work experience.

"Ms. Stone," said Ailes, "please tell this courtroom what your role is with MHC."

Smiling broadly, she said, "My role is two parts. I manage a sales team, and I supervise quality control through face-to-face visits with pharmacies and doctor clinics in West Virginia."

"In other words," said Ailes, "you are hands-on in understanding how your customers make their purchases, and how proper and correct records of those purchases are kept by every one of the businesses you service in West Virginia."

Suzie readily agreed, just as she readily agreed to every one of Ailes's inquiries over the next fifteen minutes. Jake watched as Ailes did his best to build his case. The attorney took great pains to try and establish that every purchase of every opioid sold by distributors such as MHC was easily traceable by reviewing the records that the DEA required every purchaser to keep. Ailes, using Suzie's words, stressed that between the distributors and the businesses, they could account for the number and type of every pill dispersed.

When Ailes finished with Suzie, he looked much more confident. That might have given Jake some discomfort, if not for the smile he saw on Deke's face. Now it was their side's turn.

"Ms. Stone," he said, "can you please tell the court how many years you've worked for MHC?"

"For almost twenty years," she said.

"A long time," said Deke.

"I was very young when I started," she said, batting her eyes.

"You're very good at your job, aren't you?" he said.

"How sweet of you to say that."

"I think I'm being more accurate than sweet," Deke said. "The average MHC sales rep makes one hundred and sixty thousand dollars a year, which is about thirty-five thousand dollars more than the national average for sales reps. However, in all your years with MHC, you have far exceeded that average. How do you explain that?"

Doing her best to act innocent, Suzie said, "I love my job!"

"Based on your paycheck, it's a mutual admiration society. Where you seem to have done particularly well, Ms. Stone, is on your annual bonus. Can you tell me what that bonus is based upon?"

"We're rewarded for sales," she said.

"There were five years in a row where you received bonuses of one hundred thousand dollars, which is the maximum amount that MHC pays out. In fact, during that time period, you were the number-one field rep for all of MHC."

"I worked very hard," she said.

"I'm sure you did," said Deke. "But I suppose it didn't hurt that during those five years in question, more opioids were distributed than at any other time in history."

"I wouldn't know about that," she said.

Ailes got to his feet. "Objection, Your Honor. This line of questioning is far beyond the scope of my questioning."

"Judge," said Deke, "this line of questioning is intended to show exactly why we need the ARCOS data."

"You may continue, Mr. Deketomis, but I expect you to tie up the relevance. Your objection is overruled, Mr. Ailes."

"Ms. Stone," said Deke, "I'm sure you are aware of what is commonly referred to as the Oxy-Express."

"I've heard of it," she admitted.

"The area you worked around West Virginia was pretty much ground zero for the Express."

Suzie shrugged. "I'll have to take your word for that."

"Is it your position, Ms. Stone, that you were unaware of the opioid epidemic going on all around the area you lived and worked?"

"As you pointed out," she said, her smile now removed from her face, "I was successful at my job. That didn't leave me time for much else."

"For most of your years at MHC—in fact, for the last dozen years—you've lived at the same address in Huntington, West Virginia, isn't that true?"

"Yes," she said.

"Are you aware, Ms. Stone, of the many pill mills located within three miles from where you live?"

She looked over to Ailes; he didn't meet her gaze.

"I'll rephrase the question for you, Ms. Stone," said Deke, "but I will remind you that you are under oath. In the past five years, are you aware that at least three pill mills, located fewer than three miles from where you live, were shut down?"

Suzie nodded, and Deke said, "Is that a yes, Ms. Stone?"

"Yes," she said.

"I would like to show you a short video and get your reaction to it."

At Deke's signal, the lights were dimmed, and a video began to play. There was a line of people going halfway down the block awaiting admittance to a pharmacy. Some of the individuals were wearing bathrobes and pajamas. The image suddenly changed when DEA agents swarmed the clinic.

"Do you recognize this video, Ms. Stone?"

"Yes," she said.

"I imagine you would, as that DEA raid took place two years ago not far from where you live. The pharmacy that was raided was one of those exemplary businesses that was supposed to be keeping great records. Would it surprise you to know that they weren't, Ms. Stone?"

Ailes was standing and objecting.

"Enough," said Judge Sargent, shutting Ailes up. Then he turned to Deke. "And enough from you as well, Mr. Deketomis. I get it. We all get it. This witness would have had to be blind to not know what was going on in her hometown, even without the attendant publicity. If it was supposed to be a secret, then it was one virtually everyone in Huntington was in on. And I'm sure, Mr. Deketomis, that you can produce many more videos and pictures that drive home your point even further. However, the narrow question I need to answer in this hearing involves only the ARCOS data."

"As I am sure I don't need to tell Your Honor," said Deke, "from what we surmise, the pharmacy records don't align with the ARCOS data, and that is yet another good reason for their being released. That being said, I have no more questions for Ms. Stone."

"I'm glad to hear that," said Judge Sargent. "Are you ready with your witnesses?"

"We are, Your Honor," said Deke.

❖❖❖

Yin and yang, thought Jake, watching the proceeding carefully. Paul's style was very different from Deke's, but just as effective. Deke was more in your face; Paul was ever affable. But in his time questioning Carol, he was able to make the points their team wanted.

First, Paul and Carol offered up an overview of the Oxy-Express. They explained what it was and how it operated. Their history lesson revealed that there was no system in place in Florida that tracked prescriptions, and because of that, doctors in Florida had prescribed what was believed to be ten times more oxycodone pills than every other state in the country combined.

Even Judge Sargent looked surprised by that figure.

Carol also explained what "doctor shopping" was, and how every day there were troops of people going from pill mill to pill mill until they found a doctor who'd prescribe them the opioids they wanted without asking too many questions.

"And what happened to all those pills?" asked Paul. "These were addicts who just had a ball?"

"Some of them were. But the rest was a massive pill diversion," said Carol. "Not surprisingly, many criminal enterprises took advantage of the ease of purchasing pills, and they bought massive quantities to resell on the black market. It's believed that billions of pills made their way up the I-75 corridor that way. The diversion of opioids became a huge profit center, not only for the cartels reselling them but for the drug companies fulfilling this demand, which went far beyond what they could have sold in legitimate prescriptions."

Paul opted to limit his questioning, keeping it focused on the ARCOS data and why it was necessary. When he announced that he had no more questions for Carol, Ailes stepped up to the witness stand and began what should have been his cross-examination. It didn't take long for him to digress from a classic cross-examination and begin rambling on about the dangers of making it difficult for doctors to manage their patients' pain. Jake could see Judge Sargent becoming ever more impatient.

"Am I going to hear an actual question, Mr. Ailes," he asked, "or just more closing commentary?"

Ailes turned to Judge Sargent, pretending to look surprised and hurt. "Judge, it seems to me you let Mr. Vogel and Ms. Morris give this court a history lesson."

"The background they offered regarding the Oxy-Express was well within the court parameters," said the judge. "I will remind you that you are supposed to be conducting an actual cross-examination. You have moved beyond that in talking about doctor-patient care that has no relevance to this court, as far as I can determine. Do you wish to use your limited amount of time for the cross-examination of this witness, or for some other purpose?"

"I will continue with my cross-examination, Your Honor," Ailes promised.

A second later, he broke that promise. "Are you aware, Ms. Morris, that the prescribing of oxycodone is trending downward, and has so for several years. There have even been a number of recent studies that show that statistically—"

"Objection, Your Honor!" shouted Paul, his normally affable face red and angry. "What is it about the term 'cross-examination' that Mr. Ailes doesn't seem to understand?"

"Let me try this again," said Judge Sargent, his voice slightly frayed. "The objection is sustained, Mr. Ailes, for the same reason that has been explained to you three times now by this court. Later in this hearing you can voice your arguments, but for now, please continue with your *cross-examination*."

"No, I don't think I will, *Your Honor*." Ailes was unsparing in his disdain. "I believe I'll just choose to wait for an appellate court to hear my arguments. Thank goodness in America there are courts of appeal to oversee the conduct of lower courts."

Most federal district judges would have had Ailes removed from the courtroom in chains. Judge Sargent merely smiled at the lawyer's temper tantrum. Judging by Ailes's red face, the judge's composure—and especially his smile—was more galling to him than a scolding or rebuke.

"As you wish, Mr. Ailes," he said. "Now please take your seat and we will continue."

Paul Vogel's mouth was open. Jake would bet that in his many years of practicing law, he had never seen a lawyer show such disrespect for a federal trial judge.

Paul and Deke exchanged glances. It was clear that the two men were thinking the same thing Jake was. Their side could only benefit from Ailes's lack of composure and professionalism. All three of them did their best to hide their smiles.

33

SMARTER THAN THE AVERAGE DOG

Deke and Paul both concluded it would be better not to call their second witness after Nathan Ailes's courtroom meltdown. They'd planned to call Gordon Ferris, a county controller from Ohio. Ferris could discuss all the costs, many hidden, that had fallen upon counties in the wake of the opioid epidemic. Because Judge Sargent had limited the parameters of the hearing, they opted to not overstep the boundaries he had set. It was their thinking that they had already either made their case, or not made it. The judge seemed pleased by their decision that less was more.

Judge Sargent scanned the courtroom, making eye contact and smiling at the fewer than a dozen people in attendance. He looked at his watch and announced, "It's four thirty, but then I suspect most of you are well aware of the time."

There was laughter in the courtroom.

"This hearing is concluded. However, I would ask that before this day is out, the legal teams supply me with all the briefings they want me to review. If I'm not overwhelmed by new and cogent material, you should have my ruling by Thursday morning."

He paused for a moment, removed his glasses, and leaned back in his chair before continuing. "Last week I was asked to give a speech about some of the more interesting statements made by Justice Oliver Wendell Holmes while he was on the bench. One especially telling statement Holmes made was this: 'Even a dog distinguishes between being stumbled over and being kicked.'

"I would like to think that I have more judicial insight than the average dog, and over the next few days I am confident I will be able to look at the bigger picture in front of me and determine that which was inadvertent, and that which was purposeful and hurtful and perhaps even vicious. Does the ARCOS data show a deliberate diversion of drugs was afoot, and that blind eyes were purposely turned to that, or did things just fall through the cracks, as they are often wont to do?"

Judge Sargent stood up, and those in the courtroom rose. With a backward wave, the judge made his way toward chambers.

"How does an early Italian dinner sound to everyone?" asked Deke.

On the recommendation of the concierge, all seven members of the plaintiff's party decided to dine at a long-established family Italian restaurant in downtown Columbus. Jake had never dined in such a fancy restaurant. He wished Anna were there with him. If she had been at his side, everything might not have felt so anticlimactic. The excitement and ebullience that had carried him through the day had vanished. Maybe it was the uncertainty of the future that made him feel weighed down, or it could have just been the ebb and flow of his recovery. Intellectually, Jake knew that opioids had altered his brain chemistry, but that knowledge didn't make his reality any easier.

Over the course of the meal, starting with antipasti and lots of red wine, the hearing was rehashed. Even the judge's final words were considered. Deke focused on the judge's dog analogy.

"What could be more *purposeful* and *hurtful* than circumventing safeguards and distributing billions of pills?" he asked. "And in the end, what could be more vicious?"

"And doesn't Nathan Ailes strike you as the kind of human being who would kick a poor dog?" said Paul.

There seemed to be unanimous agreement on that.

Deke couldn't help but notice how quiet Jake had been throughout the meal. "So, how's that pork ragout with that pasta's name I can't pronounce?" he asked.

"Pappardelle," said Jake, "but don't ask me what it means. I've never had the dish before and didn't know what to expect, but the server steered me well. It's really good."

"I was twenty-five when I learned there were other Italian dishes besides pepperoni pizza and spaghetti and meatballs," said Deke.

"That's pretty much my knowledge and experience with Italian food," said Jake.

"So is the food here better than Mom's?" asked Deke.

Jake ran his hand along the white linen tablecloth. "The food is equally good," he said. "But this white linen is a bit more appetizing than Mom's vinyl tablecloths. I'm pretty sure some of those tablecloths are older than I am."

Deke smiled. "So now that you're a bona fide lawyer, Jake, what do you think of practicing law?"

Jake pursed his lips and gave the question some thought. "I'm afraid I don't feel like a bona fide lawyer," he admitted. "Maybe I'll think differently when I get the monkey off my back."

"As I've told you," said Deke, "and I hope you're hearing me, whatever rehab clinic you choose will be paid for by our firm."

"That's very generous of you," said Jake.

"There are some treatment facilities that have gorgeous ocean views and serve spa food," said Deke. "In fact, there's one just like that in Spanish Trace."

Spanish Trace was Deke's waterfront hometown in the Florida Panhandle. Jake nodded and offered a polite if noncommittal smile.

Paul decided to get in on the conversation. "You're not trying to steal my fellow West Virginian to work at your firm, are you, Deke?"

"The thought had crossed my mind," said Deke.

"Jake's a Mountaineer through and through," said Paul. "West Virginia is in his blood. When this is over, I see his future in Huntington at a certain boutique law firm. How does that sound, Jake?"

"It sounds better than I deserve," Jake said. "Especially since lately I've been wondering if I was really cut out to be a lawyer."

"You're too young to be having a midlife crisis," said Deke.

Jake tried to smile, and did his best not to look or act glum. "Maybe it's the Naltrexone talking," he admitted. "Maybe when I'm off it, I'll be reinvigorated and back to my old self. But I never imagined practicing the law would be so cumbersome. It's hard to believe we're still a ways from the finish line in this case, but just to get to this point has taken so much longer than I thought. That sure wasn't what I expected."

"I'm afraid the term 'speedy justice' is invariably an oxymoron," said Paul.

"If we get our MDL," said Deke, "I guarantee you that things will speed up. And one day you'll look back and realize that by jumping through all the hoops that you did, you might very well have made the difference in our being able to establish an MDL. And if we get there, we will absolutely bring an end to all this. I'm convinced, Jake, that nothing has better potential to help mitigate the damage caused by the opioid crisis at the city and county and personal level than an MDL."

Jake was reluctantly nodding. "I guess I've always known that time was not on our side," he said. "Every day's opioid body count is a reminder of that."

He thought about Blake. Every unnecessary opioid death was a reminder of his own painful loss.

Later, Jake ordered tiramisu for dessert. He had never eaten it before and was looking forward to trying it, but only when he was looking at an empty plate did Jake realize he'd finished the dessert without even being aware of how it tasted.

Thursday morning, Judge Edward Sargent's decision was emailed to both legal teams. From his office in Spanish Trace, Deke scanned the pages. His first call was to Jake, but it went immediately to his voice mail. After leaving him a quick message, Deke called Paul.

"See the decision?" he asked, his voice triumphant.

"I'm just looking at it now," said Paul, who sounded equally exultant.

"Judge Sargent's office must have contacted the DEA's office with his ruling yesterday so as to expedite matters," said Deke. "Because of that, we're supposed to get all the requested ARCOS data this morning. Judge Sargent has made it clear that there will be no kicking of the can. They'll be in contempt if they don't comply."

"As far as I can see," said Paul, "the judge's only concession to Jazz Hands is that the ARCOS data is for our eyes only for the next sixty days."

What that meant was the information couldn't be disseminated to any other parties, especially the media.

"That will give Jazz Hands two months to prepare his take on the data," said Deke. "He'll probably use that line about how there are three kinds of lies: lies, damn lies, and statistics."

"Don't give him any ideas," said Paul.

"Let's just use the sixty days to our advantage," said Deke. "Even though Judge Sargent sealed the data, we can still use the ARCOS information to take the first steps to draft the pleadings and briefings we'll need to launch an MDL. I don't think we're being premature in this, what with Judge Sargent discussing the connection between ARCOS and the foundation of an MDL in his decision. Starting tomorrow, I'll get to work building a team of lawyers from coast to coast who have the talent, financial ability, and courage to jump into this project. Because Ohio was essentially ground zero for the start of the opioid epidemic, it would be my first pick as an MDL jurisdiction. If that occurs, either Cleveland or Columbus is the likely choice of venue. I'd like you to identify the best local law firms based in and around those cities."

"I'll make some calls," said Paul. "We can start building bridges, even if for sixty days we can't be specific about the materials we're using."

"Exactly," said Deke.

"Did you get a chance to talk to Jake this morning?"

"Not yet," said Deke. "What about you?"

"I left a message on his voice mail," said Paul.

"So did I," said Deke. He tried not to sound worried, but he was.

Just before noon, the DEA complied with Judge Sargent's directive, emailing files with the ARCOS data to the legal teams. Deke spent an hour poring through the figures. He wasn't a forensic accountant, but he could add two and two. The numbers were showing a systematic diversion of opioids on a scale hard to imagine.

In the middle of crunching numbers, Deke suddenly remembered that Jake still hadn't called him back. That wasn't like him.

He checked his cell phone for messages and texts but saw nothing.

Maybe Jake is just studying the ARCOS data, Deke thought. It was a logical explanation, but Deke's gut told him something wasn't right. Once again, his call went directly to voice mail.

There was an explanation for that as well, Deke told himself. Whenever he forgot to charge his cell phone, he knew that his calls always went straight to voice mail. It was possible Jake hadn't even noticed his phone needed charging. Deke hoped that was the case, but he wasn't buying it. He called Alison. She and Ron had remained behind in Huntington.

"Congratulations!" Alison said. In the background, Deke heard Ron joining in.

"And congratulations to you and Ron," he said. "I also want to bring Jake in on this group hug. Have you seen or heard from him?"

"No," she said.

Deke didn't want to alarm Alison, but she was apparently perceptive to the undertones of his inquiry. "Is anything wrong?" she asked.

"I wouldn't worry," he said. "It's just that I haven't been able to reach Jake this morning, and I wanted to make sure he knew about the ruling."

"He was on Judge Sargent's email list," she said. "And wasn't he also on the approved sender list for the ARCOS files?"

"That's right," said Deke, pretending to be reassured. "I'm sure he's out celebrating with Anna."

Alison agreed with him, and the two said their goodbyes. Deke wished he believed his own story, but he knew something else had to be behind Jake's falling off the radar. Had he relapsed? Was he back on opioids? Was he in some other kind of danger? Despite the ongoing investigation, they still didn't know who had ordered Jake's abduction.

Deke sat at his desk thinking. He should have been more closely monitoring Jake. After all, he was undergoing drug treatment and had acknowledged to everyone that he hadn't been himself since escaping from captivity.

Think like Jake would, thought Deke. The kid was as impetuous as he was smart. Like anyone in their twenties, Jake was impatient. And he was driven by the death of his brother. That had motivated everything he had done.

"Dammit," said Deke.

Was that the answer? And if it was, what was Jake's response? It had been Jake's hope that the ARCOS data would make a huge splash. He wanted the figures to be used as a platform for reform. Jake had wanted to explain the opioid plague that had claimed so many lives. Waiting, in his mind, was not an option. The judge had ordered the ARCOS data to not be released for two months. Sixty days didn't seem too long a wait for someone Deke's age, but to his friend that time frame must have seemed like an eternity. Jake's passion demanded he act. The idea of perhaps as many as ten thousand deaths over the course of those sixty days was enough to compel him to act. Jake had made the choice to be a lightning rod—to call people's attention to the crisis, even though doing so would get him burned.

Deke was certain he was right. He hit Paul's cell number, and as soon as he heard his voice, began talking.

"I'm afraid Jake is about to throw himself on his sword," said Deke. "My guess is that he's decided to release the ARCOS data to the media."

"Shit," said Paul. "What can I do?"

"Call Jake. If your call goes to voice mail, leave a message and say it's imperative that he contacts you immediately. After that, text him. Tell him he needs to talk to us before he acts rashly and unnecessarily throws his career away. And then get in touch with some of those media contacts of yours. See if Jake has scheduled some sort of news conference. If we're lucky, you might be able to head him off at the pass before he starts singing. After we finish this conversation, I'll call Ron and Alison and tell them they're to be on call to do whatever you might need them for. Then I'll start a Team Jake group text and include Carol and Bennie in it. They might have some ideas on how to find out where Jake is. Let's all keep each other in the loop."

"Will do," said Paul.

"Good luck," said Deke.

Jake finished his email to Judge Sargent and sent it from his cell phone. There were dozens of emails in his in-box, and even more texts. He purposely didn't read any of his friends' messages. He wasn't going to be deterred.

His email to the judge explained what he'd done, and why he'd done it. Naturally, Jake had exonerated all of his coworkers by stating they had no knowledge of his plans. He'd apologized to the judge for disseminating the ARCOS data sixty days early and said he understood there would be consequences for his actions, and that he would not contest whatever punishment the judge deemed fit.

It was time, Jake thought. No—it was past time. He walked forward and stood at a microphone. He'd promised the media a big story, and a handful of news cameras and reporters were waiting to see if he'd deliver.

"I was responsible for a media dump that just occurred," Jake said. "I'm no Edward Snowden or Julian Assange, and I have no political ax to grind. The media dump was ARCOS files provided by the DEA. This data is essentially an accounting of all controlled substances from their point of manufacture to their distribution. This tracking takes place in the twenty-eight DEA distribution warehouses throughout the United States, and covers the last decade.

"Right now, I see some eyes glazing over. Many, if not all of you, believe the tracking of pills sounds rather boring, even if I put it into perspective by noting that in 2016 over six billion hydrocodone pills and five billion oxycodone pills were distributed throughout our country. If you don't find those numbers compelling, perhaps these are more to my point: in that same year, there were more than forty-two thousand deaths from opioid overdoses, as well as thirteen thousand deaths from heroin overdoses.

"Today I made the decision to release the ARCOS data, even though I knew full well it was illegal to do so. If I had merely waited another sixty days, I would not have committed professional suicide. To many of you, I am sure that seems ridiculous, and yet this morning after an inner debate, I decided I couldn't wait. To not act would mean that over the next two months as many as ten thousand people would needlessly die of an opioid overdose directly and indirectly caused by corporate drug dealers. My twin brother, Blake, was one of those victims, and I decided if there was any way I could prevent one father or mother, or wife or husband, or sister or brother, from experiencing the pain that I did, it would be worth it to release the data early.

"Justice delayed is justice denied, especially when delay means death. I have also chosen to speak out now because of what happened to me. As many of you know, I was abducted, held captive for more than a month, and unwittingly consumed enough opioids to make me an addict. Someone must have seen me as a threat and decided to silence me. But guess what? I'm still here, and I'm still talking. And for today, at least, I'm still a lawyer, but one who has never had a chance to offer up closing arguments.

"I'd like to take the opportunity to do that now, and I hope you will do me the courtesy of listening to me for a few minutes and being my jury."

Jake took a deep breath and blinked away a few tears. *This one is for you, brother,* he thought. When he'd been imprisoned, Jake had worked on his opening comments to the jury. Jake had known that most of those opening arguments could never be used in court, but that hadn't stopped him from incorporating those thoughts into what he was about to say now.

With a heartfelt smile on his face, Jake began the most important closing argument of his life.

34
STAND BY YOUR MAN

It was an almost perfect closing argument, thought Deke. If not for Jake's having to sacrifice his career, it would have been considered textbook quality.

Or maybe that was what made it the perfect closing, but Deke was too invested in the career of his protégé to see that.

During the many years of the opioid crisis, the battleground had somehow never been personalized, despite the deaths of such actors as Heath Ledger and Philip Seymour Hoffman, and musicians Prince and Tom Petty. The public didn't identify opioids with a face, or an event. But Jake somehow made it a big story. Few people would have cared about the ARCOS data; what caught their attention was a young, penitent lawyer who essentially was willing to give everything for his cause. Becoming an addict wasn't enough; he'd also had to throw away his career.

Jake was the car crash that people stopped to observe. His was the story that finally gained enough traction for progress to be made in dealing with the grievous wounds caused by opioids.

Of course, all of that didn't prevent Jake from being disbarred. There was always a price for martyrdom. It was a ramification that seemed to bother Deke and Paul much more than it did Jake. But then again, Jake had been busy getting clean. The Naltrexone was a godsend, and had allowed Jake passage through the rocky shoals, but Jake hadn't wanted to be dependent even upon that.

He'd chosen a private rehab facility with a view of the mountains and not the ocean. He'd eschewed villas in Malibu and Miami, and instead got clean in a log cabin in West Virginia. Anna visited him every day.

Jake's friends also checked in with him. When Paul and Deke called, they invariably updated him on the goings-on of the MDL. Together they were keeping the unwieldy beast on its proper course. The MDL was one of the largest in legal history.

Carol and Bennie were also frequent callers. Sometimes they just wanted to see how he was doing; on other occasions, they called with news. Deke heard how much Jake enjoyed these calls. Carol and Bennie said he was fascinated with the way they tracked down leads and accumulated evidence. Deke suspected that Jake felt as if he were working the case with them.

The U.S. military's Warrior Ethos is: "I will never leave a fallen comrade." Deke was a believer in that same ethos, as was the law firm of Bergman/Deketomis. That was why Carol and Bennie continued to pursue whoever had abducted Jake. They weren't going to forget the assault, nor were they going to let West Virginia law enforcement forget it either.

After Jake left rehab, Deke hired him part-time to help them review the millions of documents that had been produced by the MDL. The work seemed to be good for Jake. Reading the emails, memos, and clinical data that the distributors were finally forced to hand over confirmed everything he had always believed about those who had helped facilitate the deaths of so many people. During one of their conversations, though, Jake had told Deke that he was ready to move on from the MDL work.

"I know I won't be able to escape the sanctions for what I did," he said. "That means my trial-lawyer days are behind me. It's about time I stopped playing at the law."

He'd told Deke that he wasn't sure what was ahead, other than knowing that Anna would be part of that future. The two had become a loving couple. As for what Jake would ultimately do, he'd told Deke that he was "letting the universe decide."

That wasn't good enough for Deke. Behind the scenes, he *worked* with the universe.

"So," Carol asked Jake one day, "have you made a decision on the job?" Deke stayed in the background, letting Carol do most of the talking. Jake and Anna, he knew, were sitting together at the Rutledge house—because they'd moved in together, the couple was now referring to it as "our" house.

Jake had been offered the position of assistant director of Complex Investigations at Bergman/Deketomis. That meant he would act as a combination investigator/lawyer. His legal background—disbarred though he was—and his investigative knack made him an ideal candidate for the position. But now it was up to Jake, not the universe, to decide.

"In case you're wondering," said Deke, "Paul said that West Virginia would miss its native son, but you had his blessing to take your leave for a time."

Jake laughed. "We actually talked to him. Anna got his blessing as well."

"We know you're a package deal," said Carol. "And we're hoping Anna might be amenable to considering a few open positions we have in mind."

"Thank you," said Jake. "However, before we make a final decision, Anna and I think we should spend a few days in Spanish Trace."

"How about I book both of your airline reservations and hotel accommodations?" Carol said.

"That sounds great," said Jake.

"Tomorrow too early for you?" she asked.

Both Anna and Jake agreed that tomorrow was great.

"You should tune in to the news," Carol advised. "We're still working on catching the big fish, but the little fish are being pulled in right now."

"I'll do that," he said. "Thanks for everything, Carol and Deke."

"Our pleasure," said Deke. "And I do mean that."

Eva Whistler stood on the Davis County Courthouse steps. She had made sure her mascara was running. The smudged makeup didn't detract from her beauty but bespoke her inner turmoil for the world to see. She wanted to make sure the public knew how distraught she was. After all, her beloved husband, Danny, had been arrested.

To all appearances, Eva was doing a great Tammy Wynette impression. She was standing by her man. Or at least that's how it seemed.

In reality, she was walking a perilous tightrope. The deputy Danny had been working on those Oakley properties with had flipped on him after being confronted by the Bergman/Deketomis investigators, who'd gathered plenty of damning evidence. The clincher was an affidavit from the Mexican drug dealer, who told a story very different from the one concocted by the deputy and Danny. Because the deputy was willing to testify against Danny, Dunn would get no jail time. He'd been the first domino, but others were already clicking. County officials throughout West Virginia were now letting loose with their sobs of "mea culpa" at being caught subverting due process in their blight and condemnation schemes.

Eva knew there was no way her husband was going to walk. Luckily for Danny, the police had not yet found the man that Jake Rutledge referred to as "Screech." And, Eva was sure, they never would. Screech was distant kin, and blood looked after blood. It was possible Danny would escape kidnapping charges. If he was lucky, he might get off with ten years.

Of course, Eva had to make Danny think it wouldn't be that bad, and that she would be waiting for him on the other side of whatever he had to face. She had to look loyal and pretend to be in great pain, but still make it clear that she was yet another of his victims. If she played her cards right, Danny would never get it into his head to point his finger her way.

Some of those trying to pull her down had made it clear they suspected her involvement, or even more. The worst of them had been that woman named Morris, an investigator who worked for that ambulance chaser Deketomis. Carol Morris had outright told Eva that she believed her guilty of pulling Danny's strings while leaving hubby holding the bag.

Luckily for Eva, few others suspected her of such a thing, and she needed to keep it that way. Eva wiped her eyes for the cameras and sniffed loudly into the microphones.

She pointed to one of the reporters who had his hand raised. Her apparent anguish didn't stop him from calling out, "Are you saying you knew nothing about your husband's criminal enterprise?"

"*Alleged* criminal enterprise," said Eva, "and I most certainly did not."

The reporter continued. "Your husband didn't say anything or do anything to make you believe something might be suspect about his businesses?"

Eva squeezed her nose with the hankie. "I'm sure Danny is guilty of nothing more than bad judgment," she said. "No doubt the incident of Whistler's Mother will be brought up again, and Danny will once more be dragged through the mud."

She pretended to ignore their snickering, even though she had purposely raised her husband's sketchy past. What the public didn't know was that it was Eva who had always reminded Danny that he couldn't treat his mother any better than he did the other residents. It was Danny, though, who'd tried to hide his mother away in a closet. His stupidity had made them the laughingstocks of West Virginia.

And that was something Eva would never forgive.

"Will you be resigning your job as prosecuting attorney?" another reporter yelled.

Eva shook her head emphatically. "As far as I know, it's not a crime to love your husband, and that's the only thing I'm guilty of. That said, I have no plans to resign."

A few crocodile tears ran down her face. She dabbed at them with her hankie.

35

OVER THE RAINBOW

Teri Deketomis crept out of the bedroom where her husband, Deke, was sleeping. When they'd first married, Teri had resisted calling him Deke, and instead had addressed him as Nick or even Nicholas. It hadn't been long, though, before she'd given in. The nickname just seemed to fit him.

Deke had arrived home just before midnight. He'd been so tired that Teri had insisted he go directly to bed. Deke had tried to argue that he had a pile of work he needed to attend to, but she'd overruled his every objection.

He should have known resistance was futile, but he had continued arguing even after he fell into bed. He was halfway into a sentence—and an appeal—when he'd fallen asleep. After Teri was sure he was down for the count, she'd removed his business suit and hung it up.

Deke's long hours were nothing new, but Teri hoped this MDL business would be over soon. She knew how important this case was to him, though. To Deke, it wasn't a case so much as a cause. Some lawyers chased dollars signs, but not her husband. It wasn't the money that motivated him, as much as it was the hope that he could help return a little balance to the world. When Deke spoke about the need for lawyers to focus their skills in places that would "even the playing field," Teri knew it wasn't Pollyanna pabulum. What her husband loved most about his work was being able to speak for the have-nots.

Over the course of their relationship, time and again Teri had pulled Deke back from the brink of exhaustion. Sometimes she felt like a battlefield nurse. It was up to her to patch Deke up so that he could once again engage in the fight. This MDL case had been particularly tough on him. As the lead counsel, Deke was orchestrating a case whose outcome would reverberate nationally. It was a responsibility he embraced, despite its physical toll. It was rare for a boxer to enter into a heavyweight fight and leave the ring unscathed.

Of course, it was understandable that Deke had forgotten what day it was. Thirty years ago today, the two of them had exchanged vows. They'd been little more than kids at the time. Deke was a first-year law student. Back then he'd dreamed of being a criminal prosecutor. Teri had supported the two of them during those early years of their marriage.

I won't give him his anniversary gift, she thought, *until he remembers. It's better that he gets as much sleep as he can while he's here.*

Teri had looked up the appropriate gift for a thirtieth wedding anniversary and found that it was pearl. She'd considered getting him fine pearl cuff links but then thought better of it. Deke didn't like wearing finery.

That hadn't stopped her from finding the perfect pearl present for him. She had located an antique Colt Single Action Army Peacemaker with mother-of-pearl handles. This was the gun that had supposedly won the West. There was a crack in one of the pearl handles, but Teri learned that was the price of beauty. The seller had told her there were very few antique mother-of-pearl stocks available on Colt Peacemakers because of their propensity to crack or split when fired. That was fine with her. Deke wouldn't be firing this weapon. It would go in a display case in his man cave.

Teri finished dressing in the bathroom. When Deke awakened, she planned to spoil him with a pancetta-and-cheese omelet, along with fruit. The only thing missing was the croissant Deke liked with strawberry jam. In downtown Spanish Trace, there was a wonderful French bakery where they brought out fresh, warm croissants on the hour. Terri was sure Deke would still be asleep when she returned. She took care, though, not to make any noise as she opened the front door and stepped out onto their patio.

"What?" The word came unbidden out of her mouth. She turned her head from right to left, taking in the colors. That's what kept her mouth open.

How had all these flowers magically appeared? There were so many flowers filling their patio that there was barely a pathway out. Teri felt like Dorothy stepping into OZ. Around her were vibrant colors of all shapes and sizes.

It wasn't only flowers, though. Atop a stand was a necklace rack. Hanging from one of the displays was a three-strand pearl necklace. Next to it was a card.

Teri ran to it, ripped it open, and pulled out a handwritten note. Deke had written: *Thank you for being my rainbow. Love, Deke.*

It was like being in a rainbow, Teri thought. All the colors were overwhelming. With tear-filled eyes, she read Deke's postscript.

P.S. Did I happen to mention to you that we are now half owners of a flower farm?

Teri wasn't sure whether to laugh or cry, so she did a little bit of both.

36
A STROLL INTO THE FUTURE

Jake and Anna walked along Navarre Beach, the crown jewel of Florida's Emerald Coast. The nickname hadn't been idly earned. The water was a striking emerald color, and clear enough to see colorful fish moving along in its shallows.

The two of them were barefoot and walked along the surf line. It was their first day in Spanish Trace, and both of them were enchanted. The beach was clean, and the white sand was pristine.

"It's like walking on newly fallen snow," said Anna, "except that it's warm and inviting."

She ran ahead and scooped up another sand dollar. She'd discovered the trove of seashells along the high-tide line, and now the pockets of their shorts were overflowing with her "treasures."

"Isn't this incredible?" she asked.

"It's like a postcard," Jake admitted.

"The weather's here," she said. "Wish you were fine."

Jake laughed at her transposing of words.

"Can we do this every day?" she asked.

"We could try," said Jake. His tone changed, becoming suddenly serious. "What do you think about committing to living here for a few years?"

"I'm willing to give it a go if you are," she said.

"The temperature isn't this perfect every day," said Jake. "It's hot and humid during the summer, and let's not forget that hurricane season goes from June to November."

"You think the weather here will scare me away?" she said. "I've spent my life in West Virginia."

"You're okay with being away from your dad?" he asked.

Anna nodded. "I think we could both use the separation. And there's a widowed neighbor woman who I could pay to make meals and look after him. Truth be known, I think they're a little sweet on one another, and probably would have gotten together already if I hadn't been in the way."

"Truth be known," said Jake, repeating her words, "I think I'm a little sweet on you."

"A little?" said Anna, kicking some sand his way.

Jake offered her his hand. After pretending to deliberate about accepting it, she took it into her own, and the two of them continued their walk.

"Did you know there's a paralegal program at the community college in Spanish Trace?" she asked.

"No, I didn't," he said. "What of it?"

"Remember that job you gave me where I was sorting through all that Freedom of Information material related to your case?"

Jake nodded.

"At the time, you mentioned that was the kind of work that paralegals did, and that sort of stuck in my mind. I was surprised at how interesting that job was. That's when I began to seriously consider the possibility of working as a paralegal."

"You never mentioned anything to me," said Jake.

"You were kind of preoccupied with being a prisoner, and an addict, and then working on the most important trial of your life. And that doesn't even take into account your being disbarred and getting clean."

The two of them started laughing. It had been an interesting few months. "Now that you frame it that way," said Jake.

Their walk continued as the sun sank lower and lower on the horizon. Without needing to consult, both of them stopped walking. A minute passed, and the sun finally disappeared from view. The clouds were red and purple and looked altogether too stunning to be real.

"Did you ever see anything so beautiful?" Anna asked.

She offered up an "Oh" of contentment and awe. With his hand, Jake smoothed a strand of her hair, and then he lightly touched her cheek.

"I believe I have," he said, and kissed her.

It was a long time before either of them came up for air. Anna didn't think the moment could be more perfect. She was wrong.

"What are you doing for the rest of your life?" asked Jake.

ABOUT THE AUTHOR

MIKE PAPANTONIO is a senior partner of Levin Papantonio, one of the largest plaintiffs' law firms in America taking on Big Pharma, tobacco companies, and the automotive industry. The firm is taking legal action against the wholesale distributors and manufacturers of opioids in order to recover the immense damages more than 400 cities, counties, and tribes have sustained as a result of these companies creating the current opioid epidemic.

Papantonio has handled thousands of cased throughout the nation involving tobacco and pharmaceutical drug litigation, securities fraud actions, and many of the nation's largest environmental cases. He is one of the youngest trial lawyers to have been inducted into the Trial Lawyer Hall of Fame.

In 2012, Papantonio became president of the National Trial Lawyers Association, which represents forty thousand trial lawyers nationally. For his trial work on behalf of consumers, he has received some of the most prestigious awards reserved by the Public Justice Foundation, the American Association for Justice, and the National Trial Lawyers Association.

He is the author of the legal thrillers *Law and Disorder* and *Law and Vengeance*, as well as four motivational books for lawyers. He is also the coauthor of *Air America: The Playbook*, listed by the *New York Times* as a "political best seller."

Papantonio is the host of the nationally syndicated radio show *Ring of Fire*, along with Robert F. Kennedy Jr. and Sam Seder. In addition to the radio show, Papantonio hosts *America's Lawyer* on the RT America network. He has also served as a political commentator who has appeared as a regular guest on MSNBC, Free Speech TV, the RT America Network, and Fox News.

Just as this novel is being published, Papantonio is heading the most important legal trial in the history of America against those responsible for the opioid epidemic.